THE CRAZED

HA JIN

THE CRAZED

Ha Jin left his native China in 1985 to attend Brandeis University. He is the author of the internationally bestselling novel *Waiting*, which won the PEN/Faulkner Award and the National Book Award; the story collections *The Bridegroom*, which won the Asian American Literary Award, *Under the Red Flag*, which won the Flannery O'Connor Award for Short Fiction, and *Ocean of Words*, which won the PEN/Hemingway Award; the novel *In the Pond*; and three books of poetry. He lives in the Boston area and is a professor of English at Boston University.

INTERNATIONAL

THE CRAZED

THE CRAZED

A NOVEL

HA JIN

VINTAGE INTERNATIONAL

Vintage Books

A Division of Random House, Inc.

New York

FIRST VINTAGE INTERNATIONAL
OPEN MARKET EDITION, JULY 2003

Copyright © 2002 by Ha Jin

The Library of Congress has cataloged the
Pantheon edition as follows:
Jin, Ha, 1956–
The crazed / Ha Jin. — 1st ed.
p. cm.
ISBN 0-375-42181-5
1. Teacher-student relationships — Fiction. 2. Cerebrovascular
disease — Patients — Fiction. 3. Literature teachers — Fiction.
4. Graduate students — Fiction. 5. College teachers — Fiction.
6. China — Fiction. 7. Psychological fiction. 8. Political fiction.
I. Title.
PS3560.I6 C73 2002
813'.54 — dc21   2002022427

Vintage Open Market ISBN: 1-4000-3214-8

www.vintagebooks.com

Printed in the United States of America
10 9 8 7 6 5 4 3 2 1

FOR LISHA

THE CRAZED

Everybody was surprised when Professor Yang suffered a stroke in the spring of 1989. He had always been in good health, and his colleagues used to envy his energy and productiveness — he had published more than any of them and had been a mainstay of the Literature Department, directing its M.A. program, editing a biannual journal, and teaching a full load. Now even the undergraduates were talking about his collapse, and some of them would have gone to the hospital if Secretary Peng had not announced that Mr. Yang, under intensive care, was in no condition to see visitors.

His stroke unsettled me, because I was engaged to his daughter, Meimei, and under his guidance I had been studying for the Ph.D. entrance exams for the classical literature program at Beijing University. I hoped to enroll there so that I could join my fiancée in the capital, where we planned to build our nest. Mr. Yang's hospitalization disrupted my work, and for a whole week I hadn't sat down to my books, having to go see him every day. I was anxious — without thorough preparation I couldn't possibly do well in the exams.

Just now, Ying Peng, the Party secretary of our department, had called me to her office. On her desk an electric fan was whirring back and forth to blow out the odor of dichlorvos sprayed in the room to kill fleas. Her gray bangs were fluttering as she described to me my job, which was to attend my teacher in the afternoons from now on. Besides me, my fellow graduate student Banping Fang would look after Mr. Yang too; he was to take care of the mornings.

"Well, Jian Wan," Ying Peng said to me with a tight smile, "you're the only family Professor Yang has here. It's time for you to help him. The hospital can't provide him with nursing care during the day, so we have to send some people there." She lifted her tall teacup and took a gulp. Like a man, she drank black tea and smoked cheap cigarettes.

"Do you think he'll stay in the hospital for long?" I asked her.

"I've no idea."

"How long should I look after him?"

"Till we find somebody to replace you."

By "somebody" she meant a person the department might hire as a nurse's aide. Although annoyed by the way she assigned me the job, I said nothing. To some extent I was glad for the assignment, without which I would in any case go to the hospital every day.

After lunch, when my two roommates, Mantao and Huran, were napping, I went to the bicycle shed located between two long dormitory houses. Unlike the female students, who had recently all moved into the new dorm building inside the university, most of the male students still lived in the one-story houses near the front entrance to the campus. I pulled out my Phoenix bicycle and set off for Central Hospital.

The hospital was in downtown Shanning, and it took me more than twenty minutes to get there. Though it wasn't summer yet, the air was sweltering, filled with the smell of burning fat and stewed radish. On the balconies of the apartment buildings along the street, lines of laundry were flapping languidly—sheets, blouses, pajamas, towels, tank tops, sweat suits. As I passed by a construction site, a loudspeaker mounted on a telephone pole was broadcasting a soccer game; the commentator sounded sleepy despite the intermittent surges of shouts from the fans. All the workers at the site were resting inside the building caged by bamboo scaffolding. The skeletonlike cranes and the drumlike mixers were motionless. Three shovels stood on a huge pile of sand, beyond which a large yellow board displayed the giant words in red paint: AIM HIGH, GO ALL OUT. I felt the back of my shirt dampen with sweat.

Mrs. Yang had gone to Tibet on a veterinary team for a year. Our department had written to her about her husband's stroke, but she wouldn't be able to come home immediately. Tibet was too far away. She'd have to switch buses and trains constantly—it would take her more than a week to return. In my letter to my fiancée, Meimei, who was in Beijing cramming for the exams for a medical graduate program, I described her father's condition and assured her that I would take good care of him and that she mustn't be worried too much. I told her not to rush back since there was no magic cure for a stroke.

To be honest, I felt obligated to attend my teacher. Even without my engagement to his daughter, I'd have done it willingly, just out of gratitude and respect. For almost two years he had taught me individually, discussing classical poetry and poetics with me almost every Saturday afternoon, selecting books for me to read, directing my master's thesis, and correcting my papers for publication. He was the best teacher I'd ever had, knowledgeable about the field of poetics and devoted to his students. Some of my fellow graduate students felt uncomfortable having him as their adviser. "He's too demanding," they would say. But I enjoyed working with him. I didn't even mind some of them calling me Mr. Yang, Jr.; in a way, I was his disciple.

Mr. Yang was sleeping as I stepped into the sickroom. He was shorn of the IV apparatus affixed to him in intensive care. The room was a makeshift place, quite large for one bed, but dusky and rather damp. Its square window looked south onto a mountain of anthracite in the backyard of the hospital. Beyond the coal pile, a pair of concrete smokestacks spewed whitish fumes and a few aspen crowns swayed indolently. The backyard suggested a factory—more exactly, a power plant; even the air here looked grayish. By contrast, the front yard resembled a garden or a park, planted with holly bushes, drooping willows, sycamores, and flowers, including roses, azaleas, geraniums, and fringed irises. There was even an oval pond, built of bricks and rocks, abounding in fantailed goldfish. White-robed doctors and nurses strolled through the flowers and trees as if they had nothing urgent to do.

Shabby as Mr. Yang's room was, having it was a rare privilege; few patients could have a sickroom solely to themselves. If my father, who was a carpenter on a tree farm in the Northeast, had a stroke, he would be lucky if they gave him a bed in a room shared by a dozen people. Actually Mr. Yang had lain unconscious in a place like that for three days before he was moved here. With infinite pull, Secretary Peng had succeeded in convincing the hospital officials that Mr. Yang was an eminent scholar (though he wasn't a full professor yet) whom our country planned to protect as a national treasure, so they ought to give him a private room.

Mr. Yang stirred a little and opened his mouth, which had become flabby since the stroke. He looked a few years older than the previous month; a network of wrinkles had grown into his face. His gray hair was unkempt and a bit shiny, revealing his whitish scalp. Eyes shut, he went on licking his upper lip and murmured something I couldn't quite hear.

Sitting on a large wicker chair close to the door, I was about to take out a book from my shoulder bag when Mr. Yang opened his eyes and looked around vacantly. I followed his gaze and noticed that the wallpaper had almost lost its original pink. His eyes, cloudy with a web of reddish veins, moved toward the center of the low ceiling, stopped for a moment at the lightbulb held by a frayed wire, then fell on the stack of Japanese vocabulary cards on my lap.

"Help me sit up, Jian," he said softly.

I went over, lifted his shoulders, and put behind him two pillows stuffed with fluffy cotton so that he could sit comfortably. "Do you feel better today?" I asked.

"No, I don't." He kept his head low, a tuft of hair standing up on his crown while a muscle in his right cheek twitched.

For a minute or so we sat silently. I wasn't sure if I should talk more; Dr. Wu had told us to keep the patient as peaceful as possible; more conversation might make him too excited. Although diagnosed as a cerebral thrombosis, his stroke seemed quite unusual, not accompanied by aphasia — he was still articulate and at times peculiarly voluble.

As I wondered what to do, he raised his head and broke the silence. "What have you been doing these days?" he asked. His tone indicated that he must have thought we were in his office discussing my work.

I answered, "I've been reviewing a Japanese textbook for the exam and —"

"To hell with that!" he snapped. I was too shocked to say anything more. He went on, "Have you read the Bible by any chance?" He looked at me expectantly.

"Yes, but not the unabridged Bible." Although puzzled by his question, I explained to him in the way I would report on a book I had just waded through. "Last year I read a condensed English version called *Stories from the Bible*, published by the Press of Foreign Language Education. I wish I could get hold of a genuine Bible, though." In fact, a number of graduate students in the English program had written to Christian associations in the United States requesting the Bible, and some American churches had mailed them boxes of books, but so far every copy had been confiscated by China's customs.

Mr. Yang said, "Then you know the story of Genesis, don't you?"

"Yes, but not the whole book."

"All right, in that case, let me tell you the story in its entirety."

After a pause, he began delivering his self-invented Genesis with the same eloquence he exhibited when delivering lectures. But unlike in the classroom, where his smiles and gestures often mesmerized the students, here he sat unable to lift his hand, and his listless head hung so low that his eyes must have seen nothing but the white quilt over his legs. There was a bubbling sound in his nose, rendering his voice a little wheezy and tremulous. "When God created heaven and earth, all creatures were made equal. He did not intend to separate man from animals. All the creatures enjoyed not only the same kind of life but also the same span of life. They were equal in every way."

What kind of Genesis is this? I asked myself. *He's all confused, making fiction now.*

He spoke again. "Then why does man live longer than most animals? Why does he have a life different from those of the other creatures? According to Genesis it's because man was greedy and clever and appropriated many years of life from Monkey and Donkey." He exhaled, his cheeks puffy and his eyes narrowed. A fishtail of wrinkles spread from the end of his eye toward his temple. He went on, "One day God descended from heaven to inspect the world he had created. Monkey, Donkey, and Man came out to greet God with gratitude and to show their obedience. God asked them whether they were satisfied with life on earth. They all replied that they were.

"'Does anyone want something else?' asked God.

"Hesitating for a moment, Monkey stepped forward and said, 'Lord, the earth is the best place where I can live. You have blessed so many trees with fruit that I need nothing more. But why did you let me live to the age of forty? After I reach thirty, I will become old and cannot climb up trees to pluck fruit. So I will have to accept whatever the young monkeys give me, and sometimes I will have to eat the cores and peels they drop to the ground. It hurts me to think I'd have to feed on their leavings. Lord, I do not want such a long life. Please take ten years off my life span. I'd prefer a shorter but active existence.' He stepped back, shaking fearfully. He knew it was a sin to be unsatisfied with what God had given him.

"'Your wish is granted,' God declared without any trace of anger. He then turned to Donkey, who had opened his mouth several times in silence. God asked him whether he too had something to say.

"Timidly Donkey moved a step forward and said, 'Lord, I have the same problem. Your grace has enriched the land where so much grass grows that I can choose the most tender to eat. Although Man treats me unequally and forces me to work for him, I won't complain because you gave him more brains and me more muscles. But a life span of forty years is too long for me. When I grow old and my legs are no longer sturdy and nimble, I will still have to carry heavy loads for Man and suffer his lashes. This will be too miserable for me. Please take ten years off my life too. I want a shorter existence without old age.'

"'Your wish is granted.' God was very generous with them that day and meant to gratify all their requests. Then he turned to Man, who seemed also to have something to say. God asked, 'You too have a complaint? Tell me, Adam, what is on your mind.'

"Man was fearful because he had abused the animals and could be punished for that. Nevertheless, he came forward and began to speak. 'Our Greatest Lord, I always enjoy everything you have created. You endowed me with a brain that enables me to outsmart the animals, who are all willing to obey and serve me. Contrary to Monkey and Donkey, a life span of forty years is too short for me. I would love to live longer. I want to spend more time with my wife, Eve, and my children. Even if I grow old with stiff limbs, I can still use my brain to manage my affairs. I can issue orders, teach lessons, deliver lectures, and write books. Please give their twenty years to me.' Man bowed his head as he remembered that it was a sin to assume his superiority over the animals.

"To Man's amazement, God did not reprimand him and instead replied, 'Your wish is also granted. Since you enjoy my creation so much, I'll give you an additional ten years. Now, altogether you will have seventy years for your life. Spend your ripe old age happily with your grandchildren and great-grandchildren. Use your brain wisely.'"

Mr. Yang paused, looking pale and exhausted, sweat glistening on his nose and a vein in his neck pulsating. Then he said dolefully, "Donkey, Monkey, and Man were all satisfied that day. From then on, human beings can live to the age of seventy whereas monkeys and donkeys can live only thirty years."

He fell silent, but was still wheezing. I was bewildered by his version of Genesis, which he had poured out as spontaneously as though he had learned it by heart. As I was wondering about its meaning, he interrupted my thoughts, saying, "You're puzzled by my story of Genesis, aren't you?" Without waiting for my answer, he went on, "Let me tell you its moral."

"All right," I mumbled.

"Comrades," he resumed lecturing, "entangled with Monkey's and Donkey's lives, Man's life cannot but be alienated from itself. In his first twenty years, Man lives a monkey's life. He capers around and climbs trees and walls, doing things at will. This period, his happiest, passes quickly. Then comes the next twenty years, in which Man lives a donkey's life. He has to work hard every day so as to carry food and clothes to his family. Often he is exhausted like a donkey after a long, arduous trip, but he has to remain on his feet, because the load of his family sits on his back and he has to continue. After this period Man has reached forty, and human life begins. By now his body is worn out, his limbs are feeble and heavy, and he has to rely on his brain, which has begun deteriorating too, no longer as quick and capable as he thought. Sometimes he wants to cry out in futility, but his brain stops him: 'Don't do that! You have to control yourself. You still have many years to go.' Every day he presses more thoughts and emotions into his brain, in which a good deal of stuff is already stored but none is allowed to get out so as to accommodate new stuff. Yet day after day he squeezes in something more, until one day his brain becomes too full and cannot but burst. It's like a pressure cooker which is so full that the safety valve is blocked up, but the fire continues heating its bottom. As a consequence, the only way out is to explode."

I was amazed by his wild interpretation — it was as though he'd been talking about his own life and about how he had gone out of his mind. He tilted his head back and rested his neck fully on the pillows; he was exhausted, but seemed relieved. Silence fell on the room.

Again I thought about his biblical story, whose source baffled me. Probably he had made it up himself, combining some folktale with his own fantasies. Why was he so eager to tell me it? Never had he shown any interest in the Bible before, though in secret it must have occupied his mind for a long time.

He began snoring softly; his head drooped aside. I went over, removed the pillows from behind him, and slid him carefully back into bed. He moaned vaguely.

Soon he sank back into sleep. I picked up my Japanese vocabulary cards and started to review them. Despite not enjoying Japanese, which sounded to me like ducks' quacking, I had to fill my brain with its words and grammatical rules for the Ph.D. candidacy, which required a test in a second foreign language. My Japanese was weak because I had studied it for only a year. English was my first foreign language, in which I was much more proficient.

A bent old nurse came in to check on Mr. Yang. She was a mousy woman with a moon face, and her bony hands suggested gigantic chicken feet. She introduced herself as Hong Jiang. Seeing that my teacher was sleeping, she didn't feel his pulse or take his temperature and blood pressure. I asked her if he could recuperate soon, and she said it would depend on whether a blood clot in his brain could be dissolved. If not, no treatment could really cure him. "But don't worry," she assured me, leaning down to pick up the spittoon by the bedpost. "Lots of people have recovered from a stroke. Some have lived more than twenty years afterward. Your teacher should be able to get well."

"I hope so," I sighed.

"For now, what's most important of all is to keep him calm. Don't disturb him. If he gets too excited, he may break a blood vessel in his brain. That'll cause a hemorrhage." Holding the white spittoon with one hand, she with her other hand piled together the soiled plates, bowls, and spoons on the bedside cabinet, then placed a pair of lacquered chopsticks on top of them. I stood up to give her a hand.

"Don't bother. I can manage this," she said, and unwittingly tilted the spittoon toward my belly. I stepped aside and barely dodged a blob of the yellowish liquid that fell to the wood floor.

"Whoops! Sorry." She grinned and lifted the stack of bowls and plates carefully. With a stoop she gingerly turned to the door. She was so skinny, she reminded me of a starved hen. I opened the door for her.

"Thank you. You're a good young man," she said, shuffling away down the hall. I took a mop from behind the door and wiped the blob off the floor.

Her explanation of Mr. Yang's stroke consoled me to a degree. I used to think a brain thrombus was caused by a ruptured blood vessel. Thank heaven, his case was merely a blockage.

2

Once again I bicycled to the hospital to relieve Banping Fang. Thanks to the scalding sun, the asphalt street had turned doughy; automobile tires had left tracks on its cambered surface, from which a bluish vapor rose, flickering like smoke. I felt drowsy, not having slept well the night before. I pedaled listlessly. If only I could've taken a nap at noon as I used to do every day.

On arrival, I heard somebody speaking loudly inside the sickroom. I stopped at the door to listen. It was Mr. Yang's voice, but I couldn't make out his words. He sounded strident, panting and shrieking by turns, as if he were arguing with someone. I opened the door and went in noiselessly. Seeing me, Banping nodded and put his forefinger to his lips, his other hand supporting our teacher's back. It looked like he had just helped him sit up.

"Kill them! Kill all those bastards!" Professor Yang shouted.

Banping's mouth moved close to his ear, and he whispered, "Calm down, please!"

Mr. Yang's head hung so low that his chin rested on his chest. "Why did you interrupt me?" he asked with his eyes still closed. "Hear me out, will you? When I'm finished you can raise questions." He sounded as if he were teaching a class. But whom had he yelled at just now? And who were the people he wanted to wipe out? Why did he hate them so much?

Banping smiled at me with some embarrassment and shook his head. I sensed the meaning of his smile, which showed sympathy for me probably because of my relationship with the Yangs. He gestured me to sit down on the wicker chair and then turned to make our teacher lean back against the headboard.

The moment I sat down, Professor Yang broke into speech. "All the time he has been thinking how to end everything, to be done with his clerical work, done with his senile, exacting parents, done with his nagging wife and spoiled children, done with his mistress Chilla, who is no longer a 'little swallow' with a slender waist but is obsessed with how to lose weight and reduce the size of her massive backside, done with the endless worry and misery of everyday life, done with the nightmares in broad daylight — in short, to terminate himself so that he can quit this world."

I was shocked. Banping smiled again and seemed to relish the surprise on my face. Mr. Yang continued, "But he lives in a room without a door or a window and without any furniture inside. Confined in such a cell, he faces the insurmountable difficulty of how to end his life. On the rubber floor spreads a thick pallet, beside which sits an incomplete dinner set. The walls are covered with green rubber too. He cannot smash his head on any spot in this room. He wears a leather belt, which he sometimes takes off, thinking how to garrote himself with it. Some people he knew committed suicide in that way twenty years ago, because they couldn't endure the torture inflicted by the revolutionary masses anymore. They looped a belt around their necks, secured its loose end to a hook or a nail on a window ledge, then forcefully they sat down on the floor. But in this room there's not a single fixed object, so his belt cannot serve that purpose. Sometimes he lets it lie across his lap and observes it absentmindedly. The belt looks like a dead snake in the greenish light. What's worse, he cannot figure out where the room is, whether it's in a city or in the countryside, and whether it's in a house or underground. In such a condition he is preserved to live."

I couldn't tell where he had gotten this episode. When did it happen? And where? Was it from a novel, or was it his own fantasy? Since the man's mistress had a rather Westernized name, Chilla, the story might be set in a city. That was all I could guess. Professor Yang was so well read that I could never surmise the full extent of his knowledge of literature. Maybe he had made up the whole thing himself; otherwise he couldn't have poured it out with such abandon.

He interrupted my thoughts, speaking again. "All the time he imagines how to stop this kind of meaningless existence. Mark this, 'all the time.' He can no longer tell time because there's no distinction between day and night in this room. He has noticed some kind of light shimmering overhead, but cannot locate its source. He used to believe that if he could find the source, he could probably get out of his predicament by unscrewing the lightbulb and poking his finger into the socket. But by now he has given up that notion, having realized that even if he identified the source, the light might not be electric at all. He's thus doomed to live on, caged in an indestructible cocoon like a worm." Mr. Yang paused for breath, then resumed: "The only hard objects in the room are the plastic dinner set — a bowl, a dish, a spoon, and a knife. There's no fork. He's deprived of the privilege of piercing his windpipe with a fork. Time and again he picks up the knife, which is toothless and brittle. Stropping it on his forefinger, he grunts, 'Damn it, I can't even cut my penis with this!'"

Banping chuckled, but stopped right away, his buckteeth on his lower lip. He straightened up and put his notebook and fountain pen into his breast pocket.

I didn't find anything funny in Mr. Yang's story, which actually saddened me. My throat was constricting as I avoided looking at Banping.

On leaving, he whispered almost in my ear, "Come over for dinner tonight, will you? We'll make dumplings. Weiya's coming too."

I nodded to agree. He and I were classmates and friends of sorts, and his one-room home in a dormitory house near the campus was a place where we often got together. Weiya Su was the other graduate student who had Professor Yang as her adviser. This year our teacher directed only the three of us in our graduate work, though he was on almost every master's thesis committee in the department.

In his delirium Mr. Yang continued making noise. He was unusually agitated today. His head jerked as he went on groaning and gnashing his gums. In addition, the rhythm of his respiration changed drastically — one moment he breathed evenly, and another moment he panted as though running a race. What's more, he seemed frightened by something or somebody, whining piteously every now and again. He mouthed some unintelligible words, which sounded like complaints or curses. His right hand kept rubbing his thigh, and his motion made the bed shake a little.

He might hurt his brain if he continued like this, so I decided to put him into bed, hoping he could fall asleep after he lay down. I went over and inserted my left arm under his legs, wrapped my right arm around his thick waist, and slowly moved him down. He didn't seem to feel the downward movement and never stopped muttering and squirming.

It took me about five minutes to slide him back into bed. Sitting on the chair again, with my right leg over its arm, I began to review Japanese vocabulary. Hard as I tried, I couldn't concentrate on the flash cards, distracted by Mr. Yang, who seemed to be quarreling with someone now. He sounded bellicose and from time to time gritted his teeth, which I knew indicated he was holding back his temper.

Despite my effort to focus on my work, I couldn't help but observe his sweat-streaked face. Half an hour later, out of the blue, he burst into song. His singing baffled me, because to my mind he was born to teach seminars and deliver lectures. Who could've expected that Professor Yang would be singing this particular nursery rhyme?

> To wear a flower
> You pick a big red one,
> To ride a horse
> You mount a sturdy steed,
> To sing a song
> You praise great deeds,
> To obey orders
> You listen to the Party.

The song jolted me, and I felt the hair on the back of my head bristling. I hadn't heard it for a long time. In spite of his gusto, Mr. Yang was no singer and sounded more like he was crowing.

No sooner had he finished singing than he added a shrill operatic chant, imitating drums, gongs, and cymbals: "Dong — chang, dong — chang, dong — dong — chang, chang — chang — chang, dong — dong — chang . . ." He then let out a resounding belch, and his stomach growled as he clacked his tongue against the roof of his mouth. He seemed to be enacting a snatch from a Beijing opera, which had no bearing on the nursery rhyme.

I was actually more disturbed than baffled, as I remembered singing the rhyme with other children in the kindergarten over twenty years before. At that time it had been commonplace for us to chant such a song in raptures, but Mr. Yang's singing now was so anachronistic and so out of context that it sounded ludicrous. Luckily for him, nobody but I had heard it.

Then, as if mocking my discomfort, he hit on another song. Eyes ablaze, he boomed:

> *The Proletarian Cultural Revolution*
> *Is good, is good, is good, is good!*
> *Workers are masters again.*
> *Landowners, rich peasants,*
> *Reactionaries, evildoers, rightists*
> *Have no place to hide —*
> *All will be swept away.*

He bellowed the whole thing out as if he were under some kind of spell. His ferocious voice seemed to belong to someone else. I couldn't imagine that an equable scholar like him would have anything to do with such a silly song. His singing made my scalp itch as I remembered hearing Red Guards chant it in my hometown. By so doing, those big boys and girls had contributed their little share to the revolution; but that had been two decades before, and now the song was no more than an embarrassing joke.

How had Mr. Yang learned this piece? I had been told that when the Cultural Revolution broke out, he was turned into a Demon-Monster, a target of the struggle, who would not have been entitled to sing such a progressive song together with the masses. Perhaps he had learned it on the sly, or he had heard others chant it so many times that it stuck in his mind.

Eyes shut, he resumed crooning the tune of the song, though its words were now disjointed and garbled. His singing sickened me. I put the flash cards on top of my bag that leaned against the leg of the chair, wondering how to stop him. He gave me the creeps. I looked at my watch — it was just past two o'clock. This was going to be a long afternoon.

"My heart is still good, pure and warm!" declared Mr. Yang. Without a pause he started another song. This time he not only was caroling but also seemed to be dancing around. His body wriggled a little as he mimicked a feminine voice:

> *There's a golden sun in Beijing.*
> *It brightens whatever it shines upon.*
> *Ah, the light does not come*
> *From the sky but from*
> *Our Great Leader Chairman Mao!*

While singing he flexed his toes, heaved his belly a little, and twisted his lips into a puerile smile. The instant he was done, he cried cheerfully, "See, I can sing it as well as any one of you. I can dance to it too. Let me show you."

I went to him and placed my palm on his forehead, which was sweaty and burning hot. I patted his shoulder, but he turned his head aside and shouted ecstatically, "Don't get in my way! Look, I can do it!" His right leg kicked, though he couldn't raise it.

Should I wake him up? Though ridiculous, he seemed happy, grinning like a half-wit and licking his parched lips to wipe away the foam.

I decided to let him enjoy his hallucination for a while and returned to the wicker chair. By now he had calmed down a little, but he went on humming the tune of the song through his pink swollen nose. I remembered that about twenty years ago some kids, who were Small Red Guards and five or six years older than myself, had often performed the Loyalty Dance to this very song at restaurants, bus stops, inns, department stores, and the train station in my hometown in the Northeast. Chanting those words, they capered and sidled about, waving their hands above their heads; they kicked their heels, swung their legs, and bent their waists. Too young to participate, I watched them enviously. In hindsight they looked like crazed frogs wearing red armbands; yet at that time some of the kids were so sincere that, if asked, they would have sacrificed their lives for Chairman Mao without second thoughts. But Mr. Yang was a reactionary intellectual then and must have been forbidden to join the revolutionary masses in any celebration and propa-

ganda activities. Could he really know such a dance? I didn't
think so.

"Ah, who can tell I always have a loyal heart!" he said and
smacked his lips. "Come, just watch me." He started the tune
again, his legs kicking slowly and his arms jerking on the
crumpled sheet. Not only the bed but also the floor, whose
boards buckled in places, creaked now. He wiggled more and
more rhythmically while a radiant smile broke on his face. He
seemed beside himself with joy.

"Yes, I can raise my legs higher than that, no problem," he
said with a wide grin. "I always love Chairman Mao. For him
I dare to climb a mountain of swords and walk through a sea
of fire. Why don't you believe me? Why?" His head rocked
from side to side.

I was puzzled by his assertion of loyalty to the Great
Leader. When he was in his right mind, Mr. Yang had never
expressed any deep feelings for Chairman Mao in front of
me. Did he really love him? Was this a subconscious emotion
that had at last surfaced once his mind failed? Chairman Mao
had died twelve years ago; why was Mr. Yang still obsessed
with him? Did he really worship him in his heart?

Whatever the truth was, I thought I'd better stop him from
hallucinating. He might damage his brain. I shouted, "Hey,
Professor Yang, wake up. We're in the hospital now."

He made no response and kept singing and "dancing." I
went over, held his wrists, and clapped his hands a couple of
times, hoping this might wake him. But it didn't. He paused,
then yelled, "Long live the Communist Party! Down with
warlords! Long live the New China!" My mind boggled and
I let go of his hands. He must have been imagining himself as

a revolutionary martyr being dragged to an execution ground by the police like a hero in a propaganda movie. He was hopelessly crazy.

I hurried out, heading downstairs to the nurses' station. I knew Dr. Wu often prescribed sedative-hypnotic drugs for Mr. Yang.

I expected to find Hong Jiang in the office, but the small woman wasn't there. A nurse in her mid-twenties sat on a broad windowsill, her unbuttoned robe revealing her sea-green dress. Her hands were busy embroidering a butterfly on a white tablecloth. On her right, toward the corner and against the baseboard, stood a line of scarlet thermoses containing boiled water, their mouths emitting tiny hisses. She recognized me but didn't budge, as if I were one of the nurse's aides hired to do cleaning. Her large eyes were fixed on the needle-work in her long, rosy fingers; the butterfly, as large as a palm, was still missing a wing. Ignoring her slight, I walked up to her and asked if she was in charge of Mr. Yang's medication.

"Uh-huh," she said without lifting her eyelids. Overhead a fluorescent tube was blinking with a faint ping-ping-ping sound.

"My teacher has gone berserk today," I told her. "He's been singing and raving like a madman. Can you sedate him?"

She only half listened and didn't respond, so I repeated my request. After a few more stitches, she placed the tablecloth on the sill. She yawned but immediately clapped her narrow hand on her mouth. "I'm so tired," she said, smiling feebly. "You know what? We tried to give him a sedative pill this morning. I mean your classmate Comrade Fang and I tried, but your teacher thought we were going to poison him and yelled for all he was worth. We couldn't force him to take the medicine, you know. That would've agitated him more."

"Can you give him another tablet now?" I asked.

"Well, I have no right to give him anything."

"But Dr. Wu often prescribes drugs for him, doesn't he?"

"Yes, but he's not here."

"Please help me calm him down, I beg you. I'm afraid he'll hurt his brain if he goes on like this."

"Well, maybe we can put a pill into his porridge at dinner."

She squinted her left eye, then winked at me, as if asking, Isn't this a smart idea?

"But he's running wild now," I said. "Dinner's still three hours away. Can't you give him an injection or something? Help him, please!"

"You're a pretty good student," she said dryly. She came down from the windowsill and went over to the long desk, on which sat a few shiny metal cases and a row of amber bottles containing drugs, all with glass stoppers in their mouths. She picked up the phone and called the doctor.

I felt relieved to see her jotting down a prescription. She hung up, selected two ampules of medicine, and wrapped up an injection kit. Together we headed out. On our way upstairs, she told me that her name was Mali Chen and that she had just graduated from a nursing school in Shanghai. A metropolitan girl, I thought, no wonder she looks frail and anemic.

Opening the door of the sickroom, I was surprised to see Mr. Yang sitting on the bed with one foot tucked under him. Strands of gray hair stuck out above his temples, making his face appear broader. How could he sit up by himself? Had somebody slipped in when I was away? Impossible. He must have done this on his own.

Mr. Yang was still humming something that I couldn't make out at first. Then lifting his voice, he chanted in gasps, "How powerful the tall cranes are! They can pick up tons of steel easily . . ."

I realized he was impersonating the retired stevedore in an aria from the revolutionary opera *The Harbor*, praising the brawn of some newly installed cranes, but his voice was too smooth and too thin to express the proletarian mettle. I hadn't known he could sing Beijing opera. He had seldom gone to the theater and must have learned the snatch from the radio.

"See, the pill is still here," Nurse Chen said to me and pointed to a small cup on the bedside cabinet. It contained a large yellowish tablet, probably barbiturate.

While she was preparing the injection, I removed the quilt from Mr. Yang's legs and got hold of the string of his pajamas, which was a long shoelace. He stopped short. Before I could untie his pants, he opened his eyes — only to see the syringe spurting a white thread of liquid. His face turned horror-stricken, though Nurse Chen forced a smile and said enticingly, "Well, Professor Yang, it's time to have some —"

"Help! Help! Mur-der! They want to poison me!" he screamed, his eyes glinting. He kicked his right leg but was unable to raise his arms. He was gasping, agape like a spent fish.

The nurse looked scared, her eyebrows pinched together. She turned to me and asked, "Do you think we can still make him take the needle?"

I didn't answer. Mr. Yang kept howling, "Save me! They're assassinating me!"

"Stop this, please!" I begged him in an undertone.

"Help me!"

"You're making a spectacle of yourself."

"Don't kill me!"

Nurse Chen took apart the syringe, dropped the needle back into the oval metal case, emptied the medicine into the spittoon, and wrapped everything up. "I think we'd better leave him alone," she said with a toss of her head. "Let him cool off by himself. Every time we try to put him to sleep, we only upset him more."

I said nothing. Anger was surging in my chest, but I checked my impulse to yell at him.

"Well now, I must be going," she continued. "Don't disturb him. It'll take a while for this one to become himself again." She put the injection kit under her arm and said to me casually, "Bye-bye now." She left, her heels clicking away toward the stairwell.

Professor Yang started sobbing; tears leaked out of his closed lids, trickling down his cheeks and stubbly chin. He whimpered something incoherently. I listened for a moment and felt he seemed to be begging mercy from someone, who might be an imagined murderer. He went on wagging his head and grunting like a piglet; his words had turned to gibberish.

This mustn't continue. I decided to give him the sedative pill no matter how hard he resisted. With a spoon I set about grinding the tablet in the porcelain cup until it became powder. On the cabinet stood an opened bottle of orangeade. I poured some of it into the cup and stirred the concoction for a minute, then sat down beside him. "Mr. Yang, drink this please," I pleaded and raised the cup to his lips.

He opened his eyes and saw the juice. He said, "You want to poison me, I know. I refuse to take it."

"Come on, it's just orangeade. See, I also drink some myself." I lifted the spoon to my mouth and made a gurgling sound as a parent would do to convince a child. "Ah, it's so delicious. Please try it, just a small cup."

He said, "You slipped ratsbane into it, didn't you? I know your dark fat heart."

"No, you're wrong. Please have some!"

"I won't."

Hesitantly I used the spoon to pry his mouth open, but his teeth were clenched, and the steel scraped them noisily. I was afraid this might hurt his gums, so I stopped, wondering what to do. He jabbed his elbow at the cup in my hand, and a splash of the drink fell on the sheet and left a yellow stain. His mouth was sealed up like a startled clam.

I wouldn't give up and raised half a spoonful of the orangeade to his lips again, begging him, "Please try this. It will do you good. I just want to feed you and won't hurt you."

"No, I won't. You cannot cajole me anymore."

"Please, just a sip."

"No, that will be lethal."

Out of patience, I shouted, "Look at me! You don't recognize me? Do I look like a murderer? I'm Jian, your future son-in-law." I said the last word diffidently, but thrust my face in front him. His eyes opened a crack, then fully.

"Oh," he muttered, "I didn't know I had a son."

"This is Jian Wan, remember me?"

"I didn't know it was you. What is it that you want?"

"I'd like to feed you. Here's a small cup of orangeade, please open your mouth."

Miraculously, he obeyed me like a well-behaved child. I carefully put the spoon into his mouth and turned it over. Slowly he swallowed the juice, his Adam's apple bobbing.

"I like the tangy flavor. It tastes excellent," he said.

"Sure it does," I agreed.

"What did you put in it?"

"Nothing."

With less than ten spoonfuls I emptied the cup. I told him, "Don't be afraid. I'm here with you and won't let anyone hurt you. Now you should have some sleep."

Shamefacedly he watched me as I tried to move his half-paralyzed body; he even tried to shift his hips a little to facilitate my effort. Still, I had to exert myself hard. When I had finally put him back into bed, I was huffing and puffing.

A few minutes later he went to sleep.

3

I didn't expect that Banping and his wife, Anling, would make flounder dumplings. This was the first time I had eaten this dish, which my host told me was a delicacy in some coastal areas for celebrating spring. The stuffing was juicy and toothsome, tasting like prawn. It made me miss the fat catfish, long pike, and stout carp from the lower reaches of the Songhua River in the Northeast, where my parents lived.

While we were eating, Banping bragged about his cookery. He had prepared the filling, seasoned with leeks and crushed sesame seeds. He even described to us how to debone the large flounder, how to peel its skin, and how to get rid of its blood so as to reduce the fishy taste, but Anling accused him of "cooking only with his mouth."

"Come on, don't be so mean," Banping said to her. "Didn't I work the whole afternoon?"

"You help only when we have good stuff to cook."

"That's because I'm like a chef."

"So I'm just a kitchen maid who only chops vegetables and does dishes in this home?"

"Uh-oh," I stepped in, "you're both chefs, of the first rank, all right?"

We all laughed.

"Don't you have other music? This is too loud," Weiya said to Banping, referring to the Beethoven that his cassette recorder was playing. I too felt uncomfortable; the symphony was so overpowering it seemed to be urging us to compete in wolfing down the food. Banping worshiped Beethoven and regarded Romain Roland's *Jean-Christophe* as his bible. Inspired by the biographical novel, he often talked about the joy of life. To my thinking he was too optimistic.

He got up and put a tape of popular songs into the player. Things eased up immediately.

I noticed that under the washstand, welded of iron bars, sat a new electric stove, at least 1,500 watts strong, which was strictly prohibited in the dorms because of the drain on the electricity. In fact, a top school official, Vice Principal Huang, was in charge of catching users of electric stoves, teapots, immersion heaters, and cookers. He would personally spot-check dormitory houses and buildings, especially in the late afternoons.

"Boy, you want to appear on the honor roll again," I said to Banping, alluding to the list of "electricity thieves" often posted on the bulletin board at the front entrance to campus.

"I told him to be more careful," Anling picked up.

"As long as they don't fine me, I won't mind," Banping said, exhaling smoke.

"My roommate was caught last Friday," put in Weiya.

"Was she fined?" I asked.

"No, she's a first-time offender."

In reality, Banping was afraid of being caught. On the back of his right foot was a burn scar in the shape of a tangerine segment, caused by a splash of boiling broth. One afternoon the previous fall, as he was stewing chicken and taros on an electric stove, suddenly somebody had pounded on the door. "Open it!" came Vice Principal Huang's raucous voice. Hurriedly Banping hid away the stove under his bed, pushed the window open, then went to answer the door. The leader stepped in, sniffing the meaty air. At the sight of the wire and plug on the floor, he bent down and pulled the whole thing out from under the bed. The pot overturned. "Ouch!" Banping yelled, hopping on one leg; some broth had spattered on his foot. Chunks of chicken and taros were scattered on the concrete floor, and the room at once became steamy. Though the "electricity thief" was in pain, the vice principal dressed him down and confiscated his stove. Later Secretary Peng interceded for Banping with Huang's office, saying his scalded foot was already an indelible lesson to him; otherwise, by rule, he'd have been fined fifty yuan.

Weiya sat opposite me at the square table and looked pensive. Throughout dinner she seldom smiled; her mouth closed without showing her eyeteeth as she would do when she was happy. Her luxuriant hair, held by two orange barrettes, was slightly tousled. Her egg-shaped face had lost its usual pink, though she was wearing a cherry-red shirt that should have given her cheeks more color. I had never seen her eyes so lazy. She had a high nose and almond-shaped eyes, which usually were vivid and bright but today were bleary with sadness. Even her voice sounded cheerless and rather whispery.

Our teacher's stroke must have affected her deeply. Although already thirty-one, she looked to be in her early twenties; some people in the Literature Department often referred to her as an old maid; I often wondered why she didn't have a boyfriend and why she never seemed in a hurry to look for one. With her looks and intelligence, she should have had no difficulty in finding a suitable man.

Upset as we all were, we felt lucky in a way, because we were going to graduate soon; if not, with Mr. Yang hospitalized, the three of us would have been transferred into other professors' hands as "foster children." We also talked about the prognosis in Mr. Yang's case. Banping said that normally it would take a whole year for a patient with cerebral thrombosis to convalesce, that most stroke victims couldn't recover completely, and that some had to move around with the aid of a crutch for the rest of their lives.

After we were done with the dumplings and cleared the table, Banping brewed a pot of jasmine tea. We started talking about the possible causes of Mr. Yang's stroke. We believed that apart from his pathological condition, something else might have set off his collapse. We all offered our guesses. Weiya suggested something I hadn't thought of before. She told us that Secretary Peng had pestered Mr. Yang continually ever since he had returned from Canada. "I've heard that the school demands he pay the money back," she said rather mysteriously.

"What money?" I asked.

"The dollars he spent for his Canadian trip last winter."

I was surprised. As his prospective son-in-law, why hadn't I gotten wind of this? Before I could say anything, Anling piped in, "How much did he spend?"

"About eighteen hundred dollars," said Weiya.

"Goodness, who can pay off such an amount!" Anling turned to me and went on, "How much does he make a month?" At last her hands stopped folding a toffee wrapper into a crane.

"One hundred and ninety yuan," I answered.

"That translates into how many dollars?"

"About thirty," Weiya told her.

With his chin propped on his hand, Banping said, "But I heard that Secretary Peng tried to persuade the school not to make him pay it back. She said she had helped Mr. Yang out."

"I don't believe a word of it," Weiya brought out.

"Neither do I," I agreed.

Five months ago Mr. Yang had gone to Canada for a conference on comparative literature. He had arrived at Vancouver too late to give his talk; yet seizing the opportunity, he visited San Francisco on his way back. Indeed, such a "sightseeing trip" was inappropriate, yet making him pay for the fare and the hotel would ruin his family financially. Many leaders of our university had visited North America, Japan, Hong Kong, Africa, and Europe without accomplishing a thing, but they had never bothered about the expenses. And they often reminded us of how much the country spent for our education, saying it took at least seven workers or twenty-four peasants to support one college student.

Banping sighed and said, "Anyway, it's so hard to live a scholar's life nowadays — you always have too much to accomplish and too little to live on." He lifted his cup and sipped the piping hot tea. "Worst of all, as a poor scholar your fate is never in your own hands. That's why I don't want to stay here." He looked me in the face and sighed again.

I well understood his gaze. Unlike him, I would stay in academia. If I couldn't get into the Ph.D. program at Beijing University, I'd soon begin teaching here. Truth be told, I didn't mind what he said. He only meant to justify his decision to pursue an official career; also, he couldn't help but lament our teacher's collapse.

Banping had decided to serve as a junior clerk in the Provincial Commerce Department after graduation. The position could be lucrative, but I felt he had made a mistake, because he, gauche and slightly dense, might have a tough time surviving in official circles and might never rise to a high post. Our graduate program had admitted him mainly because he had memorized some classics and excelled in the political exam that required no thoughts of one's own. Some people considered him a complete blockhead. He really ought to remain at the university, where he could at least hold a secure job. I asked him half jokingly, "Did you get Anling's permission to enter government service?"

"You bet I did. If I weren't going to the Commerce Department, she'd divorce me for sure."

Both his wife and he laughed. "Get out of here," she said, raising her small fist to shove his shoulder. Her smile revealed her lopsided teeth and made her eyes almost disappear.

"Why would you go to the Commerce Department?" I asked Banping. "You'll have to grow another pair of eyes on the back of your head if you want to survive there."

"I have my reasons."

"What are they?" I asked.

"Yes, tell us," Weiya urged.

"All right, number one, the Commerce Department has housing. They've promised me a three-bedroom apartment with a big balcony, all together more than a hundred square yards, which none of the young faculty here can even dream of. Number two, that department controls most of the merchandise produced in this province, so it's a temple where companies and factories have to pay tribute — I'll have lots of stuff to eat and drink. Are these two reasons not enough?"

"More than enough," I said, nodding while thinking, *He's so materialistic. He shouldn't have studied literature and written a thesis on ancient ballads.*

"How big is the balcony?" I asked him.

"About the size of this room."

"Wow, you can grow a kitchen garden on it."

"Exactly."

"We plan to do that," added Anling.

"Yes, we'll get some earthen pots," Banping said.

"And a few sacks of fertilizer too," I echoed.

Weiya tittered, then asked him, "Why don't you go to the Policy Office? Doesn't it want a graduate student from our school too?"

"It must have more advantages," I said.

"That office is a bigger temple," he explained. "In fact, it has some kind of control over all the departments at the Provincial Administration. Every clerk in that office is powerful because he works directly for the top leaders, who are lazy and depend on the clerks to think for them." He pointed his thumb at me as if I were to become such a clerk. "You write their speeches, suggest ideas, and even handle small matters on their behalf. So you rub elbows with those big shots every day. If one of them is pleased with your work or just takes a shine to you, within a couple of years you'll be an official of considerable stature. On top of that, you'll learn about the workings of the government and gradually you'll know how to run the province."

"Well"—I snapped my fingers—"brother, if I were you I'd snatch the opportunity, to become an expert in governance."

Without catching my mockery, he replied, "I don't want to work there, though. So far I've only talked about the bright side of the picture. Let me tell you about the downside. If a leader happens to dislike you, or if any of your colleagues informs your superiors against you, or if you get involved in one of the factions, which is unavoidable, then you're done for. Sooner or later they'll kick you out of the office and banish you to a godforsaken region. They may even stick a criminal name on you and slam you into jail. Ah, it's hard to protect your ass at a place like that."

"How come you know so much about this?" I asked, quite impressed.

"A fellow townsman of mine told me about it. He works at the Provincial Administration."

Weiya picked up, "If the Policy Office wanted a woman, I'd definitely go."

Her serious tone surprised me. She looked at me with a straight face. I couldn't tell whether she was expressing her genuine wish or just trying to enliven the conversation.

"That's not a place for me, though," Banping continued. "I don't have the ambition or the charming personality, and my mind is too slow. I wouldn't survive in the Policy Office. My goal isn't high—all I want is a stable, comfortable life, which the Commerce Department can give me."

I was amazed by his self-estimation. Obviously he was not as dense as I'd thought. I had sensed he possessed some kind of peasant cunning, but never had I expected he knew so clearly his place, needs, objects, and limitations. I bantered, "Come on, of course you have a great personality, or how could Anling have chosen you as her groom?"

"He tricked me!" his wife exclaimed. "You don't know what a big liar he was. He made all sorts of promises. He said he'd take me to Golden Elephant Park every month after we got married. But he's done that only once in a whole year."

"She's not very smart either," her husband said flatly.

We all laughed, including Anling. She pinched the leathery back of his hand.

Having taken leave of Banping and Anling, I walked Weiya back to her dormitory. We didn't talk much on the way; we were both deep in thought. The traffic was still throbbing in the west; now and then an automobile honked. The sidewalk was almost covered by broad sycamore leaves. Here and there moonlight filtered through the trees, casting dappled patches on the asphalt. Scabby-barked poplar trunks shimmered in the damp air while insects chirred. As we reached the eastern part of the campus, our shadows, mine almost twice as large as hers, collided time and again on the ground.

I glanced at her. She looked pale in the moonlight, but her face glowed with a soft shine. Her footsteps were springy and vigorous. For some reason I was suddenly gripped by the desire to touch her, my right hand, so close to her waist, trembling a little. I thrust it into my pants pocket and focused on watching our shadows mingling on the ground. Probably it was the grief and madness jammed into my chest during the afternoon that drew me closer to her. Walking with her made me feel less lonely. To me, she was quite attractive, but I liked her also because she was reliable and well read and had her own opinions. She could paint almost like a professional, and was especially good at portraiture. I was glad she would remain in the department as an instructor in classical fiction.

We said good night at the ilex bushes about fifty yards away from her dormitory building. I turned back without waiting for her to disappear from the dimly lighted doorway as most men would do for their female friends. It was safe on campus.

4

It was well past midnight, and my roommates were sleeping soundly. Outside, the drizzle rustled through the leaves of trees. The room was dank and fusty. A mouse scuttled across the ceiling; there were at least a dozen mice in the roof. Mantao murmured something and let out a curse in his sleep. He went on grinding his teeth, which, according to folk medicine, indicated that he might have roundworms in his stomach. I envied the way he slept — day or night, the moment his head touched a pillow, he'd begin to snore loudly. Sometimes my other roommate, Huran, would shout at him and beg him to roll on his side so that he would stop snoring for a while. Tonight I couldn't sleep, missing my fiancée and puzzling over the possible causes of my teacher's stroke.

According to Banping, it was Professor Song, the chairman of the Literature Department, who had crushed our teacher. Indeed, Mr. Yang and Professor Song had often locked horns. The animosity between them culminated in a quarrel over the birthplace of the great poet Li Po a year ago.

In his paper on Tang poetry, Professor Song had adopted a recent claim that the poet was born in Kazakhstan, somewhere south of Lake Balkhash. In fact, this "biographical discovery" might have been intended to validate the patriotic view that China's map in the Tang Dynasty was much vaster than today, so as to refute the Russian assertion that the Great Wall used to be China's borderline. Mr. Yang believed this was pseudo-scholarship, so he insisted that Professor Song change the poet's birthplace to Szechwan if the paper was to be included in *Studies in Classical Literature*, a journal he was editing. Professor Song refused and asserted that nobody was really clear about this issue. Separately the two scholars looked it up in a number of books, which gave at least seven places as Li Po's birthplace, including Shandong Province and Nanjing City, both in eastern China, probably because the poet was peripatetic all his life. "I wouldn't even alter a dot," Professor Song declared to others. So Mr. Yang turned down his paper. The chairman was outraged and told everyone that he had withdrawn it by choice. A few days later the altercation resumed. This time they both lost their temper, calling each other names and banging their fists on the pinewood desktop in Mr. Song's office. They pointed at each other's faces, as if each was trying to thrust his own idea into his opponent's head. There might have been a scuffle if their colleagues hadn't separated them.

Eager to retaliate, Professor Song prevented Mr. Yang from being promoted to full professor and even said he'd get the journal transferred to "reliable hands." In recent months he seized every opportunity to criticize Mr. Yang. For this reason, Banping believed it was the pressure from Professor Song that had crushed our teacher.

I didn't take this to be the main cause. Though the two professors disliked each other, their enmity had originated from their common interest — literary scholarship. The chief obstacle to their reconciliation might be that Professor Song was the chairman and that if Mr. Yang had apologized first, he'd have appeared to stoop to power. Even if their falling-out were irreconcilable, Professor Song could hardly have destroyed my teacher. During the Cultural Revolution, Mr. Yang had been paraded through campus as a Demon-Monster once a week for more than half a year; if he had survived that kind of torment, a few skirmishes with a colleague shouldn't have driven him out of his mind.

But what Weiya had said at the dinner might be a matter of ugly consequences. A year ago Mr. Yang had received an invitation to speak at a conference in Vancouver. For a long time he couldn't get funding for the trip. The Canadian side assumed he might never make it, so they replaced his talk with another one. Meanwhile, Mr. Yang wrote letters to our school leaders and even to officials at the Provincial Administration, begging for dollars. To be fair, our college did take the invitation seriously, because this was the first time a faculty member in the humanities here had been invited to lecture abroad. To Mr. Yang, this must have been a once-in-a-lifetime opportunity; never having gone abroad, he was naturally eager to visit Canada. Yet not until a month before the conference did he obtain enough funding from our school. Despite the tardiness, he set out anyway, probably knowing he was no longer on the panel. He didn't give his talk in Vancouver, but met some foreign sinologists there.

On his way back he stopped at San Francisco for two days to see a friend of his, a philosophy professor at UC-Berkeley.

He returned unhappy and slightly fatter, but with a two-door refrigerator, which kindled a great deal of envy among the faculty and staff here. Soon people began to whisper that he had gone to North America just for sight-seeing and so that he could pocket the foreign currency (he had been given an allowance of thirty-four dollars a day, which he saved for the refrigerator of Chinese make). He couldn't exonerate himself from such an accusation. If the school now demanded the $1,800 back, Mr. Yang couldn't possibly pay up such a debt.

Although I could accept Weiya's explanation, I wouldn't exclude overwork as a major cause of his stroke. Since the previous year he had been compiling a textbook of Tang poetry for graduate students. It was a critical edition, so he needed to supply comments and notes on the poems. Every night he stayed up late at his tiny desk, with books spread on his bed and on the floor, working until three or four in the morning. During the day he had to teach, meet students, and attend meetings. How could he hold out for long if he worked like a camel, sleeping only four or five hours a night? The publisher in Shanghai had pressed him several times, and Mr. Yang had promised to deliver the manuscript by the end of May. I often said to him, "When can you slow down a little?" He would answer with a smile, "I'm a harnessed horse. As long as I'm on my feet, I have to pull the cart." He slapped his belly to show he was strong.

Besides working and writing, he had to take care of himself, since his wife and daughter were not around. He ate lunch in the school's dining hall, but cooked a simple dinner for himself in the evening, always cornmeal porridge or dough-drop soup mixed with vegetables. He hand-laundered his clothes himself. I helped him clean his apartment twice.

Three weeks ago he and I together planted a dozen sunflower seedlings in his small backyard.

There could be another cause of his stroke, which was probably more ruinous than those I have described but which I was reluctant to reveal to my fellow graduate students, namely that his marriage might have been floundering. I couldn't put my finger on the problem, but was certain that Mrs. Yang had gone to Tibet not just for professional reasons. Last May, three months before she left, I had happened to witness a scene. I went to his home to return his volume of *Book of Songs,* an anthology compiled by Confucius 2,600 years ago. Mr. Yang's copy of the book was filled with comments in his cursive handwriting at the tops, margins, and bottoms of the pages. I was the first person he had ever allowed to read his marginalia. At the door of his apartment I heard Mrs. Yang yell from inside, "Leave! Get out of here!"

Mr. Yang countered, "This is my home. Why don't you go?"

"All right, if you don't, I'm leaving."

As I wondered whether I should turn back, the door opened slowly and Mrs. Yang walked out. She was a small angular woman with deep-socketed eyes. Seeing me, she paused, her face contorted and sprinkled with tears. She lowered her head and hurried past without a word, leaving behind the rancid smell of her bedraggled hair. Her black silk skirt almost covered her slender calves; she had bony ankles and narrow feet, wearing red plastic flip-flops.

Mr. Yang saw me and waved me in. On the concrete floor were scattered a brass pen pot and dozens of books, most of which were opened and several with their spines loosened from their sutures. He grimaced, then sighed, shaking his head.

Silently I handed him his book. Though I didn't know why they had fought, the scene unnerved me as I replayed it in my mind later on. Whenever I was with the Yangs I could sense an emotional chasm between my teacher and his wife. I was positive they had become estranged from one another. For some time I couldn't help but wonder whether my fiancée had inherited her mother's fiery disposition, or whether her parents' fights had disturbed her emotionally. But my misgivings didn't last long, as I was soon convinced that by nature Meimei was a cheerful girl, even more rational than myself.

A locomotive blew its steam whistle in the south like a mooing cow. The night had grown deeper and quieter. Having considered these happenings in Mr. Yang's life, I felt none of them alone could have triggered his collapse. Perhaps they had joined forces to bring him down.

5

Nurse Chen put a thermos of hot water on the bedside cabinet in Mr. Yang's room and asked me, "Was your professor educated abroad?" She looked perkier than two days ago.

"No, he's a genuine Chinese product, homebred like you and me."

"I heard him speak foreign words last night."

"Really, in what language?"

"I've no clue, but it was definitely not English or Japanese. It sounded strange."

"Was it like this, *'Wer, wenn ich schriee, hörte mich denn aus der Engel Ordnungen?'*"

She shook her head in amazement, then giggled. "What language is that? You sounded like an officer rapping out orders."

"It's German."

"What does it mean?"

"It's the beginning of a book of poems Mr. Yang often

quoted, *Duino Elegies*. It means 'Who, if I cry, would hear me among the angelic order?' Something like that."

"My, that's deep, I'm impressed. Tell you what, he might have spoken German."

Her praise embarrassed me a little, for that line was the only part of the long poem I had memorized. We often committed a passage or a few lines to memory not only because we liked them but also because we could impress others with them. That's one of the tricks of the academic game.

Mr. Yang had never spoken foreign words during my shift. He could read German and knew some French. He loved Rilke and had once made me read *Duino Elegies* in a bilingual edition after he came to know I had studied German for a year. But I didn't like the poems that much, perhaps because I hadn't read them carefully.

Mali Chen raised her hand, looking at her wristwatch. "I should be going, the doc must be here already. Bye-bye now." She fluttered her fingers at me as she made for the door. She left behind a puff of perfume like almond.

I knew she had come to see Banping, who had left fifteen minutes before. Although Banping appeared clumsy and dull, he had a way of getting along with others, especially with women. We had started caring for our teacher just a few days before, but already he was mixing with the nurses as chummily as if he had known them for months. I wondered whether this was due to his rustic looks and manner, which might tend to put most women at ease — they would drop their guard without fearing any emotional entanglement with him. By comparison, I must have seemed like an eccentric to them, a typical bookworm, high-strung and a bit morose.

Mr. Yang was quiet and stationary. I took out my textbook, *Contemporary Japanese*, and began reviewing some paragraphs marked in pencil. The exams were just a month away, and I had too much to study. Japanese would be a jinx on me; if only I had taken it up a few years earlier.

As I tried parsing a complicated sentence in my mind, Mr. Yang snickered. I raised my head and saw his lips stir murmuring something. I averted my eyes and made an effort to concentrate on the textbook, but in no time his words grew clear. He chuckled and said, "They look like peaches, don't they?" He smacked his lips, his face shining.

My curiosity was piqued. What did he compare to peaches? I put down the book and listened attentively. He beamed, "I'm such a lucky man. He-he-he, you know, your nipples taste like coffee candy. Mmmm . . . ah, let me have them again." His lips parted eagerly.

I was amazed. He was talking to a woman! No wonder he looked so happy. He chuckled, but his words turned ragged.

Who was the woman? His wife? Unlikely. They two had been aloof toward each other in recent years; besides, she couldn't possibly have that kind of breasts. In my mind's eye I saw Mrs. Yang's chest flat like a washboard. She was as thin as a mantis, so the peachy breasts must have belonged to another woman. Could he be having a fling with someone? That was possible. There was a fortyish woman lecturer in the Foreign Languages Department, named Kailing Wang, who had recently collaborated with him in translating Brecht's *Good Woman of Szechwan*. She was quite busty, soft-skinned, and convivial. Mr. Yang and she had been pretty close and often teased each other playfully. Several times I had seen them together in his apartment working on the translation.

They laughed a lot and seemed to enjoy each other's company. Once I saw them chatting over a bottle of plum wine; another time I found her cooking a sausage dinner for him in his apartment. Besides her, a few women faculty members in the Literature Department were also close to him, though they dared not show their friendship overtly for fear of Professor Song's notice.

On the other hand, the peachy breasts could belong to his wife, if Mr. Yang had in his mind an intimate moment from their early years. She might have had a full body when she was young. Or perhaps this erotic episode had occurred only in his dream, not in reality.

"Sorry, there's no chamber pot in here," Mr. Yang said. "He-he, you'd better peepee into the washbasin under the bed . . ." Gleefully he imitated the urinating sound: "Pshhhhh, pshhhhh, pshhhhhh —yes, yes, use the basin."

The thought came to me that he must have been in a dormitory or a guesthouse, since every home would have a chamber pot or a toilet.

"I can see you," he piped, then grinned, baring his tobacco-stained teeth.

Who was the woman he was talking to? She might not be his wife, because the Yangs had a toilet in their apartment, which she could use at night. When did this happen? Long ago?

Then I began to revise my reasoning, since it was entirely possible that he and his wife had stayed a night somewhere other than their home and had had to resort to a washbasin in place of a chamber pot.

"My goodness," Mr. Yang said with increasing relish, "how I adore your hips. Gorgeous, like two large loaves of bread fresh from a steamer." He paused, chuckling, then went on,

"Yes, I'm shameless, can't help it, shameless and crazy. Come on, give me one on the mouth."

I was all ears, but his voice was dwindling, though he still smiled mysteriously. I listened for another minute without understanding a thing, so I returned to my textbook.

But soon he started moaning. His voice suggested a sheep bleating and jarred on my nerves. In my heart I couldn't help but blame him: *Come on, stop speaking in riddles. If you want to say something, spill it out. I have to work. If I flunk the exams, I won't be able to go to Beijing and taste Meimei's nipples there.*

To my astonishment, he shouted without opening his eyes, "Forget it! I know you just want to ruin me."

I held my breath, wondering what this was about. He went on angrily, "I have no savings. Even if you kill me, I cannot come up with that kind of money." After a pause, he resumed, "I never knew you were so sneaky. Why did you encourage me to go abroad in the first place? You set a trap for me, didn't you? Now go away. I cannot bear the sight of you."

Undoubtedly he was talking about the $1,800 he had spent. Weiya was right—the university must indeed have demanded that he pay the money back. But who was he talking to? A school official? That seemed implausible, because his familiar tone of voice indicated that he knew the person quite well. According to Weiya's account, it was Secretary Peng who had pressed him for the money. The unidentified person could be she, but how had she set a trap for him? Ignorant and almost illiterate, she couldn't possibly have known how a Canadian conference operated and that Mr. Yang, though already taken off the panel, would go to North America merely for sight-seeing. This made no sense to me.

"Let me tell you, I shall never knuckle under to you," he sneered. His face, flushing, expanded with rage while his lips turned blue and sweat beaded on his cheeks. Never had I seen him so angry. Could he be arguing with Secretary Peng? I wasn't sure. He had always been polite to her, at least in appearance, though I knew he despised her at heart. The words he had just uttered sounded more like something he would spit in Professor Song's face. Could Song be the schemer?

Mr. Yang interrupted my thoughts, declaring in a raspy voice, "Nobody can destroy my soul!"

I was perplexed. This seemed irrelevant to what had gone before. Where was he now? With the same person?

Then his face began twisting, his stout nose red and crinkled. He looked in pain, groaning, "Oh, don't hurt my children, please! Don't separate them! I beg you to leave them alone." He began sniveling, tears gathering at the corners of his eyes. His flabby chin kept shaking as if stung by something. Yet I couldn't tell whether he was really heartbroken or just shamming.

This was crazy, beyond me. Having only one child, why did he mention his children and beg his tormentor not to separate them? Apparently he had mixed things up. On second thought I wondered if he had another daughter or a son I didn't know of, in other words, an illegitimate one. This was hardly plausible. To my knowledge, Meimei had always been her parents' only child.

Now Mr. Yang was wailing, tears wetting his cheeks. I went over and waved my hand before his glazed eyes, which gave no response. He seemed at another place, dealing with a different person. He cried out, "I don't want a full professorship anymore! Give it to anyone you like. I don't need a larger apartment either, I'm completely satisfied with what I have. Oh, please don't be so mean! Have mercy! I've a family to keep. Don't separate my children. For heaven's sake, can't you leave me alone?" He had to stop to catch his breath. With a warm towel I wiped his face, which went on shaking.

Although he sounded stubborn and grief-stricken, he now looked obsequious, as if making an effort to smile ingratiatingly. His jaw muscles were tight, trembling. He resumed speaking, but his voice grew weaker and weaker, his words again unintelligible. Hard as I tried, I couldn't figure out anything. Meanwhile, the look on his face became more and more fawning. He smiled and moaned alternately. Never had I seen such an eerie face, which raised goose bumps on my forearms.

I was confused and upset. When I took over from Banping, I had expected a relatively quiet afternoon, like the day before, so that I could review a few chapters of the textbook, but again Mr. Yang spoiled my plan. My desire for work was all gone. Stretched out on the wicker chair, I closed my eyes and gave free rein to my thoughts about his secret life.

6

I was still gloomy after dinner. Having no desire to study, I didn't go to Mr. Yang's office as I had planned, and instead returned to the dormitory. Fortunately on my bed was a letter from Meimei. I brushed a winged ant off my sheet, lay down, and opened the envelope. She obviously hadn't received my letter about her father's condition yet. She said:

April 19, 1989

Dear Jian,

How is everything? Have you quit smoking? Each year four million people die of smoking-related diseases in our country. Please follow my advice and quit. You know I cannot stand the smell of tobacco.

It's getting hot in Beijing, and sometimes windy and dusty. My school is kind of chaotic at this moment, because every day thousands of students take to the streets to demonstrate against official corruption. They're especially angry at the top leaders' children who have made fortunes by taking advantage of their offices and connections. Many students are talking about marching to Tiananmen Square. I have heard that this is a joint effort of the students from several colleges in Beijing. They demand rapid political reform and that the government take drastic measures to stop corruption and inflation. I don't believe their demonstrations can change anything, so up to now I have avoided participating. I am going to take the exams in less than five weeks. For the time being, nothing is more important to me than getting ready for them.

How is your preparation going? If you run into any difficulty, feel free to ask my dad for help. Try to concentrate on foreign languages and politics. These are the areas where people tend to stumble. Of course you know this, and I have more confidence in you than in myself. You will definitely score high points in all the subjects. You're one of the best rising scholars, as my dad often says.

I guess you haven't yet figured out what I like most about you. I won't tell you now, but I may in the future. I have enclosed my kisses and hugs. Take care.

Yours,

Meimei

I had heard of the students' demonstrations in Beijing, but hadn't thought they would reach such a large scale. These days I rarely listened to the Voice of America or the BBC. My roommate Mantao, who had followed the news, often mentioned the demonstrations. But every evening, after dinner, I would spend several hours in Mr. Yang's office reviewing textbooks; when I came back, my roommates would have gone to sleep, so we seldom talked. I had to devote myself to the preparation for the Ph.D. exams. Such a degree would eventually place me among the top literary scholars in China. Currently there were only a few thousand doctoral students in the whole country, and less than ten percent of them were in the humanities.

Meimei was right to shun political activities. My parents had always urged me to steer clear of politics. My father had once been an editor in Tianjin City, in charge of a column on women's issues. Because he publicly criticized the Party secretary at his newspaper, he had been branded a rightist and banished to Fujin, a frontier town in Heilongjiang Province, where he worked on a tree farm for over thirty years. Meimei was smart and coolheaded and would never entangle herself in politics. She planned to specialize in pediatrics after getting her bachelor's degree, and had applied to a medical program in Beijing. She would not consider going elsewhere because she loved the capital. In fact, only by becoming a graduate student, who didn't need a job assignment that might take her anywhere, could she be allowed to remain in Beijing legally.

I got up from my bed, dropped my cigarette butt on the concrete floor, and stamped it out. I had quit smoking for two months, but after Mr. Yang collapsed, I had started again. These days I'd smoke almost half a pack a day.

Feeling grimy all over, I picked up my basin and went out to the washroom. The long corridor was dark, reeking of mildew and urine thanks to the toilet at its east end. Mosquitoes and gnats were flickering like crazy. I had nothing on but my green boxers. These dormitory houses were inhabited only by male students except for three or four graduate students' wives, so most of us would walk naked-backed to the washrooms and even to the bicycle shed outside.

After scrubbing myself with a towel and cold water, I felt refreshed. I sat down at the only desk in our bedroom and began a letter to Meimei. My roommates hadn't returned yet, so I had some privacy. I wrote:

April 25, 1989
Dear Meimei,

I wasn't happy today, but your letter came like a breath of fresh air and made this evening different. You are very wise not to join the political activities at your college. Politics is a ground too treacherous for small people like us to tread. It's as poisonous as acid rain.

These days I have been cramming for the exams. Japanese is debilitating me; however hard I try, my mind cannot get into it. There are so many other things going on here that I can hardly concentrate. But I shall apply myself harder, to conquer Japanese. I understand that this may be the only opportunity for me to join you in Beijing, and that I must cherish it.

I assume that by now you have received my previous letter. Your father is doing poorly, though his condition has stabilized. Don't worry. There is no need for you to rush back; I am here with him. Good luck with your preparation. I miss you, a lot.

Your hubby-to-be,
Jian

Having sealed the letter, I turned on my Panda transistor radio and listened to the Voice of America. To my astonishment, there came the sound of people singing songs and shouting slogans. The woman reporter announced in slow, simple English that a throng of students from the People's University were on their way to Tiananmen Square, to join those already there. Through the sputtering static I could hear hundreds of voices shouting in unison, "We shall not return without a full victory!" "Down with corruption!" "It's everyone's duty to save the country!" "Give us freedom and democracy!"

7

To my surprise, Meimei came back the next afternoon, but she could stay only a day because she wouldn't disrupt her study. For a whole evening she was in the hospital with her father. Her presence pacified him and he stopped talking nonsense. All the sulkiness and the idiot grin had vanished from his face. When she fed him dinner, he didn't make any noise, but instead opened his mouth compliantly and chewed the steamed apple with relish. The thought occurred to me that if she had been with him all along, his condition might have improved much more.

Although animated, Meimei was tired, her eyes clouded and her hair a bit straggly. The previous night she hadn't slept, taking the eleven-hour train ride back to Shanning. After dinner, I urged her to go home and have a good sleep, but she wouldn't leave.

Soon Mr. Yang began to have the fidgets, apparently bothered by something on his back. Meimei inserted her hand underneath his shirt and scratched him a little; still he wouldn't stop squirming. She unbuttoned his shirt and found a festering boil below his left shoulder blade, about the size of an adzuki bean. She was unhappy about the discovery and said I should have rubbed him with a clean towel at least once every other day. True, I hadn't done enough to help him with his personal hygiene, not because I was lazy or careless but because I didn't know what to do. By nature I was an absent-minded man and often neglected small things. That might be why people called me "the Poet," though I had never written a poem. I had wiped Mr. Yang's face with a warm towel every day and had bathed his varicosed feet once, but had done nothing else. I was sure that Banping didn't even bother about our teacher's face. Usually he would just sit in the room reading a book or stand in the corridor chatting with a nurse or a patient. Now I felt ashamed that I hadn't cared for my teacher the way I should have.

Meimei removed a tiny safety pin from the waist of her pants and pierced the head of her father's boil to drain the pus. She then wiped the abscessed area for a good while with a cotton ball soaked with alcohol. After that, she went on to squeeze a few pimples on his back. Following her orders, I fetched two thermoses of hot water. Together we took off Mr. Yang's pajamas and set about scrubbing him with warm towels. Lying facedown, he moaned with pleasure while steam rose from his pinkish flesh.

Done with his back, we turned him over to rub his front. His eyes narrowed as a contented smile emerged on his face.

After we helped him into clean clothes, Meimei began brushing his teeth. He opened his mouth, displaying his diseased gums, which were ulcerated in places and bleeding a little. His tongue was heavily furred. "Good heavens," Meimei said to me, "what have you been doing these days? You could at least have kept him clean."

"I'm sorry, nobody told me what to do."

"This is common sense."

"Sorry, if only I had known."

"Every three or four hours we should turn him over, let him lie on his stomach for a while, otherwise he'll grow bedsores."

"I'll remember that."

"The nurses should be fired."

"Yes, they haven't done much to help him either."

"What do they do when they're here?"

"They just sit around knitting or thumbing through magazines."

She brushed his teeth twice, saying his gingivitis was severe. If only there were a way to treat his gum condition. Most dentists in town merely pulled or filled teeth, and few were good at dealing with periodontal disease. As Meimei was busy working on her father, I fetched more water. Together we began washing Mr. Yang's head over a basin. With both hands I held the nape of his neck, which felt squishy, while Meimei soaped his gray hair. A whiff of decay escaped from his insides, and I turned my face with bated breath. Meimei scooped up water with her palms cupped together and let it fall on his head to rinse the suds away. In no time hundreds of hairs floated in the bluish foam, and the inside of the white basin became ringed with greasy dirt. If only I had washed his hair before Meimei had returned.

After the washing, I shaved him and with a pair of scissors trimmed his mustache and clipped his nose hair. He looked normal now, his face glowing with a reddish sheen.

I took Meimei home after ten o'clock, when the streets were full of people who had just come out of night schools. She sat sideways at the rear of my bicycle, her face pressed against my back and her arm hooked around my waist. The warmth of her body excited me so much that I continually cranked the bell on the handlebar and even ran a red light.

Afraid she might find out that I had started smoking again, I had brushed my teeth and tongue after dinner, using her father's toothbrush with its flattened bristles, since I didn't have mine with me. Still, when we were alone in her parents' apartment and in each other's arms, she detected tobacco on my breath. "You stink," she said and sprang to her feet. She moved away and sat down on a chair, leaving me alone on the sofa. Abashed, I looked at her, my face burning.

She began lecturing me, and I listened without talking back. She said, "Your breath makes me sick. How many times did I tell you to quit smoking? Why did you take my words as just a puff of meaningless breath? Look, even your fingers are yellow now. Why can't you keep your promise? You know tobacco will blacken your lungs and give you tracheitis, but you just smoke to show how cool you are."

"Sorry, I couldn't help it," I mumbled.

"If you continue to be a smoker, how can we live together in the future? Besides, this is playing ducks and drakes with money . . ."

I felt ashamed and remained tongue-tied, just letting her fume at me. After she was done, I promised her that I would quit smoking this time and wouldn't use her father's illness as an excuse again. I had planned to take her to bed, but now intimacy was out of the question because her temper hadn't subsided yet. Also, she was utterly exhausted, unable to keep her eyes open. So I urged her to go to bed. She washed her face and bathed her feet, then padded into the bedroom and closed the door. I slept on the sofa in their living room, not daring to disturb her during the night.

The next morning she and I went to the hospital again. Banping was happy when we relieved him. After combing Mr. Yang's hair and brushing his teeth, we both sat down, she seated on my lap as there wasn't another chair in the room. The night's sleep had refreshed her thoroughly; her features were vivacious again, mischievously mocking at times. Her checkered dress was rather homely, washed out, hanging on her loosely, so I didn't have to worry about rumpling it. She was visibly excited, her eyes radiating a soft light and her full lips slightly curled. I couldn't help nuzzling her hair to inhale its hazelnutlike scent. Now and again I'd kiss her neck or gently twist her small silken ear despite fearing that her father might notice what I was doing.

We chatted about the students' demonstrations in Beijing while Mr. Yang listened quietly. Gradually our topic shifted to preparations for the exams. For one of the six slots in a graduate program in pediatrics, Meimei would have to compete with over a hundred applicants.

"We've formed a group to study political economy and the Party's history," she told me.

"Does it help?"

"Of course, a lot. We test each other with the questions that may appear in the exam. This method can make us remember the answers better, and also gives us some fun when we're working on the questions together. Besides memorizing all the answers, there's no other way to prepare for the political exam." She smiled and her chin jutted.

"That's true," I agreed. "But what a waste of time. Each year some of the answers differ from the previous year, especially in the history of the Chinese Communist Party. All depends on who is in power now—the winners always revise the history to make the losers look like a bunch of criminals."

"Don't be so cynical," she said. "We've no choice but to give the expected answers."

"I can't spend too much time on politics. The other subjects make more sense to me."

"You ought to take the political exam seriously. Last year a student in my school scored the highest in all subjects except politics. He flunked it miserably, only got forty-six points. That gave him a terrible time, although he was really smart, fluent in both English and Russian."

"Did he get into a graduate program eventually?"

"Yes, but only after a lot of trouble. The Shanghai Military Medical University was determined to have him and sent a team of three people to our school. They held meetings and asked the other students about his political attitude and activities. Everybody said something in his favor, so he was admitted as a special case two months later, approved by the Ministry of Education."

"Lucky for him."

"Yes, only because he was absolutely phenomenal. We may never have that kind of luck, so work hard on the Party's history and dialectical materialism." Somehow she left out political economy and current events, each of which would constitute a quarter of the exam as well.

"I will, don't worry," I said. "To tell the truth, I fear Japanese most. In the political exam, even if you don't have a definite answer to a question, you can bring your imagination into play, especially when writing the short essays—just make up some sentences. But in a foreign language test, every answer is fixed and there's no room to waffle."

"You know English better than most applicants, so even if you don't do well in the Japanese exam, you'll still have an edge over others. Don't lose heart."

Suddenly Mr. Yang chimed in, "She's right. Also bear in mind that you have a strong recommendation from me. The professors at Beijing University will take my words seriously. So don't waste your time looking after me here. Concentrate on your study. I want to see you two get married and settle down in Beijing. That will make me happy."

I was amazed that he spoke so rationally. Meimei stuck out her tongue, which was red, thin, and narrow. Her face grew naughty, rather boyish. She was so charming that I couldn't help touching her forearm and stroking her legs, though we dared not neck too much in her father's presence. She had a little leg hair, which was brownish and would turn lucent in sunlight. If only we could have stayed outside in the open air.

She had to catch the 12:30 train back to Beijing. She wouldn't let me buy her lunch, saying she could eat in the dining car, which would be a good way to pass the time on the train. Before leaving, she asked me to forgive her for blowing her top the night before. I was not really bothered by that, I told her. I promised to do a better job in taking care of her father—I would sponge him, brush his teeth, and rub his sore with cotton balls soaked with alcohol or peroxide. I would do those every day. Also, I'd bathe his feet and clip his nails regularly, and make sure he didn't get bedsores.

I couldn't go to the train station to see her off, so she left alone.

In the spring of 1987, three months before I met Meimei, a Hong Kong trade company had come to Shanning University to recruit employees. They wanted only graduate students who knew both English and Chinese well, and they gave the applicants written tests in both languages. Dozens of people applied for the jobs, which paid at least ten times more than a regular college graduate could earn in mainland China. I took the tests and somehow came out second, probably because my English was better than the others'. So the company was eager to hire me. The head of the recruiting group talked to me twice, promising me subsidies for housing and even for my future children's education; he also mentioned I'd receive a generous bonus at the end of every year. Most people here coveted this opportunity. After hearing of my test results, Banping congratulated me, saying he wished he had studied English devotedly. He hadn't even attempted the tests. Yet I was unsure whether I should go to Hong Kong. I asked Weiya, who couldn't say for certain either; she too thought this was a rare opportunity, though she believed I was not cut out to be a businessman. Numerous faculty members said to me in private that I shouldn't hesitate to grab the offer. One of them whispered to me, "Don't just have a one-track mind, Jian. Whatever we do, teaching or writing, in essence we all struggle to make a living. That job pays so well that you'll become a millionaire eventually."

Yet the more I heard from others, the more uncertain I became. I dared not seek Mr. Yang's advice, fearing he might scold me. I knew he disliked the idea of my going into business.

One late afternoon, as I was leaving the classroom building, my teacher caught sight of me and called to me. I froze in my tracks at the side door.

Coming up to me, he said, "Going home?"

"Yes," I answered, then together we resumed walking. Silently we strolled toward the street outside the campus. On the dusty playing field some undergraduates were chasing a soccer ball and two stout women were practicing the shot put. A group of students in sweat suits were drawing lines for a sports meet, dribbling liquid whitewash from kettles to the ground on the outskirts of the field.

Mr. Yang said to me, "I've heard you want to go to Hong Kong to become a businessman." His tone was rather sardonic.

Disconcerted, I replied, "They are interested in me, but I haven't decided yet."

"Do you think you're good at handling imports and exports?" His voice turned serious.

"I don't know."

"Can you dispense with the study of poetry? Maybe you can, and I have been wrong about you."

"That's what I've been thinking about. Honestly I don't feel like going into business. I love poetry, you know that, but everybody wants to get rich nowadays."

"Well, you are not everybody." He slowed down his pace and pointed at a thirtyish man pulling a cart loaded with cinders and garbage, the man's naked back dripping sweat. "Look at that fellow over there," Mr. Yang went on. "No matter how much money he has, I bet he will sleep on the street tonight. Even if he makes tens of thousands of yuan someday, he will never become a man who is really rich. He won't want to stay at a hotel or fly to Shanghai. He was born poor and will remain so."

"What do you mean?" I muttered, uneasy about the superiority he felt over the trash collector.

"If you are determined to study literature, spiritually you must be an aristocrat. Many of us have been poor all our lives, but we are rich in our hearts, content to be a Don Quixote."

I didn't know how to respond to that and kept walking silently.

Placing his hand on my shoulder, he added, "Think about this matter carefully, Jian. I won't make you do anything against your heart, but it's time for you to choose your way of life."

It took me a few days' soul-searching to make up my mind. When I told Mr. Yang about my decision to abandon the lucrative opportunity, he said with his eyes shining, "Jian, I knew you would be clearheaded about this. If you were someone else, I wouldn't have bothered to talk to you about it. From now on, I'll make you work harder."

"I'm looking forward to that."

I was moved by my own choice, which I regarded as a sacrifice. On the other hand, once the decision was made, I suddenly felt at peace, and even my dinner tasted better. Gradually I could see that Professor Yang treated me differently from the other graduate students; he often assigned books and papers for me to read alone.

Half a year later, his daughter and I got engaged.

8

I apologized to Banping for being late, delayed on the way by traffic.

"That's all right," he said.

"How was he this morning?" I asked about Mr. Yang.

"Awful."

"What happened?"

"He sang a lot of songs."

"What did he sing?"

"All kinds of stuff, from revolutionary chants to opera snatches." Banping shook his head, smiling facetiously.

His smile evoked a strange feeling in me, a mixture of sadness and aversion. In my head a voice suddenly said about our teacher, *He'd be better off if he lost his speech*.

Meanwhile Mr. Yang was asleep, his nose making a tremulous sound.

Banping walked out, holding a battered black umbrella and a bulky book, *An Omnibus of Spy Stories*. He had been writing a detective novel, which I wasn't sure he'd ever finish.

I had noticed that his feather bookmark was moved toward the back of the book about a hundred pages a day. He still could read quite a bit while attending our teacher, whose rigmarole didn't seem to bother him at all. Today I had with me only a pocket English dictionary. I sat down and began reviewing the word entries I had underlined.

About half an hour later Mr. Yang stirred and muttered something. I tried to ignore him, but couldn't help glancing at him from time to time. His flabby face, less puffy today, was duck-egg green, and his hair looked shaggy despite the fact that I had washed and combed it the previous afternoon. His lips quivered weirdly. For a moment I couldn't understand his odd facial expression—the corners of his mouth jerked while he breathed noisily.

Was he crying? He didn't look so. He must be smiling at someone. I knew that whenever he was in good spirits, his tongue would lick his upper teeth. He had often smiled like this in class. I averted my eyes. As long as he kept everything to himself, I'd go on perusing the dictionary.

But soon he started speaking aloud. I couldn't help but crane forward listening. He seemed to be reciting something. He definitely looked happy, pinkish patches rising on his face while his lungs labored wheezily. All of a sudden words poured out of his mouth:

> *Oh glorious stars, oh light infused with*
> *Divine Power, to you I owe all my genius —*
> *Whatever be its worth.*
> *Born with you and hidden with you,*
> *He who is the father of mortal life,*
> *When I first breathed the Tuscan air.*

And far away, as I was granted the grace to enter
  The high wheeling sphere in which you roll around,
  Your very region was assigned to me.
Devoutly my soul sighs to you now
  So that it may gain the strength
  For the hard journey leading to the final end.

He paused, beaming, but his mouth, its corners twitching, reminded me of a rabbit that had just bitten hot pepper. "You cannot trap my soul, nobody can!" he cried stridently.

What poem is that? I wondered. Its joyful, sonorous tone and its fluid cadence suggested a foreign poem. The heavenly vision was definitely not something that would occur in Chinese poetry. Then I realized it must be a passage from *The Divine Comedy.*

He recited again:

"You are so close to the ultimate bliss,"
  Beatrice began, "that you must purify your passion
  And keep your eyes clear and keen.
Before you go further into it,
  Look down and see how much of the world
  I have spread beneath your feet,
So that your heart, with full joy,
  May show itself to the triumphant throng
  Who comes rejoicing through the surrounding air."

He stopped, as if to think about the words voiced by Beatrice, whose name enabled me to locate where Mr. Yang was in *The Divine Comedy*. He was in *Paradiso,* because only in that book did Beatrice meet Dante.

As he went on reciting, his face became more relaxed, but his words were disordered and unintelligible at times. I made no effort to follow him. Even if I had understood everything he uttered, I couldn't have shared Dante's heavenly vision. I was on earth, in this hellhole, whereas he was led by Beatrice through the divine domain and basked in the chaste love and the celestial light. Perhaps only a deranged person could enjoy such a sublime illusion.

Then I curbed my irreverent thoughts as I remembered what *The Divine Comedy* meant to Mr. Yang. The poem had once saved his life.

Two years ago, on an early-summer morning, I had gone to his office and found him hunched over his desk reading a well-thumbed book. Stepping closer, I attempted to sneak a look at its title. He realized my intention and raised the book to show me its front cover, which contained a picture of numerous fists, of various sizes, all stabbed upward into the air. It was *Inferno*. "Have you read Dante?" he asked me in a nasal voice. He had a stuffy nose as a result of a cold.

"No, I haven't." Unable to say yes, I was somewhat embarrassed.

"You should read *The Divine Comedy*. After you finish it, you will look at the world differently."

So I borrowed all three books of the poem from the library and went through them in two weeks, but I didn't enjoy the poem and felt the world remained the same. On the other hand, I was horrified by the filth and torture to which the damned are subject in *Inferno*. When I told Mr. Yang that I had read the poem, he asked me to comment on it. Taken by surprise, I had little to say and just summarized some grisly scenes in hell. My thoughts rambled, and I even talked about the austere woodcut illustrations.

I was making a fool of myself, because he knew those scenes by heart. A copy of *Purgatorio* was lying on his desk. He must read Dante every day.

"Where are we now?" he asked me.

"What do you mean?"

"Which one of the three worlds described by Dante are we in now? We're certainly not in paradise, are we?"

Somehow a popular song came to mind, so I quoted its last line with a straight face, "Our life is sweeter than honey."

He burst out laughing. "You have a sense of humor, Jian. That's good. Humor can make one detached. I wish I had it." Then his face went somber again. "We're neither in paradise nor in hell. We're stuck in between hell and purgatory, don't you think?" He smiled enigmatically, chewing his lip.

"Maybe. I'll think about it," I mumbled, unable to understand his bizarre notion. I wanted to end our conversation there. There was enough Tang poetry for me to work at, and I had no need for such a huge Christian poem to clutter my mind. I turned my head. On the wall hung a painting Weiya had done for him. In it a tubby, smiley monk was eating a gourd ladle of figs while fanning his naked paunch, on which were stuck a few scraps of fig skin.

Mr. Yang resumed, "This is my favorite poem. It saved my life."

"How?" My interest revived.

"When the Cultural Revolution broke out, I came under attack as a Demon-Monster because I had translated some foreign poems and once argued that Goethe was a great poet. Sometimes the Revolutionary Rebels on campus planted on my head a dunce hat with my family name written on it. Sometimes they tied a bucket filled with water around my neck to bend my body and keep my head low. Sometimes they made me kneel on a washboard. Even when my knees began bleeding, they wouldn't allow me to get up. But during the torture I would recite to myself lines from *The Divine Comedy.* They could hurt me physically, but they could not subdue my soul. Whenever I closed my eyes, I saw the scenes in *Inferno.* If they forced me to open my eyes, I'd imagine that the crazed people below and around me were like the blustering evildoers, devils, and monsters cast into hell. They were cruel and desperate because they were hopeless. While reciting *The Divine Comedy* in my heart, I felt that my suffering was meant to help me enter purgatory. I had hope. Suffering can refine the soul. Beyond purgatory there's paradise."

"Are you a Christian?" I blurted out, unable to see why he had taken pains to memorize such a long poem.

"No, I've never been truly religious. But at that time, under torture, I often wished I were a Christian so that I could have prayed to God wholeheartedly. Religion is spiritual opium, as Marx has taught us. No doubt about that, yet once in a while human beings need some spiritual narcotics to alleviate pain. The flesh alone cannot sustain us. In any case, this poem helped me, comforted me, encouraged me, tided me over many moments when I thought of ending my life." With a grimace he lifted his hand and clutched his throat, sticking out his fat tongue. He then picked up the copy of *Purgatorio* from his desk and waved it at me, as if to convince me of the boundless power the flimsy paperback possessed.

Now his body was confined to this hospital bed while his mind roamed the empyrean, as though the Christian divine spheres could also admit pagans as long as they had been humble and virtuous in their lives. I kept quiet, not to disturb his hallucinatory journey so that he could enjoy the bliss a little longer.

I turned a page of my dictionary and resumed reading while his mouth writhed and a smile broke out on his face. From time to time I'd watch him.

Outside, a siren started screaming. There must be a fire somewhere nearby. I couldn't tell which direction the siren came from, because the mountain of anthracite outside the window had put me out of my bearings. As the siren squealed louder and louder, Mr. Yang stirred, whispering, "Fire, fire, that's the holy fire. Burn them, burn those devils!"

I listened closely. He sighed, "Yes, fire and rose are one." He opened his eyes and looked around. He noticed me and gazed at my face intently for a moment. Then he made an effort to turn to face the window, but he couldn't move his left shoulder. I got up and went over.

"Give me a hand, please," he said.

I lifted his back and made him sit up. Supporting his back with my right arm, I grasped the pillows and put them behind him. He seemed eager to talk, so I returned to the chair, ready to give him an ear.

But before he could start, somebody knocked on the door. I went to answer it. To my surprise, Vice Principal Huang's white head emerged. Since Mr. Yang was hospitalized, no school official had ever come to see him. The tall vice principal took a step forward, holding a string bag of yellow apples, some of which had russet flecks on them. He wore a double-breasted jacket with peaked lapels, which was too large on him and made his triangular face appear thin and small. "How are you, Comrade Jian Wan?" he asked, his walleyes looking me in the face.

I was amazed he knew my name. "Fine, thank you for coming," I said and stepped aside to let him in.

He went up to Mr. Yang. Although over sixty, he looked well preserved, his waist robust but not rotund, and his legs so thin that he was hipless. He said heartily to my teacher, "How are you doing, Old Yang? Do you feel better?" He patted Mr. Yang's hand.

My teacher made no reply. The leader said again, "I came to see you. Look, I brought you some fresh fruit. How are you?" He lifted the apples up and put them on the bedside cabinet.

"I'm good, won't die for a couple of hours," Mr. Yang grunted. I was puzzled by his sullenness, wondering why he showed no respect for the vice principal.

Huang turned to me and put on a smile, saying, "I'm going to talk with your teacher." I realized he meant I should make myself scarce, so I walked out and carefully closed the door.

I loitered in the corridor for a few minutes, then sat down on a long straight-backed bench. I was a bit groggy, my temples aching. The previous night I had pored over a textbook on dialectical materialism and hadn't gone to bed until 3:00 A.M. Now, eyes closed and arms folded, I soon drifted off to sleep.

I had a bizarre dream, in which Meimei and I stayed in an inn at a sandy beach. I was sick with a stomachache, lying in bed and shivering all over. Wearing a white cap and a knee-length skirt, Meimei was cooking crucian carp soup for me on a small alcohol stove we had brought along. Five of its six wicks were afire, hissing softly as the flames licked the bottom of a stainless steel pot. Turning over the fat fish gingerly with a spatula, Meimei crooned a folk song in a soothing voice. Outside, on the bulging sea, a couple of gray sails glided almost motionlessly while a conch horn was tooting somewhere on the shore.

The soup was done. It looked milky and smelled like steamed mussel, but I was too sick to eat it by myself. Meimei tried to feed me with a spoon like a small ladle, which turned out to be too broad for my mouth. She piped into my ear, "Open wide, open wide, my little groom." But my mouth was too narrow for the spoon, and a few drops of broth spilled on the front of my shirt. Tittering, she said, "You have such a tiny mouth, like a pretty girl's."

No matter how hard I tried, I couldn't open my mouth wider, as if my lips had been partly sewn together. My tongue went numb and felt like a wooden stick. I was angry at myself, my heart kicking. I told her to put away the bowl and get into bed. She shed her shirt, poplin skirt, and anklets. She was now in red panties and a white cotton bra; a birthmark the size of a mulberry was under her right breast. Her belly was almost flat; her hips were shapely, concave on the side, each hollow resembling a giant dimple. She lay down and nestled against me. As she touched my forehead, I shuddered—her hand was ice-cold.

"You have a temperature," she said, and her knees, rather warm, kept rubbing my thigh.

"I'll be all right," I muttered, still shaking.

"Uncle, please help me," broke from a voice.

Both of us froze, listening.

"Uncle, have pity," the same childlike voice said again.

I opened my eyes, only to find a scrawny girl, about four or five years old, standing in the hospital corridor between my leather shoes, her chafed hand patting my knee.

"What do you want?" I asked.

"Money." She opened her pale palm, whose edge was coated with dirt. Her dark eyes were large and fierce, sharpened by hunger or fear.

I fished some coins out of my pants pocket and gave them to her. Without a word she ran away on her bent legs, her feet in tattered sneakers. Reaching the end of the corridor, she waved her fist and gave the money to a woman, obviously her mother, who shot glances at me. I glared at the sunken-mouthed woman, cursing under my breath, "Bitch." I felt cheated, as I had thought the child was on her own.

Not knowing how long I had dozed, I rose to my feet, my right leg still sleeping. I was a little anxious and wondered if the visitor had left, so I hobbled to the door of the sickroom and put my ear to the keyhole. Vice Principal Huang was still in there. He was saying earnestly to my teacher, "Let her decide what to do herself, all right?"

"No," Mr. Yang answered.

Silence followed.

About half a minute later, Huang said again, "Okay, Old Yang, take it easy. We'll talk about this when you're well."

My teacher made no response.

Hearing footsteps coming toward the door, I leaped aside. The vice principal came out. He nodded at me, meaning I could go in now. "Take good care of Professor Yang, will you?" he said to me.

"Sure I will."

"Good-bye." Without giving me another look, he walked away. He seemed unhappy and preoccupied.

I tiptoed into the room. Mr. Yang sat on the bed with both heels tucked under him, his head hanging low and his eyes shut. I sat down and observed him closely. He looked like a sleeping Buddha, as inert as a vegetable, but with both hands cupped over his kneecaps instead of rested palm upward. A moment later he opened his eyes a crack. The look on his face showed he was alert, but why had he pretended to be drowsing just now?

"He's gone," I told him.

"Who?"

"Vice Principal Huang."

"Who's he? I don't know him."

Perplexed, I had no idea how to deal with his denial. And anger surged in my chest. Of course he knew Huang. Who else had he been talking with a short while ago? But I kept silent, thinking of the dream I'd just had. Why couldn't I eat the fish soup, my favorite food? My mouth wasn't small at all, at least as big as most people's. As if I could have smelled the delicious soup, I went on sniffing.

Meimei in fact was not a good cook. She couldn't even make steamed bread, not knowing how to use yeast and baking soda, let alone a crucian carp soup. But this didn't bother me. I had promised her that I'd cook most of the time after we married. She said she would wash dishes.

"Revenge!" Mr. Yang bawled, as though he were playing the part of an official executioner or a rowdy in an old opera. "I shall raise this nine-section whip and thrash your fat hips, pack, pack, pack — I want to taste your blood and flesh. Ah, with full resolve I shall root out your whole clan like weeds!

A debt of lives must be paid with lives!" His shrill voice was getting louder and louder.

I was totally baffled, not knowing whether he was faking or truly believed he was onstage. Holding my breath, I watched him wriggling as if he were bound by invisible chains. He looked in pain and probably imagined exchanging words and blows with an enemy.

He chanted ferociously, "I shall eliminate all the vermin of your kind, and shan't withdraw my troops until the red clouds have covered the entire earth . . ."

Dumbfounded, I listened. He enacted this militant role for about half an hour. I couldn't tell why Vice Principal Huang's visit had disturbed him so much. By no means did it seem that the official had come to press him for the $1,800. Then why did Mr. Yang go berserk like this?

9

Two days later Kailing Wang, the woman lecturer in the Foreign Languages Department, came to see Mr. Yang. She brought along a bouquet of red silk roses and a copy of *The Good Woman of Szechwan*, which had just come out from Tomorrow Press in Shanghai. She said the book was well received and there would be a review in the journal *Foreign Drama* praising the brisk, sturdy translation. Having no idea what to do with the artificial flowers, I just held them for her as she tried to talk to my teacher.

She was of medium height and wore a puce dress, which made her appear less plump and set off her full bust. Although her appearance reminded me of Mr. Yang's words about the peachy breasts, I bridled my wayward thoughts. Actually I very much respected Kailing. Ten years ago her husband, a regimental staff officer, had been killed in a border battle between Chinese and Vietnamese armies. Since then, she had raised their son alone. Today apparently she hadn't expected to see my teacher in such a wretched condition. She said to me, her voice torn, "He wasn't like this last week. Why did they tell me on the phone that he was getting better? This is awful!" She kept wringing her hands while her eyes misted up.

Indeed this afternoon Mr. Yang was too delirious to talk with anybody. Now and again his lips twisted into a puerile grin as if he were a victim of Down syndrome. The book that bore his name as a cotranslator made no special impression on him, and Kailing seemed to him a total stranger. To whatever she said he wouldn't respond. I couldn't tell whether he recognized her or not. He grunted and groaned vaguely as if having a migraine, and his upper body shuddered frequently.

Taking Mr. Yang's lifeless hand and folding his fingers, Kailing burst into tears. She went on wiping her cheeks with a white handkerchief. Her face at once looked aged, slightly sallow, as if its muscles had lost their elasticity. Her nose was clogged and a little rounded. As she sobbed, her full chin couldn't stop shaking. Observing her, I wished I could have said something to console her. Then she bent forward to peer into his eyes, which were still blank and rheumy and without any trace of recognition. On his swollen face his eyes appeared thready and his lips parted. I was fighting down the impulse to grab his shoulders and shake him out of this wooden state.

Kailing remained standing in front of him for more than twenty minutes. Now and again she looked into his eyes, eager to find out whether he still knew her, but he seemed like a senseless retardate. I told her that this was just a bad day and that usually he was much more lively and clearheaded. She nodded without a word.

At last she let go of his hand. Placing the book near his knee, she said, "Professor Yang, you must get well. I need you. You promised to work with me on Brecht's poetry." He made no answer.

"I've done a draft of some of his poems and like them very much," she added.

Still he was wordless. She looked at me, her eyes filled with disappointment, while her right thumb was massaging her temple.

On leaving, she told me to let her know if Mr. Yang needed anything. She said quietly, "When he's himself again, show him the book. He'll be pleased."

"I'll do that," I promised, putting the roses on the bed so as to see her off.

"I'm sorry to give way to my emotions like this. I'm so upset." She managed a smile.

"I understand."

"I wish I could've brought some fresh flowers. I went to several stores but couldn't find any."

"Don't worry about that. These last longer."

She smiled rather bitterly and took her leave. As she slouched out of the room, I followed her for a few steps, then stopped to watch her shuffle away until she disappeared at the corner of the stairs.

Whatever her role in Mr. Yang's life, her visit saddened and touched me. She was a widow about whom there had been a great deal of gossip, yet today, in my presence, she was not ashamed of shedding tears for him, a man she cared about deeply. It was common knowledge that after studying a foreign language for some years, some women tended to become effusive, romantic, and even warmhearted. This must be one of the reasons why the girls in the Foreign Languages Department were usually more attractive than those majoring in other fields. But this didn't explain my feelings about Kailing. I was moved by her visit because she had brought into this spooky room some human warmth, which continued to affect me after she left.

Why is *The Good Woman of Szechwan* so popular these days? The question came to mind again. I couldn't figure out a definite answer. I had read several articles on this play, none of which said anything illuminating, all in the manner of a biographical introduction. The critics, or buffs, just praised it as a masterpiece, but couldn't say why. Perhaps because the story was set in China, a place rarely presented in serious Western literature, they had rushed to write about it when Brecht's works could finally be translated into Chinese after the Cultural Revolution. To me, however, the play seemed inferior to *Mother Courage and Her Children* and shouldn't be judged his best drama as they claimed.

Mr. Yang stirred a little and opened his eyes, which seemed apprehensive, shifting. I was puzzled, wondering why he hadn't recognized Kailing just now if he was wide awake.

"Help me, please," he whispered earnestly.

"With what?" I asked in surprise.

"I—I wet my bed." He averted his face.

I touched the sheet beneath his thighs. My goodness, he had soiled his pajamas, the quilt, the sheet, and the cotton-padded mattress. The pallet must have been wet too. "Sit tight, I'll be right back," I told him, then hurried out to the nurses' station.

Hong Jiang, the old woman, happened to be on duty. She came up with me immediately. Together we pulled a rattly gurney loaded with clean bedding and clothing. To my knowledge, this was the first time Mr. Yang had lost control of his bladder, which Nurse Jiang said was common among stroke patients.

At the sight of us my teacher murmured, "I'm sorry, really sorry."

"It's all right. Don't feel bad about it," the nurse told him.

I helped him climb onto the gurney so that Hong Jiang could change the bedding. It was impossible for us to replace the thick pallet, whose rice straw had an eye-catching blotch in the middle, as big as a large lotus leaf, so the nurse spread a plastic bag over the wet spot, then went about making the bed with the things we had brought — she unrolled the thin mattress, threw the sheet over it, and unfolded the quilt. She did everything expertly.

Meanwhile, I took off his striped pajamas and flowered shorts. I crumpled them into a ball and wiped his fleshy thighs and backside with it. He reddened and kept his eyes shut all along. He was very cooperative, so without difficulty I helped him put on the fresh shorts I had taken out of the cabinet, in which his underclothes and socks were stored. Next I pulled the clean pajamas on him, then changed his shirt, whose tail was wet too.

Nurse Jiang drew away the gurney loaded with the soiled bedding and clothing while I was huffing and puffing. Quietly Mr. Yang began sobbing. He lay on his side with his face toward the window. I walked around the bed and said to him, "This is normal. Don't feel so bad."

"I never thought I could become such a nuisance," he said. "Oh, I should have died."

"Come on, nobody blames you."

"I want you to promise me never to tell anyone about this."

"Of course, I won't breathe a word."

"Thank you." He let out a heavy sigh and closed his eyes again.

I leaned my rear end against the windowsill and observed his jowls twitching and his Adam's apple jiggling. Once every few seconds he stuck out his tongue to lick his gray mustache.

I didn't sleep well that night and felt out of sorts in the morning. My temples were numb as though squeezed by a vise. Mr. Yang's ravings had distressed me palpably—my roommates complained that these days I was too irascible. Mantao once said, "Jian, you must have been stuffed with gunpowder. Any sparks can start an explosion." Indeed, my temper often flared. Aside from worrying about my teacher, I was unsure whether I could tackle the exams without thorough preparation.

It was a cool, sunny morning. Raindrops from a shower the night before still flickered on the tops of the elms and willows on campus. On the playing field a tall man in a red gym suit blew a brass whistle and stretched his limbs. Following him, a group of middle-aged men and women were doing calisthenics. Some undergraduates, books in their hands, strolled about among the lilac and cypress bushes, reviewing lessons and reciting texts in foreign languages. Their voices hummed in the air, which throbbed with the sonorous cry of a cuckoo, whose two-note calls stopped each time just long enough to let the foliage absorb the vibration. Beyond the depths of a distant poplar wood, where the bird was, mist spread billowing like a body of water.

On my way to the dining hall I ran into Professor Song. He pulled his pipe from his teeth and waved it to stop me, his other hand holding a black canvas bag on which a pair of seagulls was in flight. Apparently he had just jogged to school, his gaunt face covered with pinkish patches, a film of sweat oozing from his forehead. Mr. Yang's stroke had intensified the concern for health among the older faculty in the department, most of whom had begun exercising seriously. Some went swimming in the afternoon; some often played table tennis in the lobby of the classroom building. They would remind one another that health was their main asset and that as long as they lived long enough, eventually they could get promoted to professorship, so there was no need to work hard.

Mr. Song wore a pair of blue sneakers and a gray jacket, which was shoulderless and barrellike — a standard garment for middle-aged male college teachers at the time. I was amused to see him in such a jacket even when he was jogging.

"How's Mr. Yang?" he asked me.

"Not very well."

"I'm sorry to hear that." He paused for a moment, then went on, "Can you tell him that I'll come to see him when I have time?"

He seemed to treat me as a family member of the Yangs, sounding me out on whether his visit would be welcome. I told him he could go to the hospital anytime.

Then he switched the topic. "How well are you prepared for the exams, Jian?"

"I can't do much these days. I have to spend a lot of time in the hospital."

"Maybe our department should hire somebody to replace you. Do you know if Mr. Yang has some relatives in town?"

"I don't think he has any here."

"How about in the countryside?"

"I have no idea."

"Don't worry, I'll see to this. Our department still has some money left for this year. I'm going to talk to Secretary Peng about it. Meantime, concentrate on the exams, Jian. If the Beijing University program accepts you, that will be a great honor to our department, and Mr. Yang will be pleased too. Also, you'll grow faster as a scholar there." He cleared his throat and spat into a puddle of rainwater on the roadside.

"I'll do my best," I said, glancing at the blob of phlegm floating on the rust-red water.

"Good. If you need any help, let me know."

"I will."

As he walked away, a muffled jangle came from his flank. He always carried a large set of keys on his belt. He left behind a tang of alcohol, sweetishly sour. It was said that he would start his day with a cup of liquor. He was so fond of drink people joked that a bottle was a must if you went to him for help. It was rumored that a graduating senior had once gotten a good job assignment because he had presented Chairman Song with an expensive-looking bottle of French brandy that later turned out to be cheap champagne (another version of the story claimed it was plain water). But I don't think any student would dare to trick him that way.

I was unsure whether Professor Song's concern for Mr. Yang and me was genuine. For over a year, whenever possible, he had kicked me around; since he couldn't always lay his hands on Mr. Yang, he'd take out his anger and frustration on me. A couple of times he criticized me for listening to foreign English broadcasts. The previous summer he assigned me to join a team of faculty members in grading the college entrance exams, so that I had to stay at school two extra weeks after the summer break started. Owing to his opposition, the department had almost refused to hire me as an instructor if I couldn't get into the Ph.D. program at Beijing University. Eventually it agreed to keep me, mainly because I had just published a lengthy paper in *Poetic Inquiry*, which stirred up a debate, and because a few senior faculty argued that I was quite promising in the field. Yet despite my suspicion of Professor Song, I did have some positive feelings about him today. Perhaps he at last meant to make reconciliatory overtures to Mr. Yang.

I went on to the dining hall, which was full of people eating breakfast. There wasn't a single stool in the room, so they were all standing around a dozen tables, whose tops were covered with grease, dust, and dead flies. Most students and staff would go to a much larger dining hall at the southern end of the campus, which was cleaner and had hundreds of stools in it, but this smaller place was closer to my dormitory, so I preferred to eat here. I bought a bowl of millet porridge, a twisted roll, and two salted eggs. Holding my breakfast, I walked across to a corner and began eating.

At the door, Little Owl was delivering a speech again. I call him that because I don't know his name and because his small body, round face, yellow eyes, tufty hair, and aquiline nose always reminded me of an owl. He was known as a madman who had been a lecturer in the Chemistry Department three decades before. In the late 1950s he was branded a rightist, arrested, and sent away to a prison camp near Siberia. When he saw that the convicts were beaten every day and heard that some of them, unable to endure the torture and hard labor, had committed suicide, he started to feign madness. He shouted slogans, chanted songs, imitated animals' cries, talked nonsense, and smeared mud and human feces on himself so as to avoid beating, interrogation, and backbreaking work. He played the idiot for more than twenty years, which helped him outlive most of the convicts. But somehow this faked insanity had grown into his nature—when he was finally released, he could no longer control himself and had to continue to rave and curse every day, suffering from "mental incontinence," as some people put it. He often laughed or wept or blustered randomly; the more attention you paid to him, the more excited he would get. The dining hall was his favorite place for giving speeches.

"Comrades, George Bush is the number-one Current Counterrevolutionary," he announced, still using the outdated language. "Bush has the blackest heart and guts. We must overthrow him, beat him to the ground, and trample on him, so that he will never stand up again!" The ferocity in his voice could hardly arouse any interest from the breakfasters. This was a daily show, of which people had wearied.

Having sensed he didn't have a responsive audience today, Little Owl tried something different. He burst out singing:

> The east wind blows
> While the battle drums roll.
> Who fear whom on the globe?
> People are not afraid

Of the American imperialists,
Who actually fear people. . . .

He sang hysterically, beating time with his tiny fists, one of which had a battered knuckle. Nobody listened to the song, which had been long out of fashion. But today his crazed voice grated on my nerves, so I cried, "Shut up!"

All eyes turned to me as if I were a madman too. Little Owl yelled ecstatically, "Look, comrades, he's on the side of American imperialism!"

Several girls giggled, looking my way. One of them had a carmine dot on her forehead like an Indian woman. I picked up my bowl and started for the door. To my surprise, Little Owl followed me, brandishing his fists and shouting, "Down with this imperialistic lackey! Down with him! Down with this American running dog!" It was as if I were being paraded on the street. I could do nothing but ignore him.

I placed my bowl on the ground under a large elm tree, squatted down on my heels, and resumed eating. I peeled an egg, but no sooner had I taken a bite of it than a hand was thrust before my face. It was Little Owl's dirty, scabbed paw. He wanted to share my breakfast.

"Get lost!" I said.

He declared vociferously, "Chairman Mao has instructed us: 'We come from all corners of the country and have joined together for a common revolutionary cause. So our cadres must show concern for every soldier, and all people in the revolutionary ranks must care for each other, must love and help each other.' Now, you must give me some grub, I'm your soldier. You cannot discard me like a cracked pot just because you're a big shot now."

"Give me a break!" I snapped. Meanwhile, more than twenty people were gathering around to watch.

He wouldn't leave me alone and went on quoting instructions from Chairman Mao, as if the Great Leader were still alive. Too embarrassed to remain the target of his harangue, I put my uncracked egg in his palm. He grabbed it, whisked around, and scampered away to the hot-water room, holding the egg above his head and shouting, "Long live Chairman Mao! Long live the Communist Party!" That was an old way of expressing one's joy, but now the shibboleth sounded farcical.

Despite his pitiable condition, Little Owl ate better food than most of us. Usually people were generous to him, and he could eat his fill in the kitchen. My roommate Mantao often quipped that China was a paradise for idiots, who were well treated because they incurred no jealousy, posed no threat to anyone, and made no trouble for the authorities—they were model citizens through and through. Indeed, most of the retarded and the demented were taken care of by the state. Mantao went so far as to claim that this "pseudo-philanthropy," a word he actually used, had caused China to degenerate intellectually as a nation.

After breakfast I was so distressed that I didn't go to Mr. Yang's office to review my notes on ancient prosody as I had planned. Instead, I went to the library and spent two hours browsing through some journals and magazines. Afterward I decided to take a break for the rest of the morning to get myself ready for the afternoon. It was depressing to sit with Mr. Yang, and I'd better unwind a little.

In town there was an exhibition of artwork by some painters from the Southern coastal provinces, mainly from

Fujian and Guangdong. I had seen an advertisement for it on the side wall of the White Crane Hotel. To see the paintings might ease my mind, so I decided to go. The gallery was not far from my school, just fifteen minutes by bicycle. In a way I wished it were farther away, because I wanted to pedal longer on a breezy morning like this one.

On the way I noticed there were more police in town today. Their green vans and motorcycles with sidecars perched at the mouths of alleys and at street corners. One man held a walkie-talkie, though none of them seemed armed. The word was that some students at Shanning Teachers College planned to demonstrate downtown, so the police were stepping up security.

The exhibition differed from what I had expected. The hall couldn't serve properly as a gallery, not providing enough wall space for all the paintings. And dozens of screens were set up in the middle of the hall for some smaller pieces, which, hung on the green or sky-blue silk, looked strange, even sloppy—the colors of the backdrop interfered with those in the paintings. Though three of the artists in this group were famous as master painters of animals, there were fewer visitors than working staff members at the show.

Facing the entrance was a piece over thirty feet long horizontally, entitled *A Thousand Chickens*, which presented a scene on a poultry farm. Hundreds of chicks with yellow, fluffy down had been arranged to welcome visitors. I was not impressed by it because all the chickens looked identical, as if printed with the same mold. Moving counterclockwise, I went through paintings of country life: peasants, animals, vegetables, tractors, plows drawn by buffaloes, fields of crops, waterwheels, a pond of ducks, boats laden with splashing bass, even peacocks and peahens. Then came landscapes and seascapes, some of which were so coated with indigo and brown that they appeared muddy.

I was more interested in people than in scenery and animals, so I stayed longer in front of the human figures. I stood for a good while before a painting of a Uigur girl, who couldn't have lived in the South. The artist must have done this piece on a copying-from-life trip to the Northwest. In it the girl in a tight vest danced wildly with her numerous braids flying. Her movement and her supple limbs were well unified, pivoting from her slender but sturdy waist, below which a saffron skirt was swirling into a canopy. One of her heels kicked backward knee-high. Her lovely calves were slightly pink, gleaming with a soft sheen. I liked her long lashes best, which almost shaded her naughty eyes. There was a kind of fervent loveliness that illuminated this girl, who made me think of my fiancée. Meimei usually seemed carefree, and her insouciance gave her a peculiar charm; yet beneath her casual appearance was the fire fueled by her determination to achieve. What's more, she always liked to have things her way, right or wrong, but that was all right with me. Ever since we got engaged, whenever I saw a pretty woman, I couldn't help comparing her with my fiancée. The habit was weird, but too ingrained for me to outgrow.

I lingered in front of the Uigur girl for ten minutes solid, until I stepped closer and murmured with my nose almost touching her knee, "I love you."

"Don't touch it!" shouted a sharp female voice. I spun around and saw a fiftyish woman, her fat rump resting against a metal-legged desk, pointing her forefinger at my face. Several people paused to look at me.

I grasped the front of my shirt and gasped, "Goodness, what a fright you gave me!"

"You want to pay a fine?"

"No, no, I didn't touch anything, just wanted to study it closely." Hot-faced, I raised both hands with the palms toward her and backed away.

Absently I passed through the next three sections. Then in the corner of two screens I came on a piece called *A Poet*, with the subtitle *No, Not in the Presence of Others*. This painting fazed me. Viewed from a distance of ten feet, the human figure in it resembled a scarlet rooster. If the title had not been given, I could hardly have made out what this was about. The piece was vertically long and presented a tall, emaciated man in a tattered cloak, the end of which flapped in the breeze. Beyond him snaked a brook, along which a few people were sauntering, fishing, practicing tai chi, or blowing bamboo flutes, and two women were scrubbing laundry on flat stones. With his neck stretched, the poet seemed to be yearning to chant something, but unable to bring it out. A huge earring hung from his earlobe, casting on his throat an elongated shadow, which reminded me of a noose. A half-transparent mask almost shielded his nose and mouth. His shifty eyes and hollowed cheeks suggested a fearful ghost rather than a man. This painting made me wonder whether there had been an oversight on the part of the authorities that had allowed it to be included. Quickly I turned away.

When I reached the end of the exhibition, ready to head for the door, I came across a broad piece entitled *A Hundred Donkeys*, which served as the finale. In it many donkeys, large and small, stood on grassland. They were in various postures: some were grazing, some touched each other's necks and muzzles, and a few still carried wicker baskets. Several mother donkeys held their bodies still to suckle the young; their teats were wizened, almost invisible. The grown-up donkeys all kept their heads low, including those that were not browsing. Many of them had downcast eyes, which darkened with shyness and modesty. Their legs looked vigorous but fragile. In the right upper corner of the piece there were a few lines of verse serving as a caption. I stepped sideways and recognized the meaning of the poem. It read:

> *They endure humiliation*
> *And bear the heaviest loads.*
> *Unafraid of long trips*
> *They tread the roughest roads.*

At first I was touched by these words, which seemed to provide an allegorical focus for the painting. They emphasized the virtue of endurance and silent self-sacrifice, a virtue deemed to be a noble quality of the Chinese character. Throughout thousands of years the donkey and the ox had been eulogized as obedient, industrious, cheap to keep, mute, and enduring.

For some reason Mr. Yang's Genesis story came to mind. How these donkeys differed from that one who begged God to abridge his life span so as to reduce his suffering! Then I remembered that when I turned seven, one summer night, a starving donkey had broken into the tofu mill on the tree farm where my parents worked. A militiaman on patrol heard the noise inside the shed and shouted, "Who's there? Password!" The dumb animal, frightened, dashed out and ran away. Believing it was a thief and unable to stop it with his command, the man fired his rifle and a bullet struck the donkey down. It bled to death an hour later. The next morning my father helped the kitchen skin the carcass, so the cooks gave him a chunk of the boiled meat to bring home in the evening. That was the first time I had tasted donkey meat, which was delicious. My mother cut it into small cubes and seasoned it with mashed garlic, soy sauce, vinegar, and sesame oil.

Now, standing before the painting and thinking about the caption, I realized how people had humanized animals and animalized human beings. These creatures represented an abnormal species created purely for human needs. If man hadn't imposed his will on animals or abused his power and intelligence over them, no donkey would ever have kept its head close to the ground, not to mention have worn a humble look like these creatures in the painting. Without human subjugation, donkeys would have eaten grapes, cucumbers, melons, tomatoes, and would have borne nothing on their backs; they wouldn't have given a damn about the quality of roads. Without the iron shoes, they'd have had soft hooves, too lazy to take any trip. In short, they would have been donkeys as donkeys.

I grew dubious and angry, feeling the painting must be either false or satirical. To some extent I was perturbed by my response to it. This kind of artwork used to touch me easily, but now it had lost its impact because I had begun to look at things with doubtful eyes.

When I came out of the exhibition, it was already past twelve o'clock. The sky was grayish with smog, and the air thick with automobile exhaust and frying oil. With less than an hour before my shift started, I had to find a place to eat lunch without delay. I mustn't be late again.

11

As I opened the door to the sickroom, Mr. Yang was sitting on the bed and reading the *People's Daily*, a pair of bifocals on his nose. His left cheek still bore the marks of the wrinkles in the pillowcase. In a gray cashmere cardigan he looked casual and calm, as if he were taking a break from his work. I glared at Banping and said, "Come out, I want to have a word with you." We both turned to the door.

"What is it?" he asked the moment we were in the hall.

"Why did you give him the newspaper and the glasses?"

"He wanted to read."

"But that may hurt his brain. Why are you so careless?"

"Go easy, Jian. How come you're so crabby today?"

"Dr. Wu told us not to let him read anything, you know that."

"But if I didn't give him the newspaper, he'd cry like a little boy and even call me names. He wanted to sit up and study something. What else could I do? The paper at least can keep him peaceful. He said he must know our country's current affairs."

"Like a statesman, eh?" I couldn't help being sarcastic, then heaved a sigh.

He grinned and said, "He's like a little kid now and we should humor him."

We both went back into the room. Banping had been re-reading *Jean-Christophe* recently; he picked up the book from the armrest of the wicker chair and thrust it into the side pocket of his jacket. He looked unhappy and left without a word.

I felt bad as I realized I shouldn't have blown up at him. He might not have had a comfortable time staying with our teacher in this depressing room either.

Soon Mr. Yang began reading an editorial aloud. His voice grew stronger and stronger as he continued. The newspaper was an old back issue. The article was about a flood in the provinces on the Yangtze River. Hundreds of people had drowned; sixteen thousand houses flooded; troops were sent over to help the victims; Vice Premier Zhang was flying from place to place to express the government's sympathy and solicitude to the victims and to inspect the flood relief meas-ures. Mr. Yang was reading the article ardently as if he were an official addressing an audience of hundreds of people. His mouth was ringed with foam, and spittle darted in every direc-tion, some of it falling on the newspaper and some on the dark green blanket over his legs. He was so excited that he was trembling a little, his eyes glinting behind the lenses.

I went up to him and tried to take the newspaper away, but he gripped it tightly. So I gave up.

A few minutes later he put the newspaper down on his lap and started an official speech. "Comrades," he shouted with his eyes closed, "our country has difficulties now, what shall we do to help? Under the wise leadership of our Communist Party, we are not afraid of any natural disaster. As long as we rally closely around the Party Central Committee and as long as we help one another, we shall defeat the river and conquer the flood. We Chinese are heroic men and women, capable of holding up the sky and restoring the earth. No natural calamities can daunt us, because we live in a new society now. In the old days a cataclysm of such magnitude would toss millions of corpses everywhere and turn our land upside down. But now it cannot overcome us at all. Why? Why is everybody here still alive, well clad and well fed? Why do many of you still have smiles on your faces? Why are you still healthy and hopeful? The reason is clear and simple — because we have our greatest Helmsman Chairman Mao and the wise leadership of the Communist Party. Comrades, our Chairman is deeply concerned about our well-being. He doesn't go to bed at night. Instead, he pores over maps and holds emergency conferences to make plans. Although he's tired and sleepy, he eats oranges and smokes Ginseng cigarettes to keep himself awake. He's working his heart out to save us from this flood. There's no doubt he will save us, every one of us! Comrades, we must work ten times harder, care for the old and the young, and faithfully follow the Party leaders. Remember, solidarity is strength!" He paused, panting, then resumed: "Most important of all, we must not lose hope. If you lost your house, our country will build you a new one. If your crops are gone, our country will allocate you seeds and provisions. If your livestock are drowned, our country will supply you with money and young animals. In one word, we shall have everything back and we shall defeat nature. There's no reason to lose heart."

He lifted his right hand halfway, looking around with an air of authority; then he held the newspaper with both hands again. "Comrades," he went on, "in a time like this, we must be more alert to class struggle. Our enemies will not sleep when we are in trouble. I'm sure they will creep out of their holes and sabotage our efforts at every opportunity. They will spread rumors, fan evil fires, and sow the seeds of discontent. Comrades, keep your eyes open on those blackhearted evildoers and redouble your vigilance against—"

"Shut up!" I yelled with a shudder. He was pathetic. He had forgotten that he himself used to be maltreated as one of those so-called class enemies. Oppressed for decades, now he dreamed of ruling others. He didn't know who he was anymore. I rushed to him, seized the newspaper, threw it to the floor, and stamped on it.

He looked shocked and remained silent for a moment, still holding two tiny scraps of the paper with his thumbs and forefingers. Then he said wistfully, "They ought to have appointed me the general director of the flood relief work. I'm more capable than any of those bureaucrats, who are just rice bags and wineskins."

"You've forgotten who you are," I said deliberately.

"I'm a born official."

"No, you're just a crazy bookworm."

"I'm destined to govern."

"You can't even govern yourself."

He paused for a few seconds, then blustered, "Oh, how dare you talk to me like this! If you were not my son, I would have you hauled out and beheaded. Heavens, how can I have sired such an unfilial thing?" He began wailing, tears trickling down his fleshy cheeks.

That frightened me. No matter how furious I was, I shouldn't have disturbed him so much. I sat down on the bed and put my hand on his shoulder. I said, "I didn't mean to hurt your feelings, Mr. Yang. I just hate to see you make a fool of yourself. Don't be so heartbroken. See, I'm here to take care of you."

"Am I still an official?"

"Sure, you hold the fifth rank, the same as the provincial governor's."

"Do I have a chauffeur and a chef?"

"Yes, a dozen servants."

"And a personal doctor?"

"Of course, a complete staff."

"Including four armed bodyguards?"

"Sure, you have a squad of them."

"Also a Red Flag sedan?"

"Yes."

"No, I like a Mercedes-Benz better."

"All right, you can have that."

He calmed down, but was still sniveling. Again with a spoon I slowly ground a sleeping pill in a cup, poured some orangeade into it, and fed the concoction to him. He obeyed me like a child exhausted by crying. After that, I put him back into bed.

As he sank into sleep, I picked up the newspaper from the floor and looked through it. I was not interested in the old news, but a photo on an inner page caught my attention and gave me the creeps. It showed a young woman, eyes shut and crying with her mouth wide open as if she were laughing. She had jumped off a smuggling sampan, swimming toward Hong Kong, but a shark had attacked her and ripped a large piece of flesh off her thigh. Her femur showed, whitish like a debarked tree branch and dripping blood. A police boat had rescued her and carried her to a hospital nearby. Later she was returned, together with a pair of crutches, to her hometown in Hubei Province. Evidently the picture was intended to deter people from sneaking across the water into Hong Kong. There were other photos on the same page. One of them showed the fossil of a dinosaur egg found in the Mongolian Plain by a team of American paleontologists.

I dropped the newspaper on the red floor and thought about Mr. Yang's speech. Not until just now had it ever entered my mind that he might desire to become an official. He had often told me that he hated bureaucrats. If he really meant what he said, why did he yearn to be one of them? Probably he used to be able to quench this hankering, but now he was too ill to suppress it anymore. Or maybe this longing had been dormant in him all the time and even he himself wasn't aware of it; now when he lost his mind, it manifested itself.

On the other hand, I shouldn't be too hard on Mr. Yang. Empleomania was commonplace among the intellectuals I knew. A case in point was the provost of our university, Shengtan Bai, a renowned mathematician, who was now dying of cancer. Four months ago when he heard that he was being considered for the provostship, without delay he began to bike through the campus once every other day to demonstrate that he was in adequate health, though in reality he was suffering from rectal cancer. He was a stalwart man, weighing at least two hundred pounds. It was said that after every bicycle ride he'd lie in bed at home groaning in pain for hours on end. Eventually he did get the promotion and stopped teaching and doing research. Unfortunately, he couldn't enjoy the high post for long because his cancer had spread. He sat on the leather swivel chair in his new office only a few times, having to stay home two weeks after his appointment. Now he couldn't even attend official banquets, unable to sit anymore.

To be fair, when Mr. Yang was in his right mind, he had never appeared keen about any official position. Many times he told me to be detached and disinterested, which he believed was the only proper way of pursuing scholarship. He would say, "I'd talk of poetics only with those who have an unpolluted mind." How often he expressed to me his contempt for some pseudo-intellectuals, whose sole ambition was to enter officialdom and whose main function was to write editorials for the Party's publications, to prepare speeches for their superiors, and to attack the people the authorities disliked. In Mr. Yang's own words, "A scholar must not be a clerk or a mouthpiece of others."

The previous winter when he returned from Canada, he had told me excitedly that scholars in the West lived more like intellectuals. He and I were sitting in his living room, which also served as a dining room. He explained to me over Dragon Well tea, "My friend at UC-Berkeley said that in his department nobody coveted the chair, because they all wanted more time for research. Contrary to this darned place"—he knocked the dining table with his knuckles as if it were the desk in his office. "Here to become a departmental chair is the pinnacle of a professor's career. But scholars abroad are more detached and don't have to be involved in politics directly, so they can take up long-term research projects, which are much more valuable and more significant. Oh, you should have seen the libraries at Berkeley, absolutely magnificent. You can go to the stacks directly, see what's on them, and can even check out some rare books. Frankly, I would die happy if I could work as a librarian in a place like that all my life."

True, he might have romanticized the academia in the West, but he was genuinely moved. Later he advised me to consider attending graduate school in the United States, saying, "You can live a real intellectual's life there after you earn a Ph.D. from an American college."

His advice surprised me, because I had never imagined living in a foreign country. Although it was fashionable among graduate students to study abroad, I hadn't thought about this matter for myself. How could Mr. Yang talk of emigrating from our homeland like moving to another province? Did he make this suggestion also for the sake of his daughter? In other words, he might have figured that it was impossible for Meimei to go abroad on a scholarship in medicine, whereas I might receive some financial aid in the humanities, so only through me could she get to America. But I soon dismissed my misgivings and was convinced that he mainly had my interest in mind. Despite lacking confidence in my English, I decided to contact some schools in the United States. I applied to Yale, Columbia, the University of Wisconsin at Madison, and UC-Berkeley. Mr. Yang wrote a stunning recommendation for me, saying I was a rising scholar in poetic studies in mainland China. I was somewhat embarrassed by his excessive praise, though he meant what he said. He even offered to pay the twenty-nine-dollar TOEFL fee for me, since I couldn't come by any foreign currency myself.

A month later I sat for the test, in which I didn't do well. The written part went all right now that I had a solid grasp of English vocabulary, idioms, collocations, and syntax, but the part on listening comprehension dragged my scores down. I left many questions unanswered, not able to follow a meteorologist's forecast and the conversation between a postman and a woman customer. So my total score was merely 570, below the 600 standard most Ph.D. programs in the humanities required. To my amazement, the University of Wisconsin accepted me, though it wouldn't offer me any financial aid. Without a penny I couldn't possibly go to the United States. To be honest, I wasn't disappointed at all, because I still could not see the point of studying Chinese poetry in a foreign country. What's more, I was unsure if I could survive in America. A former graduate student of our department, an excellent calligrapher, had gone to New York to study toward a master's degree in journalism, and ever since he arrived there he had slaved as a busboy in a Cantonese restaurant in Manhattan. His parents were terribly worried that he might lose his mind, as he often complained in his letters that he had become an educated coolie, working more than fifty hours a week to earn his tuition, and might never graduate — he was too exhausted to study.

Last winter I began to prepare for the Ph.D. exams seriously. Mr. Yang once said that after I entered Beijing University, it would be easier for me to get a scholarship from an American college. He explained, "You'll hold a vintage position." His words implied that Beijing University was a prestigious school, internationally known, so foreign colleges would be more willing to accept its students. He was still bent on sending me abroad. I was not enthusiastic about the idea, still daunted by English, which I could read but couldn't write or speak. How could I accomplish any significant work in poetic studies in America without the ability to write well in English? Besides, I was not fully convinced that a foreign country could be a better place than China for studying Chinese poetry. Mr. Yang's eagerness suggested that he might indeed have his daughter's interest in mind. My doubts revived.

Now as I was sitting in this sickroom and thinking whether I should apply for a graduate program in America again, Mr. Yang yawned and said, "I must save my soul." He smacked his lips as if chewing something tasty.

I was puzzled, but tried to imagine where he was now and to whom he was speaking. Then he declared, "I'm only afraid I'm not worthy of my suffering."

I listened hard, but his voice trailed off.

12

The next evening all the graduate students in the Literature Department were gathered for a meeting, at which Secretary Peng presided. She was a macho woman with a Mongolian face, which would remain stern on such an occasion. Although she was not old, just in her mid-forties, she looked down on women who wore skirts. Even on broiling summer days she would dress in baggy pants and a long-sleeved shirt. Sometimes she put on an army uniform that had lost its green. Despite having only six years' schooling, she was well versed in officialese and tended to digress in front of an audience. Without the help of a text, she'd talk on and on, "rambling like a tumbling river," as people say about such a speaker. So at most meetings she would read from a speech or a report ghostwritten for her. Several faculty members in the department served as her "pens"; among them Yuman Tan, a man of thirty-nine and a lecturer in philology, was the glibbest one.

After everybody was seated, Yuman Tan lifted a bamboo-cased thermos and refilled the secretary's glass teacup with scalding water. The water went on roiling the soggy tea leaves for a good while in the cup, which was a jam jar. He sat down and his rabbity face began to turn right and left. He seemed to be checking to see if every one of us had shown up. What a snob. Holding no official position whatsoever, why should he assume such a responsibility? Probably Secretary Peng had told him to count heads for her. He looked quite happy today, smirking continually.

Sitting at the head of a long table formed by six desks grouped together, Ying Peng wore a yellow pongee shirt with two baggy breast pockets. Her hooded eyes made her look sleepy. Strange to say, though this meeting seemed ominous, she had no written speech in her hands. She waved us to quiet down, then started to speak in her abrasive voice.

"Comrades, you've all heard some students are making big scenes in Beijing. We just received orders from the Municipal Administration that says no demonstration will be tolerated here in Shanning City. Two weeks ago, the *People's Daily* brought out an important editorial that defined the nature of the disturbance in Beijing as 'a plotted conspiracy—a riot.' You all understand the full weight of those words. Without doubt some people are conspiring to overthrow the Communist Party's leadership, to sabotage the unity of our country, and to rattle the security of our socialist system. I know that some undergrads on campus are restless, planning to take to the streets, but you graduate students, older and more mature, must keep your heads cool and must discourage every undergrad from making trouble. Let me remind you that thirty years ago lots of intellectuals were sent to jail and labor camps just because they yammered a few words against the Party leaders of their work units. Some of them were merely college kids, still wet behind the ears, but they lost their youthful years in no-man's-land. All was due to a few rash words they let out. Comrades, please learn from the historical lesson and don't repeat the same silly mistake. Behave yourselves and tuck your tails between your legs — like a modest creature. Bear in mind that our Communist Party has never been forgetful. As long as our Party's in power, we won't let you get away with your wrongdoing. So don't go to the streets. Don't take part in any reactionary activities. Mark my words, I won't make any effort to protect you this time if you get into trouble. Even if you go down on your knees calling me Grandma, I won't. Even if you treat me to a sixteen-course dinner, I won't. Even if you present me with an eighteen-inch color TV, I won't. Even if you open a savings account for me in the bank, I won't!"

Laughter rang out. She looked amused, though her face remained tight. She went on: "Comrades, if you get arrested and become a counterrevolutionary, your whole family will suffer. Your siblings won't be able to go to college no matter how smart they are. Also, nobody will marry you, and you'll have to live as a bachelor or an old maid for the rest of your lives. Just imagine the lonesome years you'll have to go through. So think twice before you join in anything. If you can't help but poop and pee, come to my office or Chairman Song's office, and let your stuff out within our department. That'll be better than to make a big fuss on the streets, where the police will definitely whip your asses."

A few people tittered at the foot of the table. The secretary turned to order Banping to read out the brief document that had just arrived.

With his elbows on the desktop splotched with blue ink, Banping began reading earnestly with a rustic accent: "All Party branches in the local schools must propagate this document among the faculty, staff, and students. From now on, every school must strengthen its disciplines and regulations, and must educate its students to abide by the law. Every Party member must act as a model for maintaining unity and stability, and must vigorously fight against any activities that instigate disorder and undermine the Party's leadership. . . ."

Weiya Su was seated across the table from me. Since the dinner at Banping's place a week before, I had run into her only once. Today she seemed under the weather, her eyes red, rather watery, and an anemic pallor was on her cheeks. Her youthful outfit, an apple-green ruffled skirt and a white shirt with ladybugs printed on it and with a shawl collar, didn't add much life to her. I noticed she glanced at me from time to time. When Ying Peng bent down to sneeze, Weiya tossed a tiny paper ball toward me—it landed on the table. Immediately I put my palm over it, but Yuman Tan's small round eyes caught my hand and glowered at me. Disregarding him, I undid the paper ball below the table and saw these words: "Can we talk after the meeting?" I nodded yes to her.

During the rest of the meeting she looked preoccupied. We, the eighteen graduate students, were asked to promise the Party branch that we'd stay clear of any political activities against the government. One by one we vowed not to be involved. When it was Weiya's turn to pledge her word, she spoke rather absently.

The meeting lasted just fifty minutes, uncharacteristically short. After it, Weiya and I went behind the classroom building, where a footpath stretched along the back wall and led to the swimming pool, whose water shimmered faintly beyond the high, pointed paling. Two female undergraduates were strolling back and forth along the path, chatting in low voices and giggling intermittently. So Weiya and I chose to stand under a streetlamp whose lightbulb had burned out. A dog yapped from the yard of the school's guesthouse, about two hundred feet away in the north. The roof of that ranch-style house was partly obscured by young sycamores and a bamboo grove, and some rows of the ceramic tiles, still wet with rainwater, glistened in the moonlight.

"What's happened?" I asked Weiya.

"What do you think of Yuman Tan?" Her voice was slightly hesitant.

"As a colleague?"

"No, as a man."

I frowned. To me that dapper fellow was merely a truckler, "an anus-licker," as some people called him behind his back. "Well," I said, "I don't think he's impotent, though he never impregnated his ex-wife."

"Come on, I'm serious."

"Why are you so interested in him?"

"Secretary Peng has introduced him to me."

"She wants you to date him?"

The angry edge in my voice must have startled her; she lifted her face, her eyes flickering. She answered, "More than that, she asked me to be his fiancée."

"What? Do you like him?"

"I don't dislike him, to be honest."

"Can you imagine yourself loving him?"

"That's an irrelevant question. It doesn't matter if I can love him or not. Most marriages aren't based on love anyway. As long as a couple are compatible, their marriage may work."

I was nonplussed. Never had I thought she could be so practical.

"To be honest," she said after a feeble sigh, "I've already outgrown love. When I was a teenager, I believed I was born to love and would die for love. Romantic, wasn't I? Some years later, on the rubber farm, I fell in love with a man who taught me how to paint propaganda posters on billboards. But after he went to college, he stopped writing to me. He was a clever fellow, too clever to be serious about a girl's heart. He thought I got stuck in the wilderness forever."

"All right, but do you think you're compatible with Yuman Tan?" I asked. She had told me before about her life on a rubber plantation in Yunnan Province, where she had worked for several years, so there was no need for me to hear the story again.

"Well," she said, "I don't know him well enough to say that. Probably nobody really knows who he is. He seems to have different faces. But he's talented and writes well."

"So are some other men."

"He's a decent essayist, don't you think?"

"All right, he is. But we're talking about the man, not his pen. I can't comprehend why you're so interested in him. Believe me, Weiya, he's not worthy of your attention." I wanted to say, *To me he's just an unbearable horsefly that can't bite but is always annoying. You mustn't demean yourself this way.* But I checked myself.

She said with a drawn smile, "I'm already thirty-one, tired of being an old maid. If I don't get married soon, I'll become a childless woman all my life."

"So you want a home?"

"Yes. It's a shame to hear this from me, isn't it?"

"No, I don't think so." Pity rose in my chest as I realized that like me, she too must be a lonely creature in spite of her confident appearance. She too must have been starving for companionship, longing to rest in a pair of reliable arms. Nevertheless, I pleaded, "Don't do this to yourself, Weiya. I'm sure you'll find a better man."

"You don't understand."

"Understand what?"

"Secretary Peng can hurt me. If I don't obey her, there'll be disastrous consequences."

"In what way can she hurt you?" It felt odd to hear her say that; never had I seen her so apprehensive.

"Hmm, let me just say this: she can kick me out of the department easily."

"So?" I wasn't convinced. Why should she barter herself for a teaching position? This would ruin her life.

"I'm not like you," she said. "If I were a man, I wouldn't be afraid of her, and I'd go anywhere after graduation. I wouldn't even think of marriage at all."

I felt all at sea about what she was driving at. She was a well-educated woman, not only independent but also thoughtful. Why did she sound so timid? She went on, "Tell me, Yuman is just a scoundrel to you, isn't he?"

"Not only that. If you marry him, he may not be able to give you a child."

"You mean he may have physical problems?"

I nodded, unsure how to explain, though I knew for a fact that his ex-wife had never gotten pregnant.

"Well," she said, "I'm quite sure that physically he's fine."

"Did you check him out?"

Ignoring my mockery, she replied, "He entered college in 1977, after the entrance exams were reinstated. This means he had to pass the thorough physical screening in order to get admitted to college. Let me tell you a secret: one reason that most young women want to marry college students is that the men are healthy and unlikely to have major physical problems. For us it's a safer bet."

I was amazed by such a shrewd answer, yet I told her, "Whether Yuman Tan is physically all right or not, you deserve a better man."

"That's not a reasonable thing to say. We all deserve a good marriage, a happy family, and a great career, but those blessings are not for everyone. I used to dream of having a bunch of kids and a white bungalow like the one my grandparents once had, but that was just a fantasy. Besides, where could I find a better man?"

"There must be one if you look hard."

"Tell me where to find such a man." She gave a sly smile and went on, "To tell you the truth, recently I've begun to believe the feminist argument that most Chinese men have degenerated."

Without much thinking, I patted my chest and said almost flippantly, "Well, have you ever thought of someone like me? Of course I can't give you a bungalow." Although I kept my tone of voice nonchalant, my heart began pounding. My impromptu offer shocked me. Yes, I was attracted to her, but I had never intended to go this far.

Surprised, she looked me in the face, then turned away laughing as if in hysterics. "You're crazy," she said. "This isn't a novel or a movie, and I'm not a young heroine who needs a prince or a knight riding a white horse to her rescue. You're already engaged, so you can't be serious about what you just said. You probably mentioned yourself only out of pity, but I don't need your compassion in this situation. Even if you meant to help me, what made you think I'd do Meimei such a nasty turn? Besides, you're five years younger than me."

I was abashed but managed to counter, "Well, Karl Marx was four years younger than his wife Jenny, but they had a great marriage."

She laughed again, this time ringingly. "You're so funny. We're in China, and we're average people."

I realized what a fool I had made of myself, yet I said in self-defense, "Then why did you bother to ask me about Yuman Tan?"

"If Mr. Yang were not ill, I'd ask him. Other than him, you're the only man here I can trust. You're like a younger brother to me."

That shut me up. I was somewhat irritated by the word "trust," of which I had had an earful. When I was an undergraduate at Jilin University, quite a few young women had said the same thing to me: they found me honest and trustworthy. But none of them had ever thought me loveworthy. That was why they often talked to me and even confided in me. I felt like a wastebasket into which they dumped whatever they had no place for. This made me think that a harmless man must be more unfortunate than a charmless woman.

"How's Mr. Yang doing?" she asked a moment later, her voice full of concern.

"Crazy as ever."

"How bad is he now?"

"He's not himself anymore. Sometimes he blabbers like an imbecile, and sometimes he speaks like a sage. I wonder if he has some kind of dementia."

"You think he'll recover soon?"

"I've no idea."

"I'll come to see him."

I wanted to say, *Makes no difference,* but I held my tongue.

We walked to her dormitory, which was about three hundred yards away to the east, beyond a shallow pond overgrown with lotus flowers. From the murky water a lone frog croaked tentatively. All the way we remained silent. I was sulking, because it seemed to me she should never have considered Yuman Tan as a possibility. That man had divorced his wife the summer before; to be exact, she had run out on him. She used to be a singer in the Provincial Song and Dance Ensemble and always wore lipstick, eyeliner, and mascara. She left for the United States to join an American man, Alan Johnson, a widower from Chicago with muttonchop whiskers, who had taught linguistics in the Foreign Languages Department here. Alan Johnson had begun carrying on with her after a mutual acquaintance introduced them in a teahouse downtown. They often went to restaurants and the movies. Most of the time they had to meet off campus, because the old guards at the front entrance to the compound where the foreign experts lived would not let any Chinese visitor go in without official permission. One night last spring, the two of them were picked up by a police patrol in Golden Elephant Park while they were making out on a bench there. The affair was the first one in our school involving a foreigner, so a good number of officials got reprimanded for negligence, particularly those in the university's Foreign Affairs Office and the heads of the song and dance ensemble. Later the Provincial Education Department revoked its two-year contract with Alan Johnson, and he had no choice but to return to the United States at the end of his first year here.

After his wife left him, Yuman Tan wept every night for a week. Then he filed for a divorce, which was granted him within five days, so that he could legally go about wife hunting. He soon began to dress foppishly—a three-piece suit, checkered ties, patent leather boots. He even wore a pocket watch with a gilt chain. He bought a Yellow River moped, which was so expensive that only two or three faculty members in our university owned one, and he rode that thing to school every day. On this account some people called him "Little Running Bug." Rumor had it that his ex-wife had left him a tidy sum as a divorce settlement; this would explain why he had suddenly become rich.

To be fair, to many women he wasn't a bad match. Dozens of them were introduced to him. One was just nineteen, a technician in a gasworks, healthy and normal and without any family burden. Yuman Tan bragged that he had once seen three women in a single night, though we remarked behind his back that he could meet them each just for a few minutes and only in the presence of their parents or friends, under "special chaperonage." Unlike most marriage-oriented men, he had a two-bedroom apartment, which enhanced his worth considerably. Many newly married couples, without a place of their own, lived separately in their dormitories or at their parents' homes. Recently the university Party Committee had promised to give every married couple at least a room, which was an urgent measure to prevent young faculty members from leaving for other schools that would offer them better housing. I couldn't tell whether Weiya also had Yuman Tan's apartment on her mind. She might, considering she loved painting and must have longed for a room as a studio, which she had never had in her life. In addition, she wanted a home, which a man without housing could hardly give her. Some of the young women who were interested in Yuman Tan might have been impressed by his lectureship and writing, just as conventionally a man's learning amounted almost to a virtue, a virtue that would lead to a respectable position and yield more income. Besides his study of philology, Yuman Tan published personal essays regularly in reputable journals, so he had a name.

Yet to my mind, Weiya shouldn't have degraded herself by being one of his choices. It must have been the she-fox Secretary Peng who had set this trap for her. Weiya was too smart not to see through it, but why would she throw herself into the trap?

Approaching her dormitory building, I broke the silence. "Weiya, Ying Peng just wants to destroy you. Please don't play into her hands."

"It's not so simple," she said thoughtfully.

"Why plunge into the trap she laid for you? You mustn't do that."

She looked at me steadily and said, "You're a good-hearted man, Jian. Sometimes you're a bit too emotional, perhaps because you're not experienced in life yet. Meimei's lucky to have a man like you who hasn't lost his innocence. My situation is too complicated for me to explain in detail. Please don't get involved, or you'll only be hurt. Forget what I said about love just now. Keep in mind that whatever I did in my life, I've always been a virgin in my heart and I will always cherish our friendship. Good night." She turned and strode away.

I was somewhat bewildered by the sentiment she had expressed, which contradicted the pragmatic way she coped with Yuman Tan's interest. Why did she think me too green? What did this whole thing have to do with the virginity of her heart? Why was she so reluctant to tell me everything?

To be honest, I felt lucky that she had brushed aside my silly offer of myself as a potential man for her and hadn't taken me to be a jerk. How foolishly I had acted! If she had accepted my self-recommendation, I'd have found myself in a dilemma — having to choose between her and Meimei, whom I couldn't imagine jilting. Hotheadedness was my main problem; too often I was ruled by my impulses.

The wind was rising, tugging at the trees and the electric wires. It threatened rain, a peal of thunder rumbling in the northwest, followed by slashes of lightning, so I hastened back to my dormitory.

13

As I was reviewing my notes on political economics, Mr. Yang, sitting on the bed, broke out singing. He sang in a spirited falsetto:

> *Gallantly we are crossing the Yalu River.*
> *To defend peace and guard our country*
> *Is to protect our hometowns.*
> *The good sons and daughters of China and Korea,*
> *Let us unite closely — to defeat*
> *The vicious American wolves!*
> *To defeat the vicious American wolves!*

He bellowed the whole thing out as if he were among a large crowd of people on a platform in a railroad station to see the Chinese People's Volunteers off to Korea to fight the American army. I wasn't interested in the song, which had become obsolete long ago. He might just want my attention, but I wouldn't give him any. Instead, I kept perusing my notes. He seemed frustrated and lapsed into silence.

I had thought of wearing earphones during my shift, but decided not to, afraid of negligence when he really needed me. Besides, once in a while I wanted to listen to him, to glean secrets from his opened mind.

"What are you doing, Jian?" he asked calmly.

"Reading."

"Good. Have you brought me my books?"

"What books?" I was bewildered, as he hadn't asked me to bring him anything.

"All those on my bookshelf."

"Which shelf are you talking about?"

"The one next to my desk."

"I don't have the books here." He was crazy! There were at least a hundred volumes on that shelf in his office.

"Why?" he asked peevishly. "You're reading, but what am I supposed to do? Sit here idle like a turnip? Go fetch them, please."

For a moment I didn't know how to deal with this madness. Dr. Wu, a graying fat-faced man, had instructed Banping and me, "Absolutely no reading material for your teacher." Even if Mr. Yang were allowed to read, how could I have gone back to get his books while I was on duty here?

"Do you hear me?" he asked.

"Yes."

"For goodness' sake, go pronto!"

I made no reply, then hit on an idea. "You're too tired, Mr. Yang. Let me read to you, okay?" I thought I could use some paragraphs from my notes to beguile him.

"No, I want to study my books by myself. A good scholar

mustn't be a sluggard, letting others read to him, just as you can't ask others to eat for you. Do you *un-der-stand*?" He stressed every syllable of the last word.

"I do, but I don't have any of your books here," I blurted out.

"What!" he cried with a vacant look on his face. "You mean you've lost them? Oh heavens, what can I do without my books?" He broke into tears, genuinely aggrieved.

"Professor Yang, please listen—"

"Oh, how can I live without books! I'm utterly bereft. Why, why did you do this to me?" He started sobbing.

How could I pacify him? Even if I found him a book, he might be too addled to make sense of it. I had only a spiral notebook in hand. *Why not appease him with this?* I thought. *No, he could tell it's a hoax.*

Then I saw the copy of Brecht's *Good Woman of Szechwan* lying on the windowsill. I went to pick it up and put it on his palm. "Here's your book. See now, I haven't lost any of them. There's no reason for you to blow up like this."

He held the book with both hands, his fingers reddish and swollen, with fungus-infested cuticles. Clumsily he opened the soft cover and narrowed his eyes to look at the frontispiece, a photo of the play being staged by a Beijing troupe. Slowly he turned two pages to the foreword written by himself. "Yes, this is my new book," he said. "The ink smells so fresh it must have just come from the printer. I like the peculiar fragrance of this book." He paused to look at the page again, as if trying to locate a passage.

Fearful that he might demand another book and throw another tantrum, I sat stock-still. To my astonishment, he lifted his head and began to speak professorially. "Comrades, today we continue our discussion of high Tang poetry. First, let me read you a representative poem by Bo Wang." He flipped a page and then chanted:

> *Serrate walls abut the imperial land.*
> *In smoky wind we watch the ferry crossings.*
> *This parting, my friend, strings us*
> *Together despite our separate roads.*
>
> *You may reach any end of the earth,*
> *Yet I shall keep you close like a neighbor.*
> *Please don't stand at this fork*
> *Wetting your kerchief with our children.*

"A sad poem, isn't it?" he asked and let out a sigh. I didn't answer, wondering why he had picked this piece to begin his lecture with. In fact Bo Wang belongs to the early Tang period; Mr. Yang was mistaken about the date. To me, the poem wasn't really sad.

"The theme here is friendship," he announced. "Two scholar-officials appointed to posts in different provinces bid each other farewell outside the ancient city of Chang An. The parting, the spatial separation, can only tie them closer at heart. You see, people in ancient times had more amiable feelings, much more humane than we are. They cherished friendship, brotherhood, and loyalty. They wouldn't fly at each other's throats as we do nowadays . . ."

Cheap nostalgia, I thought. *Yesterday is always better than today, but who in their right minds can buy this kind of sentimental stuff?* If he had been in his senses, Mr. Yang would have commented on the poem in more analytical language. Clearly his mind could no longer engage the text penetratingly, and his critical discourse had partly collapsed.

"On the other hand," he resumed, "the poem isn't maudlin at all. The lines are robust and simple, just as the emotion is dignified with restraint. Please note that the language has a fine balance between fluidity and poise. The poem differs remarkably from most of the farewell poems written in the high Tang period . . ."

I wondered why he was interested in this poem. He must have been obsessed with the traditional ideal—the union of the official life and the scholarly life. In other words, he might still hanker for the role of a scholar-official. Then it dawned on me that about twenty-five years ago Chairman Mao, in one of his letters to the Secretary of the Albanian Communist Party, Enver Hoxha, had quoted two lines from this very poem—"You may reach any end of the earth, / Yet I shall keep you close like a neighbor." At that time, Albania was the only socialist country that supported the Chinese Communist Party's opposition to Nikita Khrushchev's condemnation of Stalin. It was China's only ally in the camp of socialist countries. Chairman Mao cited the ancient lines to praise the friendship between the two Communist parties. His quotation made the poem immensely popular among the revolutionary masses for over a decade. It was even set to music.

"Comrades, you all know Chairman Mao is very fond of this poem," Mr. Yang declared. "It's a real gem. If Chairman Mao likes it, we all must love it. We must study it, praise it, memorize it, and use it as our moral compass, because Chairman Mao's words are the touchstone of truth. Any one of his sentences is worth ten thousand sentences we speak."

I was sick of him! Why did he suddenly talk like a political parrot? He had lost his sense of poetic judgment and again revealed his sycophantic nature. Many people want the power to rule others; Mr. Yang was no exception. The fact that he was a scholar must have made him all the more eager to become an important official, so that he might utilize his learning, put his ideas into practice, and participate in policy making so as to realize his ambition and ideal; otherwise, all his knowledge would serve no purpose and would just rot away in his head. To some degree, he must still have a feudal-istic mind-set.

"Next," he announced, then broke off with a blank face. He fumbled, "What's next?" He riffled some pages and shut his eyes, as if making an effort to recall a prepared lecture. "Ah yes, here's the next poem we should discuss today." He read from an interleaf:

1
You, who come from heaven
To soothe all sorrow and pain
And fill the doubly wretched
With double consolation.
Oh, I am tired of this pursuit!
What for all the pain and joy?
Come, Sweet Peace,
Oh come into my breast!

2
Over the mountain
It's so quiet.
In all treetops you hardly

Feel a breeze.
The birds are silent in the wood.
Just wait, soon
You will be silent too.

I was impressed by the poet's longing for a peaceful ending. Mr. Yang's voice, full of pathos and choking with emotion, conveyed the inmost feelings of a tormented man. After he finished reciting it, the room seemed to be ringing, as if a voice were still descending from the ceiling. But the poetic mood was dispelled by his casual remark. "That's beautiful, isn't it?" He squinted at me, smirking.

"Y-yes," I faltered, wondering what kind of poetry this was. It sounded foreign, definitely not a Tang poem.

"Do you know who the author is?" he asked me.

"No, I don't."

"Goethe, Johann Goethe, the great Tang poet. Do you know who translated it into Chinese?" Again he got mixed up—if it was a translation from the German, how could it be a Tang poem?

"I've no clue," I said.

"Me, I did it myself. It took me a whole week." His eyes brightened while his brows tilted mischievously. "Do you know who speaks in this poem?"

"Goethe, the poet, of course."

"No, it's not Goethe who speaks. The speaker can be anyone." He lifted his face and began lecturing in his normal way. "Comrades, when we analyze a Western poem, we should bear in mind that the speaker and the poet are rarely identical. The fundamental difference between Chinese poetry and Western poetry lies in the use of the persona. In the Chinese

poetic tradition the poet and the poetic speaker are not separate except in some minor genres, such as laments from the
boudoir and folk ballads. Ancient Chinese poets mostly speak
as themselves in their poems; the sincerity and the trustwor-
thiness of the poetic voice are the essential virtues of their
poetry. Chinese poets do not need a persona to alienate themselves from their poetic articulation. By contrast, in Western
literature poets often adopt a persona to make their poetry
less autobiographical. They believe in artifice more than in
sincerity. Therefore, when we read a Western poem, we must
not assume that the poet speaks. In general the speaker is fic-
tional, not autobiographical."

I liked his comments, which seemed to make sense. At least
they brought him back to his former self, an eloquent professor. Yet I wasn't sure if his observation was accurate. Before I
could consider it further, he continued: "How did such opposite attitudes toward the use of the persona come into existence? In his paper published in *Poetic Inquiry* three years ago,
Professor Beiming Liang argues that this difference should
be attributed to the fact that the Western poetic tradition
originally had a parallel dramatic tradition, whereas Chinese
drama reached its maturity much later than Chinese poetry —
in other words, the poetry doesn't have such a parallel relationship with Chinese drama. Since the persona is essentially
a dramatic device, the predilection for it in Western poetry
must have originated from the primal connection between
the poetic and the dramatic traditions. I agree with Professor
Liang in principle. However, I believe we can go further
than his theory. To my mind, the difference between the two
poetic traditions' relationships with their respective dramatic
traditions may not be the fundamental cause of the opposite

attitudes toward the use of the persona. The cause should be explored deeper in the different social orders and cultural structures of the two civilizations.

"The essence of Western culture is the self, whereas the essence of the Chinese culture is the community. But poetry in both cultures has a similar function, that is, to express and preserve the self, though it attains this goal through different ways. In Chinese culture, poetry liberates and sustains the self despite the fact that the self is constantly under the overwhelming pressure of the community. Thus Chinese poets tend to speak as themselves, too earnest to worry about having a characterized voice to conceal their own — they desperately need the genuine self-expression in poetic articulation. In other words, the self is liberated in poetic speech, which is essentially cathartic to the Chinese poet. On the contrary, in Western culture poetry tends to shield and enrich the self, which on the one hand is threatened by other human beings and on the other hand has to communicate with others. Therefore, the persona becomes indispensable if Western poets intend to communicate and commiserate with others without exposing themselves vulnerably. In this sense, the persona as a poetic device functions to multiply the self."

He fell into silence, as if purposely leaving some time for his words to sink in and for his students to take notes. I was impressed by his thesis, which I felt might be original. But his view was too sweeping and still crude: it would have to be substantiated and thoroughly examined before it could be shared with others. Besides, there were holes in his argument. He ought to have taken into account the Romantics in the West, such as Byron and Keats, who seldom use a persona in their lyric poems. Even Dante often speaks as himself in *The Divine Comedy*. Furthermore, the notion that the concern for the self differentiated Western culture from Chinese culture sounded arbitrary and rather simplistic. For instance, Christianity — the core of Western civilization — cares about God more than about the individual. Perhaps Mr. Yang should focus on the poetry written in one Western language instead of the whole body of Western poetry, which was too colossal for him to tackle.

"Do you know I write poetry too? I have always been a poet at the bottom of my soul." He didn't mention my name, but his intimate tone of voice indicated he was talking to me.

"No. You never told me that," I said.

"You want to listen to one of my poems?"

Before I could answer, he closed the book and began chanting solemnly:

> In late August the autumn wind howls
> Peeling my roof of three-layered straw.
> The straw flies across the brook,
> Hanging on the top of the woods
> And tumbling into gullies and ponds.
>
> The children from South Village
> Bully me for my old age,
> Daring to be thieves before my eyes:
> They take away my straw and vanish
> Into the bamboo grove.
>
> Lips cracked and tongue dried
> I can no longer cry. And coming back,
> I keep sighing over my cane.

He paused and raised his head, his eyes flashing. "What do you think of that?" he asked me proudly. "A powerful beginning, isn't it?"

"Yes." I forced myself to agree. Anyone could tell that those lines were the beginning of Tu Fu's "Song of My Straw Hut Shattered by the Autumn Wind." How could Mr. Yang believe he had written the poem himself? Yet the earnest look on his face showed that he didn't doubt his authorship at all. I remained quiet. Whoever he fancied himself to be was fine with me, as long as he didn't throw a fit.

"See how simple these lines are. It's the simplicity that stirs the soul. Comrades, bear in mind that the traditional poetic theory believes there's an inverse relationship between ideas and emotions. If an idea in a poem is too complicated and too arcane, the poem begins to lose its emotional power. Conversely, if the poem is too emotional, its intelligence will diminish. A good poet intuitively knows how to strike a balance between thoughts and emotions. When I read this poem for the first time, I wondered to myself, 'My goodness, how could he write these lines? They are as sturdy and supple as green branches.'"

Now he seemed to have dropped his conviction that he himself was the author. Somehow he couldn't affix his mind to an idea for long; his thoughts rambled too much. I wondered whether there was a way to make his mind more focused and more coherent. Perhaps he should be treated by a psychiatrist; acupuncture or acupressure might help him too.

"Listen carefully," he demanded, as if he knew I was wool-gathering — thinking about his brain instead of his views. He went on reciting huskily:

Then the wind subsides, murky clouds
Thickening while the sky turns misty and dark.
Our quilts, ragged for years,
Are hard as iron. Full of cracks
They can't keep my kids warm in their sleep.

Again I fear that rain will fall in
Through the leaky roof, swaying like
Endless hempen threads and soaking our beds.
Ever since the war I've seldom slept.
How hard it is to pass such long dank nights!

He paused for breath, then commented, "I wrote these lines when I was 'reeducated' in the countryside. During the day we pulled plows in the fields like beasts of burden, or hoed soybean seedlings, or planted rice shoots, or cleaned latrines and pigsties, or shipped manure to the fields. Although the work was backbreaking, it was not as nerve-racking as at night, because the hard labor could numb and vacate my mind. I could hardly think of anything while my body was busy. Once I started working, I just went on like a machine. Besides, when the work was heavy and urgent, we were often given better food, not as in the regular time when we had to eat sweet-potato strips and bran buns — both were indigestible and gave me heartburn and stomachaches. When we gathered in crops or loaded sun-dried bricks into the kiln or carried them out of it after they had been fired, we could eat as many corn buns as we wanted, and sometimes there were even slivers of pork belly in the vegetables. We were also given mung bean soup, which we could drink to our fill. But it was horrible at night. I suffered from insomnia. So many things came to mind that I couldn't stop thinking about them. Once I didn't sleep for thirteen days in a row. I begged the farm's doctor to prescribe some soporific for me, but the leaders wouldn't let him give me any, saying, 'We ought to save the sleeping pills for the revolutionary masses. You can't sleep because you haven't worked hard enough.' In the daytime I walked in the fields as if treading the clouds. My eyes ached and my head swelled with a shooting migraine. I was frightened that I was going to lose my mind, but the more fearful I was, the more sleepless the night became. I hated all the men around me for being able to sleep at night and get up refreshed the next morning. How often I envied the pigs in the sties behind our house, because they just ate and slept until one day they were hauled out to the butcher's."

He swallowed, then resumed: "The roof of our room was full of holes, through which night after night I listened to the wind whistle and watched the moon and the clouds move by slowly. In spite of my wakefulness, I dared not make any noise. If by chance my movement in bed woke somebody, he would curse me relentlessly and wake others up. Then all the people in the room would heap abuse on me. On the one hand, I wished the night would end sooner so that I could stop thinking; on the other, I wished daylight would never arrive so that I could stay in bed longer and rest my body more. In that state of mind I composed these lines." He patted Brecht's play in his lap and continued, "Genuine poetry originates from the author's personal experience. It's something that overflows from the soul."

I prodded him, "But you once said in class that most poems came from other poems."

He looked askance at me, then admitted, "Yes, most poems are small potatoes that come from big potatoes, the real poems from original, genuine human experience. The big potatoes, the real poems, are planted by some people first. Then the children of the big potatoes are planted; then the grandchildren are planted. Year after year the great-grandchildren, great-great-grandchildren, great-great-great-grandchildren of the big potatoes grow smaller and smaller until they have shrunk to nothing. Then people must look for other big potatoes to grow."

This was crazy. His analogy was wild, though refreshing. I asked without any irony, "So you think this is a big-potato poem?"

"Of course. It's a piece in which authenticity overcomes artifice. Only after I had suffered all the miseries and abuse and the sleepless nights could I write such truthful lines. Listen, there's not a single false sound here." He recited again:

> *If only I had ten thousand mansions*
> *To shelter all poor scholars on earth*
> *And brighten their faces with smiles.*
> *Look, the mansions stand like mountains*
> *Unshakable in wind and rain!*
>
> *Ah, once before my eyes arise such mansions,*
> *I shall be happy, even though my own hut*
> *Falls apart and I freeze to death!*

"Oh, when can I see those mansions?" he cried and burst into sobs. His tears fell on the apricot-yellow cover of the book in his lap. "Where are those grand mansions?" he shouted. "Let me see them. Then I'll die happy. Where, where are they?" He was wailing now, his mouth writhing.

I was choking with mixed emotions—pity, misery, and disgust were all welling up in my chest. He hadn't written a single line of poetry in his whole life and had to rely on the ancient poem to express his aspiration, which was conventional and hackneyed, though not without lofty sentiment.

He blubbered again, "I only have a one-bedroom apartment. Give me one of those mansions! Where are they? I shall be a professor of the first rank, absolutely qualified for such a residence."

What a lunatic! He made me want to laugh and weep at the same time, and my eyes misted over.

"Oh, Lord of Heaven, isn't this a genuine poem?" he cried again. "Doesn't it have truth in it? Truth must come true sooner or later like light that drives away darkness. But when? Why am I not allowed to see it materialize before I die? Why can't I enter any of those high mansions to meet the happy faces of the poor scholars? If truth cannot come true, then what good can it do us? And what's the use of a poem like this?" He pulled his right hand onto his belly, its back stained with tears. He chanted extravagantly:

> *Before I die, my aspiration*
> *Is not yet realized—*
> *Tears often wet the front*
> *Of this hero's robe.*

He tried to reach his chest with his left hand, but couldn't lift it that high. Suddenly with his right hand he swept the book to the floor and yelled, "I don't want this stuff anymore! No, no more poetry, not a word of truth in it. It's full of lies. I've been fooled by it all my life."

"Professor Yang, stop, please!" I stepped over and shook his shoulder gently.

He said between gasps, "Damn it, the poem states clearly there are ten thousand mansions, but where are they? I wrote it and have studied it all my life, but I don't even have a decent apartment. What's the good of poetry? It just gets your hopes up." He was trembling all over and still wouldn't stop ranting. "People who don't care a damn about poetry live well and wallow in bliss and comfort. One of my former classmates, who is a nincompoop specializing only in licking his superiors' assholes, was appointed a minister in the State Council two years ago. He has so much power that he had a swimming pool constructed for himself, as easy as ordering a dish. But we, wretched scholars and fainthearted bookworms, have lain in word-hoards, feeding on paper and ink, believing in poetry, and dreaming of miracles. We are all fools! We — we —" He was panting so hard that words failed him.

I patted his back for a while to relieve his gasping. Then I began laying him down slowly. The muscles on his face twitched and twitched as though something were biting him in his mouth.

I too was sick at heart.

14

When Meimei and I became engaged, my parents came to Shanning to see the Yangs. They brought products from our hometown, such as hazelnuts, dried tree ears, and daylilies. They presented Meimei with a woolen coat and her parents each with a marten hat, which embarrassed me a little because the climate here wasn't cold enough for anyone to wear such a hat. Among their gifts was a small bag of dried hedgehog mushrooms, which my townsfolk call "monkey's heads." These were a delicacy that could rarely be found in the forest nowadays. The Yangs were very impressed by the mushrooms, which they had heard of but never seen before. Although my mother explained to Mrs. Yang in detail how to prepare and cook them — soak them in warm water for a day, tear them into slivers, and stew them with pork or chicken — Mrs. Yang kept shaking her head and said she couldn't make such a fancy dish by herself, afraid of spoiling the mushrooms. So my mother cooked some for the engagement dinner. The

Yangs were amazed that the mushrooms tasted almost exactly like the pork shoulder they were stewed with.

At the end of the dinner, my mother took out a folded envelope and said to my fiancée, "Meimei, here's five hundred yuan my old man and I would like to give you as a token for having you as our daughter."

The Yangs and I were all surprised. I hadn't anticipated that she'd follow the customs back home, which required the parents-in-law to present a sum of money to the prospective daughter-in-law, who in return must call them Father and Mother in front of everyone.

My mother remained silent, her broad face wearing an expectant smile. Meimei seemed puzzled, looking at me inquiringly. I told the Yangs, "By the customs in the Northeast, Meimei should call my parents Father and Mother when she accepts the money."

"I'm not selling myself," said Meimei in an undertone, but everybody heard her.

A prolonged hush fell on the table. I was disconcerted, not knowing whether I should take the money for my fiancée. Five hundred yuan was a large sum, equal to seven or eight months' salary for a common worker. It must have taken my mother two or three years to save such an amount. My father broke in, "Well Meimei, if you're against the old custom, we can understand. One of these days you will call us Dad and Mom anyway, so we can wait. Just take the money, okay? That will make my old wife happy."

"I can't do that," said Meimei.

My mother looked upset, puffing her lips out. Luckily no other people were at the dinner, or she'd have felt she had lost face. My father told her, "Meimei is a college student, and we shouldn't treat her like a regular bride in our small town. We should've thought of this beforehand."

Then I hit upon an idea. "Mother, please keep the money for Meimei for the time being, all right? She's wonderful with the harmonica. Can we ask her to play a tune for us instead of calling you Mom?"

To my relief, my mother agreed. "Sure, fine with me. I won't have her do anything she doesn't want to."

I turned to Meimei. "Please play a piece."

Mr. Yang chimed in, "That's the minimum you should do for your future parents-in-law."

Pouting, Meimei went into the bedroom and returned with her large harmonica. Without asking us what to play, she began blaring the music of "March Forward, March Forward!," the theme song of the revolutionary ballet *The Red Women Detachment*. The militant tune was metallic and fierce; it sounded like a pack of cats whining and growling at one another. At times one or two notes snapped out of place. The music made my temples smart. For some reason, my mother enjoyed it and even hummed along with the tune. I saw resentment in Meimei's eyes and her red cheeks bulging. When she was done, I dared not comment, but my parents clapped their hands.

Mrs. Yang muttered, "She's totally spoiled."

"You could have chosen a sweeter piece," added her father.

Meimei sat down without a word, panting a little. My mother picked up the envelope and put it back into the inner pocket of her jacket. She said, "Meimei, I'll keep this money for you. Whenever you need it, it's yours."

I was unhappy with Meimei. If she had accepted the woolen coat from my parents, why couldn't she take the money? What made her so particular? But I didn't say anything to reopen the topic.

The Yangs' apartment had just one bedroom, so my parents stayed with me in the dormitory. Huran and Mantao had gone home for the winter break, and there were enough beds, though my parents had to sleep separately. That they didn't mind. But they were accustomed to the heated brick-bed back home, the beds here were too cold for them, and they complained that there was no stove in the room.

The day before my parents returned home, Meimei, Mrs. Yang, and my mother went shopping downtown. My parents wanted to take back some fashionable clothes for friends and neighbors and also some fancy candies for children, which were not available at our local grocery stores. My mother was fond of Meimei despite my fiancée's unsteady temper, often saying it was fortunate to have a doctor in our family. At those words, Meimei would smile complacently and declare she'd handle me like a doctor treating a patient. She even warned me to expect a fishwife.

My father and Mr. Yang stayed home, smoking pipes while chatting away over black tea. They liked each other very much. My father had been a college graduate and was well read, so they had a lot to talk about. I sat in the bedroom, listening to them through the door ajar.

"Old Wan, you must have gone through a great deal of hardship all these years," said Mr. Yang.

"That's true," my father admitted. "Look at my hands, they're coarser than a peasant's. I used to write articles for a major newspaper in Tianjin. Just because of a few words of criticism about an overbearing leader, they sent me to Heilongjiang Province to be reformed."

"Did you often starve at the labor camp?"

"I didn't go to a camp actually. What happened was that before the revolution my father had been a landowner, a small one who had only five acres of land. But he helped the Communists during the war against the Japanese invaders and often gave them food and shelter, so during the Land Reform the Communists put him into a different category from a regular landowner. He was classified in 'the open-minded gentry.'"

"Does this mean you're from a revolutionary family?" Mr. Yang asked in earnest.

"No, we were treated as a lesser kind of reactionary. Some of the Communists still remembered my father when I was in trouble, so they intervened on my behalf. That's how I wasn't sent to a camp. Else God knows where my bones would've been scattered."

"I see," sighed Mr. Yang. "There has been so much gratuitous suffering in our lives."

I peeked in at them. My father's face grew more rugged, his little nose twitching. "My family suffered a lot because of me too," he went on. "Jian and his brother often got beaten up on the streets. One evening I was released by the revolutionaries and returned home, only to find that my boys both had swollen faces and broken skulls. Jian still has a scar above his eye."

True, my right eye would still blur a little in sunlight, owing to a stone a boy had thrown at me when they kicked and slapped me outside the elementary school. After that beating, for a week, my right eye could hardly distinguish two from three fingers put before my face, but later my mother fed me cod-liver oil every day and gradually my vision was restored.

Mr. Yang said, "No wonder Jian often seems sad and gloomy like an older man."

"For many years he didn't have any friends except for his younger brother. I was terribly worried about him and afraid he might be traumatized. He was more withdrawn than my other son. I wondered if he'd lost the ability to smile, but after he went to college, he seemed to become more open."

"He gets along with others well here, he's a fine young man."

"Now with Meimei, he should be all right." Father laughed.

"You have raised him well, Old Wan."

"I would say so too. I often did homework with him and the younger one together."

More than that, my father had also told stories and recited classical poetry to us. With his help, I had memorized many poems. That was the origin of my love for literature. In every way he was a devoted family man; my brother and I often slept with him so that we could hear him tell us folk tales. Although my mother, from a local peasant family, was almost illiterate, he had always treated her with respect and gratitude for her loyalty and endurance. She had seldom complained about the humiliation and hardship we had gone through. She was a strong woman and for many years had driven a mule cart selling tofu on the streets, which was the only job she could get. Her rawboned face often reminded me of that painful period of our life.

My father had dexterous hands. Several times the tree farm's leaders had wanted to transfer him to its propaganda section, but he refused to go, saying he couldn't write anymore and preferred to remain a carpenter. He was well respected for his craftsmanship, and so many people wanted him to make wardrobes, chests, and dining tables for them that he always had his hands full. He told Mr. and Mrs. Yang that when they had a more spacious apartment, he'd like to come and build some furniture for them. If they couldn't get lumber here, he could send them some before he came.

Gradually the two men began talking about poetry. My father was no expert in poetics, but he knew many of Tu Fu's poems by heart. Mr. Yang got excited as they went on. They both loved the later Tu Fu more than his early work, believing it represented the peak of classical Chinese literature.

"It's poverty that refined his poetry," remarked my father, repeating the cliché, but with genuine feeling.

"Well, for many years I thought that way too," said Mr. Yang.

"You don't think so anymore?" my father pressed on.

"Honestly, I'm not sure."

"How come?"

"Two years ago I went to a conference in Chengdu, so I had an opportunity to visit 'the straw hut' where Tu Fu spent his last years. Believe it or not, it's not a hut but a big house, much bigger than a regular cottage. Before the house there were flowerbeds filled with chrysanthemums and roses of various colors. The yard was so large that it took me a few minutes to walk across. His residence was more like a wealthy landowner's. Tu Fu seemed well provided for in his last years. He had powerful friends who gave him money and provisions."

"But didn't he starve to death?"

"That's a legend without any proof. The belief that he lived in dire poverty could just be a sentimental invention, meant to comfort poor scholars and intellectuals like us. Frankly, I don't see much connection between poverty and the refinement of poetry. I dare say that Tu Fu might have had a better life than many of us."

"That's very interesting." My father sounded dubious, but said no more.

Mr. Yang added, "In Chinese history, this must be the toughest time for us intellectuals. So many lives have been wasted and so many talents destroyed. In addition to material poverty, there's spiritual sterility too."

They both turned silent.

In class Mr. Yang would never speak so candidly. His remarks indicated that he had reservations about some of the comments in our textbooks. The notion that poverty can refine poetry is a principle in the conventional poetics, but according to my teacher, this idea could be erroneous. *Probably,* I thought, *I should write a paper on this subject if he doesn't dare to do it himself.* Later I brought this up with Mr. Yang, but he told me to forget about it.

15

On my way to the hospital for my afternoon shift, I was stopped by a traffic jam at May First Square. About six hundred students from the Yellow Plain Mining College, the City Institute of Industrial Arts and Crafts, the Teachers College, and our school — Shanning University — were demonstrating there. They held up large banners with slogans written on them, such as PUNISH CORRUPT OFFICIALS! DOWN WITH PARASITES! SAVE OUR COUNTRY! LONG LIVE DEMOCRACY! GIVE ME FREEDOM OR DEATH! Some of them wore white headbands as if they belonged to a dare-to-die team, though they were all empty-handed except a thickset fellow toting a lumpy bullhorn. As they marched, drums and gongs thundered between rounds of shouted slogans.

On the eastern fringe of the square, near the Second Department Store, stretched a line of workers, three or four deep, all in white Bakelite helmets, which had the name STEEL PLANT printed on them. Every one of these men carried a wooden cudgel across his back. They looked lighthearted and once in a while cursed the demonstrators loudly. Despite their role as law enforcers, they seemed spoiling for a fight, waiting to wreak mayhem. I had heard that the Mayor's office had sent them over to keep order, and that they were paid double for this kind of "work." Some of them smoked self-rolled cigarettes and some sucked hard candies, laughing in whoops as they swapped wisecracks and insults with one another. Meanwhile, thousands of onlookers gathered along the sidewalks; some gave the students the thumbs-up, and a few even joined the procession moving northeast. With both hands raised above her head, an old woman displayed a white neckerchief bearing the word WRONGED! Apparently she was seizing this opportunity to air her grievances.

"Down with the privileged class!" a short girl shouted in a sharp voice. People followed her, flourishing their fists or tiny flags.

"Give us democracy!" cried a boy. Again hundreds of voices roared together.

"All are equal before the law!" a male voice immediately shouted through a megaphone, but the timing was out of sync and few people responded.

To my surprise, I saw Kailing Wang among the students. She held up a small rectangle of cardboard displaying the slogan UPHOLD HUMAN RIGHTS! Her face was sweaty and tan, but she looked spirited, her abundant hair hanging down over her shoulders. As I wondered how she had gotten mixed up with these demonstrators, she caught sight of me and stepped out of the procession. She came over, saying in a fluty voice, "Hi, Jian Wan, want to join us?"

"No. I'm going to the hospital."

"How's Mr. Yang doing?" Her voice turned earnest, and her smile revealed her even teeth.

"Improving, but not a whole lot. How many students here are from our school?"

"About one hundred and sixty," she said, jutting her chin forward a little. "We tried so hard to mobilize the kids, but most of them wouldn't come, especially the graduating seniors."

"I don't blame them. The school has threatened to give them a bad job assignment if they get involved."

"Still, this isn't bad, is it?" She pointed to the demonstrators.

"No at all. Actually I'm impressed. I didn't know you were such a revolutionary."

"Or a counterrevolutionary." She giggled nervously and seemed uneasy about her own quip. She wore a white tank top and coffee-colored culottes, which had just come into fashion.

I told her, "I showed Mr. Yang the Brecht play you translated."

"Did you?" Her face lit up. "What did he say?"

"He said it smelled good."

She laughed. "Tell him I'll come to see him soon."

"I will."

Without further delay she said good-bye and hurried away to catch up with her group. She seemed to play some organizing role in the demonstration, but not a major one. In a way I was perplexed by her interest in this kind of activity, but at the same time impressed by her audacity. Even most of the undergraduates remained uninvolved. Unlike the students, Kailing had a teenage son. Wasn't she risking the boy's future as well? After this turmoil, the school would at least demand she make self-criticism. She'd be lucky if they didn't demote her or brand her with a criminal name.

I had to skirt a huge jam of onlookers to get through to Cloud Bridge Road, which led to the hospital. The air reeked of sweat, diesel oil, vinegar, soy sauce, fried garlic and scallion, roast chicken, and braised pig's feet. Dismounted cyclists kept cranking the bells on their handlebars, some yelling at one another. Fifty yards away in the west a tractor loaded with black bricks was put-putting clamorously, but had to mark time. As I pushed my bicycle past the front of an ice cream stand, a tall simian man in dark glasses, who looked like an official or an entrepreneur, said loudly to an old woman about the students, "These nitwits must've been overstuffed and have too much energy to spare. If we starved them just for a week, I bet none of them would come here to make such a fuss. We should ship them all to the vegetable farms in the suburbs and make them work the fields twelve hours a day."

"Tut-tut-tut, these brats are real spoiled," said the woman, shaking her puckered face and waving a horsehaired fly whisk. She stretched her neck and called out, "Ice brick, half a yuan apiece."

"Damn, it's so hot," cursed the man. "I screw their mothers for giving birth to these bastards!" He spat on the ground, scraping the phlegm with his boot.

I stared at him and he glared back. His dull eyes, reminding me of cooked oysters, were so ruthless that I ducked my head. Before stepping away, I caught a glimpse of the muzzle of a pistol that stuck out of the ribbing waistband of his jacket. Evidently he was a plainclothes agent. As I walked along, I noticed that among the spectators about a dozen men and women wore the same kind of dark glasses as that man's. Raising my eyes, I saw two men in white shirts and blue pants working a video camera on the rooftop of the department store. The machine panned down to follow the demonstrators. Despite the hustle and bustle, few of the vendors, sitting on their haunches or on canvas stools, had stopped crying for customers. Some people were still haggling over prices.

When I reached the corner of Swift Horse Road, a middle-aged jaundiced man appeared, waving a miniature flag made of orange paper. "Down with the Communist Party!" he yelled. No one repeated his shout, but immediately a crowd, about twenty people thick, gathered around him. He fluttered the triangular flag again and screamed, "Down with socialism!" Still, the crowd was silent, watching him in horror and confusion.

Before he could shout more, three plainclothes agents, two men and one woman, rushed over, grabbed his hair and arms, and handcuffed him from behind. "Help! Save me!" he hollered, his eyes bulging and flashing, sinews drawn tight in his neck. His mouth went agape, dripping saliva. "Don't be slaves anymore!" he shouted at us over his shoulder.

Nobody interfered. Instead, a bowlegged locksmith walked over, and wielding his long pipe, he struck the man's crown three times with its brass bowl. "Damn you, how dare you call me a slave?" he barked.

"Ow, don't hit me, Uncle!" the man screeched. At once a thread of blood trickled down his forehead. A few bystanders laughed.

"Serves you right, such an unreformable reactionary!" the old locksmith said through his teeth, and bent down to pick up his own flat cap from the ground.

"What a moron!" said a young herb peddler. "He can't see that cops are everywhere."

The three agents dragged the man away despite his blustering resistance. From time to time his legs stretched straight, his feet unyielding, yet they hauled him along. One of the agents kept thrashing his shoulders with the buckle end of a leather belt while the woman kicked the backs of his knees. Within a minute they disappeared past a barbershop door. Throughout the commotion, a gray-browed cobbler, sitting next to a toy stand, his lips clamping a few tiny nails, hadn't even once stopped hammering the sole of a leather shoe mounted on his last. All around, people talked about the arrested man, calling him a fool and saying that at least one of his family members had been executed by the Communists.

The students seemed aware of the odds against them, so they behaved guardedly, marching in good order. Now and then they shouted "Salute to the workers!" as a way to appease the hirelings from the steel plant. Slowly they headed toward the City Hall, which was a few blocks away in the northeast. Once I had threaded my way through the square, I leaped on my bicycle and pedaled away to the hospital at full speed.

16

Professor Song came to see Mr. Yang the next afternoon. As soon as he stepped into the room, I retreated to the window and sat on the sill. Seated in the wicker chair, he took his jujube-wood pipe out of a chamois pouch and absently tamped down tobacco into its bowl. He looked haggard, with dark patches under his lower lids, and his breath smelled of alcohol. Although he was given to drink, I have to admit that I had never seen him drunk. He bicycled around all the time, but somehow always eluded accidents.

"Shenmin, how are you doing these days?" he asked Mr. Yang in a hearty voice, addressing him by his first name.

My teacher raised his eyes. "I'm doing poorly, going to die in a couple of weeks."

"Come, I still need you to quarrel with me. Our graduate program depends on your guidance. You can't leave us so soon."

"No more bickering, I forgive you," mumbled Mr. Yang.

"I miss sparring with you. To tell the truth, I miss your gibes."

"It's all over between us."

A lull set in. Professor Song glanced at me, then asked Mr. Yang, "How's your appetite?"

"I still eat something."

"Try to eat more."

"I'm neither a glutton nor a gourmet."

Professor Song put the stout pipe between his teeth, about to thumb his lighter, but he paused to look at me inquiringly. Before I could say go ahead, he removed the pipe from his mouth, unloaded the tobacco into the pouch, tied the kit up, and stuffed it back into his pocket. He said again, "Shenmin, don't worry about anything and just concentrate on your recuperation, okay?" He sounded quite sincere.

"I have thought of nothing these days but how to save my soul."

"All right, don't worry about your classes and the journal. I've made arrangements, and you're still the editor in chief. I assigned a few young hands to help you with the editorial work. Everything's fine."

"You can suit yourself. I'm not interested in that sort of clerical work anymore. From this day on I shall think only my own original thoughts and shall write for nobody but posterity."

A shock crossed Mr. Song's face, but he managed to reply, "Okay, you should write like that. I also mean to tell you that our department has submitted your name for a full professorship. I'm sure there will be no problem this time. You deserve a promotion, it's long overdue."

"Give it to anyone you want. I have no need for that."

"Why?" Professor Song looked puzzled.

"I don't want to be a clerk anymore. I have quit."

"What are you talking about? Are you not our best scholar?"

"No, I've been a clerk all my life, so have you. We're all chattels of the state."

Professor Song looked at him in alarm. He said, "I don't understand this, Shenmin. Why should we look down on ourselves so? We're both intellectuals, aren't we?"

"No, we're not. Who is an intellectual in China? Ridiculous, anyone with a college education is called an intellectual. The truth is that all people in the humanities are clerks and all people in the sciences are technicians. Tell me, who is a really independent intellectual, has original ideas and speaks the truth? None that I know of. We're all dumb laborers kept by the state — a retrograde species."

"So you're not a scholar?"

"I told you, I'm just a clerk, a screw in the machine of the revolution. You're the same, neither worse nor better. We are of the same ilk and have the same fate, all having relapsed into savagery and cowardice. Now this screw is worn out and has to be replaced, so write me off as a loss."

Mr. Song bowed his head. The room was so quiet that you could hear sparrows twittering outside, one of them drumming its wings.

A moment later Professor Song said rather timidly to Mr. Yang, "Don't be so pessimistic. There's still hope."

"What hope?"

"For instance, the new generation of scholars, like Jian, will make improvements. Indeed, our lives were mostly wasted, but they'll learn from our mistakes and losses and will live a better life than ours."

"False. At most he'll become a senior clerk."

Professor Song looked at me as my heart tightened. He said again, "Shenmin, don't be so harsh on young people. You're not yourself today. I know you love them, or you wouldn't want Jian to go to Beijing University."

"Yes, I want him to do that. What else can I expect of him? He flunked TOEFL, so he blew the opportunity to study comparative literature at the University of Wisconsin. He let me down." Mr. Yang exhaled a sigh and resumed: "He'd better leave this iron house soon so that he won't end up a mere scribe here. In our country no scholars can live a life different from a clerk's. We're all automatons without a soul. You too should go before it's too late. Don't get trapped here."

"Shenmin, maybe we shouldn't continue like this—you're talking in circles. In any case, take it easy and get well soon. We all want you back in the department."

"Nobody can use me anymore."

Professor Song gave me a nod that indicated it was time for him to leave. He rose to his feet and said good-bye to my teacher. I went out of the room with him. In the hall I begged him, "Please don't take to heart what Mr. Yang said. He's not himself today."

"I know. Actually I liked our talk and will think about what he said. Your teacher has suffered a lot. Don't distress yourself about his opinion of you. He didn't mean it."

"I don't mind that." I grimaced.

As he walked away with measured steps, he fished out his tobacco pouch and began loading his pipe again.

I felt relieved that he wasn't offended. Although Mr. Yang's drivel often sickened me, there was one virtue in it which I did like, namely that he spoke his mind now. Never had I imagined that he didn't see any meaning in my effort to enter the Ph.D. program. He had obviously been disappointed by my low TOEFL score. Without question he wanted me to go abroad so that I wouldn't end up a clerk here and his daughter could avoid the fate of a technician.

I didn't return to the sickroom immediately, and instead sat on a bench in the corridor for a while. Nurse Chen came along the hall, holding an empty cream-colored pail. She stopped in front of me and smiled, saying she had just been assigned to attend Mr. Yang at night, from 6:00 P.M. to 1:00 A.M. After her shift, Nurse Jiang would take over until morning. "So we're on the same team now," Mali Chen said. "He's a well-learned man, I mean your teacher. Sometimes I like listening to him." She smiled again, fluttering her eyes.

I said, "Well, we count on your help."

"Don't say that. We help each other. By the way, did you read the book Mr. Yang translated?"

"Which one?"

The Good Woman of Szechwan.

"Oh yes, I read it a while ago."

"Why are all the people so nasty and so greedy in the play except Shen Te?"

"You mean the prostitute?"

"Yes. What a bizarre world the play shows."

"Not like ours?"

"Of course not. Doesn't the foreign playwright understand China at all?"

"He didn't mean to present China. He wanted to express his understanding of the world."

"I know, his philosophy. Still, what a world it is! Where nobody but a streetwalker is a good person."

"Perhaps it's like ours, don't you think? Tell me, where can we find a good woman or a good man?"

"That depends on how you define a good person."

"I mean someone you can absolutely trust."

"Your mother or father."

"You really think so?"

"Don't you trust your parents? My, you're such a misanthrope."

"No, I'm not, only grim."

"Like teacher, like student. Just joking." She tittered, waving her thin hand.

Somebody called to her from the stairwell, and she left in haste, the handle of the pail in her hand making rhythmic creaks.

I was still preoccupied with what Mr. Yang had said about me a moment before. Unhappy as I was about his reproach, I had to admit that he did have a point. The more I thought about some professors and lecturers at Shanning University, the more they resembled clerks and technicians. Even if someday I became a scholar as erudite as my teacher, I would have to remain in the clerical ranks. Then why should I bother so much about it all?

17

Meimei's letter arrived, and I couldn't wait to read it.

May 6, 1989

Dear Jian,

I hope my father is getting better. Tell him that I'll be back as soon as I'm done with the exams. Actually at this moment it's unclear whether the exams will be given on time. Things are in chaos here. Hundreds of students from my school have gone to Tiananmen Square a few days in a row to join the students of other colleges already there. Together they demand a dialogue with the premier. I just heard that the exams might be postponed. If so, I'll come home sooner.

But you shouldn't be disconcerted by this information. Keep working on your Japanese and reviewing the textbooks. All we can do is get prepared.

I have just heard from my mother that she will be on her way home soon. She thanks you for looking after my father.

These days I'm so busy that time passes almost unnoticed. Quite a few friends here have tried to drag me out of my room, but at this point of my life I have to sacrifice fun and excitement, so that eventually I can become a pediatrician in Beijing. I miss you, Jian. In my last letter I mentioned that I liked something very much about you. Have you guessed what? Why didn't you ask me when I was back ten days ago?

Well, I don't want to keep you guessing. To save your brain for your work, let me spill it out: I love your voice most. If only I could hear you talk to me every day.

All right, enough of this girlish stuff. I have to return to anatomy. Please be considerate to my father and keep him clean.

Good luck with your preparation.

Yours,

Meimei

My fiancée's letter bothered me to some extent, particularly her mentioning "quite a few friends" of hers. I knew there were always some young men running after her in Beijing, and they'd find ways to get her attention and spend time with her. Mrs. Yang had once told me, not without pride, that her daughter was a top beauty in her college — one of the so-called "school flowers." Even if Meimei was fond of my voice, my physical absence from her life might provide an opportunity for those men to step in.

What should I do? The question cropped up in my mind again, but it wasn't about Meimei only. For several days I had wondered whether I should take the exams, bedeviled by my doubts about the meaning of pursuing a Ph.D. The former vision of myself as one who must study hard to become an eminent literary scholar had vanished, replaced by the image of a feckless clerk who was already senile but wouldn't quit scribbling. Now I felt unable to work toward a doctorate just for the practical reason of settling down in Beijing eventually. But if I withdrew my application, I'd waste a whole year's work. More worrisome, if I changed my mind, Meimei would be so angry that she might break up with me. Since I loved her, shouldn't I just take the exams for her sake? Rationally I should do that, yet somehow my heart couldn't help revolting against such a concession.

In the evening I went to see Banping in hopes that he could help me straighten out my thoughts. His wife hadn't returned from her textile mill yet, so we two alone talked over chrysanthemum tea. Between our squat cups sat a clay teapot like a small turtle. Banping was always proud of his tea set, which he claimed was of a classic model. While we were chatting, he now and then got up and went to check a pan of eggplant cooking on his electric stove in a corner. Apparently these days the school officials were too occupied with the student movement to bother about "electricity thieves."

I described my predicament to Banping, whose hair had just been cut, cropped to his scalp. He saw my point and even said that at last I had begun to think like a man. He asked me, "If not Beijing, where would you like to go? Stay here?"

"Honestly I don't know."

"How about joining me at the Provincial Administration?"

To be a real clerk? I responded mentally.

He went on, "They still need somebody for the Policy Office. Man, you would be an ideal candidate for that position.

You're smart, trustworthy, and easygoing. If you get into that office, don't forget me. I'm sure you'll become a powerful figure in a couple of years."

"Don't they want a Party member for that job?"

"I don't think so, or I wouldn't have seriously considered it before I decided to go to the Commerce Department."

Indeed Banping wasn't in the Party, though he had applied for membership. I said, "But I'm not cut out for an official."

"Who is? You can always learn to be one. For a man of your caliber nothing's easier than holding a job like that."

"Banping, the crux of my trouble is that if I don't go to Beijing, Meimei may split up with me. You know how much I love her."

"You shouldn't worry too much about that. Is there any future in doing a Ph.D.? Look at our teacher—he collapsed out of the blue and can't stop babbling like a moron. To be honest, he often reminds me of the human insect in Kafka's *Metamorphosis* who can't communicate with others anymore. If you remain in academia, you may end up either like Mr. Yang or like one of the four middle-aged teachers in our school who died of exhaustion and cirrhosis last year."

"Come on, don't try to scare me. Just tell me your opinion. What should I do?"

"All right, let me be forthright. A real man should put his career before his woman. If you get the job at the Policy Office, Meimei may not cancel your engagement at all. Even if she does, you can always find a better girl."

"How can you be so sure?"

"Believe me, lots of good girls will want a man like you if you hold that position. Women by instinct always look for a good provider in a man, because they think of raising kids.

There's nothing wrong in this, just biological—human nature. Before I became a college student, no girls in my hometown would look at me. But after I entered college, several of them wrote to me. Imagine, a nondescript man like myself received a dozen love letters in a year, all packed with sweet words and honeyed phrases . . . Brother, I've known you for almost three years and can see a weakness in your character."

"Which is?"

"You have a broad romantic streak and tend to take a woman to be a goddess. You're so impressionable that anyone who dangles a skirt looks pretty to you."

"You imply I'm a sensualist?"

"No, you're a woman worshiper. You adore women so much that when dealing with a real woman, you don't know your own worth anymore."

"Truth be told, I do like women, a lot."

"All right, but you shouldn't worry too much about Mei-mei. Remember what Frosted Flute said about love?"

"What did he say?" Frosted Flute was a well-known local poet, though he hadn't published his first book yet.

"He said: I won't pick lilies and keep them, because along my way flowers will bloom one after another. I can't recall the lines word for word. Anyway he said something like that."

I wanted to laugh, because the quotation was altogether out of context. In his poem Frosted Flute didn't talk about love but about the gains and losses in one's life. Besides, women are not flowers that you can dump without qualms when you no longer need them. I said to him, "The fact is I don't see any meaning in becoming an official either."

"Jian, you've read too much and your brain has ossified. Why should we hold a powerful official position? My answer is, pure and simple, the pursuit of happiness. Once you have power, you'll have more comfort and pleasure. We must suck all the juice out of this life!" He said the last sentence almost ferociously.

I was amazed by the earnest look on his face, which was still weather-beaten and bronze-colored. We seemed to be talking at cross-purposes. He couldn't see that what I sought was not material gain but something significant to my being, something that could make me feel my life was properly used and fulfilled. He couldn't understand our teacher's cry — "I must save my soul!" He was only concerned with the flesh.

The door opened. In came the rear of a brand-new Flying Pigeon bicycle, gingerly pushed backward by Anling, her right hand holding the leather seat and her left the handlebar. She stood the bicycle alongside the wall. "Welcome. What wind brought you here?" she said to me pleasantly. She had on a pink dress with a cloth waistband fastened by a gray plastic buckle. The fashionable dress didn't become her and made her appear rather countrified. She looked tired despite her apparently high spirits.

"I just dropped by to see how you're doing," I said to her.

"Any news from Meimei?"

"Yes, she's well."

"Good. You and Banping go on chatting. Don't stop because of me." She went over to the washstand behind the door and began washing her face with the water her husband had prepared for her in a basin.

Banping and I talked for a few more minutes about Mr. Yang's condition and some undergraduates' planning to go to Beijing. When Anling had laid on the table the stewed egg-

plant, corn porridge, and some steamed flower buns, I took
my leave in spite of their urging me to stay for dinner. I was a
bit disappointed, as I realized I shouldn't have come to seek
Banping's advice. Granted that he treated me as a friend,
speaking with complete candor, he and I by nature were different kinds of people: I was too sensitive, too introverted,
and maybe too idealistic, whereas he was a paragon of peasant cunning and pragmatism. However filthy and ugly this
world is, a man like him can always manage to be at home in
it. People of his type have few nerves, are full of vitality, and
are more likely to endure, survive, and prevail.

Unable to decide what to do, I wrote to Meimei that
evening to sound her out.

May 10, 1989

Dear Meimei,

Your father is recuperating, though slowly. Don't worry
about him; he is in good hands now.

Recently I have been going through a crisis. I can no
longer see any point in earning a Ph.D. I love you, Meimei.
Rationally, I am supposed to take the exams, so that I can join
you in Beijing and we can build our nest there. Yet deep
down, I cannot help but question the meaning of such an
endeavor. By "meaning" I mean how this effort is significant
to my existence as a human being. I know the capital can offer
me better living conditions and more opportunities, but I cannot see any meaning in the material benefits. To be honest, I
don't care much about creature comforts.

At the bottom of my crisis lies this question: What is the
good of becoming a scholar who serves as no more than a

clerk in the workshop of the revolution? I cannot answer this question, which your father thrust on me. At times he is delirious, but at last he speaks from his heart.

For a week or so, I haven't been able to study for the exams. Now I feel reluctant to attempt them; probably I will withdraw my application. Don't be angry with me, Meimei. I will explain more when you are back. Please write to me, my love.

Yours always,
Jian

PS: Your father once suggested that I apply to graduate programs at American universities. This is infeasible now. Even if I passed TOEFL and got a scholarship from abroad, my school here would not allow me to leave. A faculty member in the Foreign Languages Department got a research fellowship from the University of Pennsylvania, but she could not obtain a passport, which is contingent on the official permission from our school, so she had to forfeit the fellowship. You may know her. Her name is Kailing Wang — she collaborated with your father in translating Brecht. I just heard that outraged, she has joined the student movement. In fact, I saw her demonstrating on the streets four days ago. She claims that her human rights have been violated.

In my crisis another question is also overwhelming, namely, what can I do?

18

When I entered the sickroom, Mr. Yang was sleeping with the quilt up to his chin. The room was brighter than the day before; a nurse's aide had just wiped the windowpanes and mopped the floor, which was still wet, marked with shoe prints here and there. The air smelled clean despite a touch of mothball. "How is he today?" I asked Banping.

"Awful." He shook his heavy chin, then motioned for me to go out.

In the corridor he said to me, "He's been sleeping since eight o'clock. At the beginning I thought it would be a quiet morning, but it turned out to be awful."

"What happened?"

"He had bad dreams, shouting at the top of his lungs and kicking his feet. He also talked about you."

"Me? What did he say?"

"He said you were studying at Beijing University. He was proud of you and praised you to somebody."

"Did he really mean that?"

"I think so. By the way, do you know who asked him for a recommendation besides yourself?"

"For what?"

"I'm not sure. Somebody asked him to write a recommendation for a young man, but Mr. Yang wouldn't do it and said, 'I know nothing about your nephew.' He was mad at that person, and they had a row."

I was puzzled and said, "He never quarreled with anyone except Professor Song." Then I remembered that the other day Mr. Yang in his sleep had begged someone to leave him and his family alone and refused the offer of a large apartment and a full professorship. But that didn't sound like a fight.

"It couldn't be Professor Song," said Banping. "He can write recommendations himself."

What confused me more was Mr. Yang's praising me in his dream. Did he really want me to become a Ph.D. candidate at Beijing University? Why this reversal of attitude? I wished he were himself so that I could ask him.

After Banping left, I began to mull over the letter of recommendation he had mentioned. Intuitively I felt it might have some bearing on Mr. Yang's stroke. The thought came to me that probably the person asking for the letter might be the same one who had promised Mr. Yang the apartment and the full professorship. What kind of recommendation was this? Perhaps it was for college admission. But what did the person's nephew want to study? For what kind of degree, a B.A. or an M.A.? In what field? Classical literature? And at what school?

Unable to figure out any answers to these questions, I began to read the current issue of *Beijing Review,* an English-language weekly, to which I had subscribed ever since I was a graduate student. It carried a lengthy article about Mikhail Gorbachev's visit to China; I could follow its general drift without consulting a dictionary.

About an hour later, Mr. Yang started to talk in his sleep. He said calmly, "Why did you turn down my proposal?"

At first I thought he referred to some departmental business, so I didn't think much of it. Gradually it became clear that he was having an exchange with a woman. I closed the magazine, trying to follow him.

"I don't give a damn about my scholarship!" he said, gnashing his teeth. "Can't you understand? I wrote you more than two hundred letters, which you discarded like trash. How much time did it take me to write them? Couldn't I have used that amount of time to make a book? Nothing but my love for you mattered to me at that time. I wanted to waste everything on you, even my life." He stopped with a catch in his throat, his lips bloodless and quivering.

He had written over two hundred love letters? Evidently this woman didn't reciprocate his love, so she couldn't be Mrs. Yang. Who was she? Was she someone I knew? Was she still alive? She must be. Did he—

He cut my thinking short. "Don't cry. I just want to speak the truth. You are old enough to take the truth now." He swallowed and bit the corner of his mouth.

Where was he now? Had the woman expressed her regret for turning down his proposal and ignoring his love letters? That seemed implausible; otherwise he wouldn't have spoken with such an unforgiving heart. Did this exchange actually take place, or was it just a figment of his imagination?

"Ah, my scholarship," he said bitterly. "After you dumped me, how could I have killed time except by reading and writing, creeping like a worm among book piles? If only I could have found another way to while away my life!" He chuckled mockingly. "Who would want to be a useless scholar and a lifeless bookworm? I'd prefer not to."

My mind was spinning. Why did the woman refuse his offer? He couldn't have been a bad-looking man when he was young. At least he must have been very intelligent and a good conversationalist.

"What do I mean?" he scoffed. "I mean I'd prefer to be a househusband, as I told you thirty years ago. Have you forgotten that? Ah, my dear, what a poor memory you have. I wanted to cook meals, wash laundry, take care of our kids and home after we got married. I promised you to do all that, didn't I? . . . I would prefer to be a happy donkey bearing the whole load of the family without a murmur. To hell with my scholarly work! To hell with my lectureship! To hell with my books! My true ambition is to become a househusband. But how many women would take such a family man seriously? Who wouldn't think of him as a weakling or a disgrace? Oh, my real dream will never come true." Although his voice was impassioned, the words were as clearly articulated as if spoken by an actor. He must have rehearsed them many times to himself.

Who was this woman? She had been with him thirty years ago, when he was twenty-nine. She must have been somebody before Mrs. Yang, because Meimei was twenty-four now and she had told me that she was born three years after her parents got married. This meant his marriage had started twenty-seven years ago when Mr. Yang was thirty-two, three years after the unidentified woman turned him down. Why wouldn't she accept his offer? He was not persecuted in the late 1950s as hundreds of thousands of intellectuals were, so it was unlikely that she rejected him for a political reason. Then why? Because she didn't love him? Or for some other personal reasons?

"Don't judge me by my appearance!" he cried. "It's true that for years I never spoke to you and treated you like a stranger. But let heaven witness how in my heart I was dying for one woman only, and that was you! If I had spoken to you, believe me, I might've collapsed at your feet. Except for avoiding you, there wasn't another way to contain my emotions and keep myself together in appearance. Now I'm too old to conceal my true feeling. It doesn't matter how you feel about me, I've always loved you—loved you. At night when I can't sleep, I'll turn in bed thinking of you, only you." He gave a long sigh.

So for all thirty years his heart had been possessed by this woman. Didn't he love his wife? Probably not. Small wonder their marriage wasn't a happy one.

He continued, "Don't cry, Lifen. Don't cry, my dear. I used to think that my heart would grow cold and exhausted as my belly grew forward. But no, in here"—slowly he drew his right hand closer to his chest—"there's always the young man's heart that desires and desires, hungrily."

He fell silent, tears spurting out of the wrinkled corner of his eye and running down toward his ear. I moved over and wiped them off with my fingers.

So her name is Lifen, but Lifen who? I wondered. Does Meimei have any idea about this woman? Mr. Yang transferred to our school from Nanjing University twenty-eight years ago, and Meimei grew up here, unlikely to have known Lifen in person, who must have remained in Nanjing. Could Lifen have been the cause of his job transfer? In other words, did he come to Shanning University, a smaller and shabbier school, so as to shun her?

"Oh, I hate you!" he roared with a contorted face. "If only I had known your cunt was never idle at home!"

His ferocious voice shocked me. Why was he so furious at Lifen? They must have gotten quite intimate, or he wouldn't have made such a crass remark. Then I remembered that three weeks ago he had mentioned some woman's nipples that tasted "like coffee candy." Maybe they belonged to Lifen.

My train of thoughts proved wrong. He croaked, "I — I believed that at least I had a faithful wife and a lovely daughter at home, but you betrayed me!" His face twisted, its wrinkles deepened into furrows.

Now he was accusing his wife! So this might have no connection with Lifen. It was almost unthinkable that Mrs. Yang could have had an affair. She was a high-cheeked woman and kept to herself most of the time; on the other hand, though rather shriveled now, she must have been quite pretty when she was young. Mr. Yang's words — "a faithful wife and lovely daughter at home" — implied that he had been separated from his family, so the conversation might have taken place soon after their reunion. When could this separation have happened? During the Cultural Revolution? It was possible, perhaps when he was sent to the countryside.

This time I guessed right. He spoke again, in a relaxed tone of voice. "In the fields we worked like beasts of burden. When we were gathering in soybeans, I had to bend so low and so long that I couldn't keep my back straight the next morning.

But I always gritted my teeth to endure the back pain. I could do that not because I recited poetry in my heart but because I saw you and Meimei in my mind's eye—you two were my hope. Little Chang couldn't stand the torment any longer, and one afternoon he slashed his wrist with a sickle, bleeding to death. We wrapped him in a reed mat, buried him on the bank of a swamp, and didn't even have time to find a stone to mark the pile of dirt. I didn't kill myself, though I thought about it many times. Why not put a period to the endless sentence of suffering? Perhaps death was no more than a long sleep from which you didn't need to wake up. Yes, why not uproot this misery once and for all? I didn't take my life because I wasn't cruel or courageous enough to desert you and our daughter. So I hoped and hoped, dreaming that someday I would come back as happy as Tu Fu when he returned home from the war-ridden land. I would shout his lines, 'My wife and children are aghast to see that I'm alive, / All our neighbors gather along our walls watching me home.' But my home was no longer the same. It's broken because of you!" He burst out sobbing.

I felt so miserable that my jaws went numb, but I wouldn't blame Mrs. Yang. Unlike many women who divorced their condemned husbands at that time, at least she hadn't left him; instead, she waited for him, raised their daughter alone, and kept the family intact. It wasn't easy to live like a widow with a husband alive who was a Demon-Monster. Meimei told me that for two years people would point at her mother's back on the streets. Besides, Mr. Yang might never have loved his wife wholeheartedly, if his love for Lifen was that deep and that hopeless.

Seeing that more tears were coming out of his eyes, I picked up a towel. As I was about to wipe them off, he wagged his head, striving to lift his hand to stop me. "Leave me alone!" he cried without opening his eyes.

I obeyed him, standing back. He went on, "You ask me to forgive you for sleeping with him? I forgive you for that, but I shall never forgive you for writing me those false letters telling me how much you loved and missed me. You deceived me. It would've been better if you had told me the truth. That would have prevented me from dreaming. I survived only because I held fast to an illusion. Oh, what a fool I was! Why was I such a coward? Why didn't I slash my wrist too?"

How had he discovered the affair? Did Meimei know anything about it? He seemed quite nasty to his wife, unfaithful though she might have been. An affair didn't have to mean she hadn't loved him. He had forgotten that he was far away from home and that a woman in her situation would need a man around.

Then I asked myself, *If Meimei two-timed you, would you still accept her as your wife?* I didn't know how to answer.

Mr. Yang sighed, "Ah, life, what an ocean of grief!"

For a moment silence filled the room. Then he declared in all sincerity, "I'm only afraid I'm not worthy of my suffering." His assertion made my gums itch.

19

It was almost midmorning. I opened the window of our bedroom to let in some fresh air. Outside, on the sun-baked ground a pair of monarch butterflies was hovering over an empty tin can, which was still wet with syrup. The colorful paper glued around the can showed it had contained peach wedges. I turned away from the window and resumed scrubbing a shirt soaking in my basin. Huran had athlete's foot, and from under his bed his shoes emitted an odor like rotten cabbage. Mantao stood in the middle of the room and repeatedly raised a set of sixteen-pound dumbbells above his head. His dark bangs, in a sideswept wave, almost covered his right eye. His face was soft and pale; a film of perspiration coated his forehead. In fact we had another roommate, a graduate student in the Philosophy Department, whose bed was next to mine, but he had never used it because his wife had an apartment in town. His absence pleased us somewhat, as we could have more space just for the three of us, although in wintertime we often wished he had slept in here at night so that his body heat could have made the unheated room a little warmer.

Having scrubbed the shirt and left it in the basin to be rinsed later, I opened my mosquito net and lay down on my bed. With my right arm tucked beneath my head, I began reading a letter from my parents for the second time. Regardless of seasons, my roommates and I all had mosquito netting hanging over our beds so that we could have some private space inside the nets.

Done with his exercise, Mantao came over and drew my net open. Waving his sweaty hand, he said to me, "Can you play volleyball with us this evening? We need you to beat the fellows in the Physics Department." He was rubbing his hands free of dirt, which dropped in tiny bits on the floor.

I put the letter facedown on my belly. "Sorry, I can't. I'm not feeling myself." I could receive and pass the ball better than most of them, but I didn't want to play today. My head was aching. Heaven knew in what state of mind I would be when I returned from the hospital toward evening.

"Just one game, please." He nudged me with his elbow.

"No."

"You miss your girlfriend again?" He smiled, his eyes turning into slits on his baby face.

"Yes, very much," I admitted.

"Ha-ha-ha, what a man!" He closed the mosquito net. I knew he would talk to others about how lovesick I was, but I didn't care.

My parents' letter said they had just renovated the north-wing house, in which there was a new brick-bed now. The walls of the bedroom were freshly papered so that Meimei and I could use it in the summer. To my parents, we two must have been like a married couple (though Meimei still called them Uncle and Aunt), because we had stayed together in their home the summer before. Several times they had mentioned they couldn't wait to hold a grandchild. I begged them not to say this in front of my fiancée. I had only one sibling, a younger brother, so they expected Meimei and me to give them a grandchild first.

Their letter made me more anxious, because I hadn't heard from Meimei yet. She must have been mad at me for giving up the exams, and I was uncertain whether we could spend this summer together.

Last July, when staying at my parents', Meimei and I had often gone swimming in the Songhua River. She wasn't a good swimmer, always floating and diving in the shallows, whereas once in a while I would swim across the main channel, where the currents were rapid and cold. One afternoon, on our way to the beach, we ran into a young couple walking over from the opposite direction. Below the broad levee birds were warbling in willow thickets; now and again a loon gave a cry like a croupy guffaw. The woman was petite, in a straw hat and a white silk blouse, which rippled slightly in the fishy breeze. She was pretty, like an actress. The man was a tall officer, bareheaded and with his collar unbuttoned, though he wore a uniform. With a wan face and bushy eyebrows, he looked urbane, rather emaciated. The moment they passed by, Meimei whirled around to observe them.

"Hey, what is it?" I asked and poked her in the ribs.

"That man's face looks so familiar." She turned back and we went on toward the beach.

"You know him?" I asked.

"No, I don't, but he reminded me of somebody."

"Who?"

"Dr. Liu, who was my mother's friend."

I felt strange about the past tense she used. "You mean this doctor isn't your mother's friend anymore?"

"No. He died when I was six, of gastric perforation."

We didn't get into the water as we had planned. Instead, we sat at the warm beach, and she continued telling me about Dr. Liu while she absently scooped a handful of white sand and let it trickle from one palm into the other. She said, "I didn't know my father until I was four. A year after I was born he was sent to the countryside. Life was hard for Mother because the nursery and the kindergarten wouldn't accept me, a child whose father was a counterrevolutionary. Dr. Liu was very considerate to Mother, and he often came to baby-sit me when Mother was away at work in the lab, where she took care of animals. They were in the same hospital at the time, but they often worked different shifts. When I was three, on a summer day, Dr. Liu took me to a small park close by, which had a pond inside with some waterfowl in it. He held me in his arms, telling me that the big white birds were called swans. I wondered if I could ride on one of them and fly away like a little girl did in a movie. Then three preschool boys appeared. They all wore slingshots around their necks and Chairman Mao buttons on their chests. They came up to us and one of them pointed at me and said, "This is the bastard of a counterrevolutionary." Another boy tweaked my toes and called me 'little slut.' I didn't understand their words, but I knew they meant to hurt me, so I broke out crying. Dr. Liu carried me away, patting my back and saying,

'They're just small hooligans. Meimei's a good girl.' When I calmed down, I saw tears on his cheeks."

She paused and narrowed her eyes, watching two pelicans flying over the other shore, one chasing the other. Then she went on, "He was an older man, in his early fifties. Mother told me that he had studied medicine in Japan and was the most skillful surgeon in the hospital. His wife died of bone cancer in the late 1950s. After that, he lived by himself. It was said that he had loved her very much. They were classmates in college. For some years I was so attached to him that I thought he was my father, although Mother often showed me Father's photos and said he was coming home soon. When Dr. Liu died, Mother and I attended the funeral. She collapsed in front of hundreds of people, crying and raving beneath his portrait and a pile of wreaths."

"When did he die?"

"Nineteen seventy-one. That same year Mother was transferred to the agricultural school."

I felt her mother's relationship with Dr. Liu might have been more than friendship, so I asked, "Did your father go to the funeral too?"

"No, he didn't. In fact Father wasn't happy about Dr. Liu's presence in our life. I remember he and Mother once quarreled over this. Mother yelled at him, 'You'll never understand!' Perhaps he was jealous."

We didn't swim that afternoon, though it was scorchingly hot. Nor did I teach Meimei how to make bird cries as I often did when we were there. I could trill, warble, and twitter like most birds, because in my early teens, having no friends, I had spent many afternoons in the thickets alone, collecting firewood and picking mushrooms.

The sun seemed very close to our heads. The water sparkled and sloped away toward the eastern sky, where herons and cranes were bobbing beneath the distant clouds. We sat there, now watching the vast grassland on the other shore with our arms around each other, now lying down and kissing passionately. From time to time a passing steamboat would blast its horn at us; some of the sailors must have been observing us through binoculars, but we were too engrossed in ourselves to care.

"Jian, we really need you to join us in the volleyball game," said Mantao before leaving for class.

"I'll try to be there, but don't count on me," I said.

"All right, see you in the evening." He walked out, humming the tune of "When Will You Come Again?," a lovey-dovey song that had come back into fashion a few years ago after being banned for three decades.

His shortwave radio was still on, giving forth crackling static. I got up and flicked it off. At once the room turned as quiet as if the whole house were deserted. Lying in bed, I tried to connect what Meimei had said about Dr. Liu with Mr. Yang's accusation against his wife in his sleep two days ago. As I was thinking about the mess of their entangled emotions, a miserable feeling came upon me. Even in our suffering, how isolated human beings can become. Mr. Yang seemed unable to stop taking Dr. Liu to be a mere third party, even though Liu had been dead for eighteen years. By nature my teacher might not be a small-minded man, but in this matter he was a picture of obstinacy.

20

I often wondered how much Banping Fang knew about Mr. Yang's private life. Had he heard about his unrequited love for Lifen? Was he aware of his marital trouble? Our teacher's mind now resembled a broken safe — all the valuables stored in it were scattered around helter-skelter. The thought bothering me most was that Banping might have known as much as I did. I was afraid he'd tell others.

The next afternoon Mr. Yang talked to a woman in his sleep again, but for a while his words were too fragmentary to be intelligible. He snickered and groaned alternately as I was leafing through the English-language magazine *China Reconstructs*. At about 4:30 he started singing. He sang in a sugary voice, impersonating a young woman:

> *Oh my ring, I lost the gold ring*
> *My groom gave me last spring.*
> *How can I get it back? Oh how?*

If an old man picked it up
I'd treat him to dinner at my house
And can accept him as my grandpa.

If a young man has it now
He can do anything with me
Except share my bridal bed . . .

Done with singing, he grinned lasciviously and said, "I can tell you're not a virgin. I don't like virgins, I want a real woman." He chuckled, his voice tapering off.

I held my breath and was all ears, but he only grinned. He seemed to be with a young woman or a girl. What was he doing? Flirting with her?

Then his voice grew audible again. "You're mine, every part of you belongs to me. No, he-he-he, I was just kidding, can't help being silly whenever I'm with you. Oh, I'm so lucky." His face was glowing.

Who was he speaking to? When did this happen? Some years ago? Time was crucial here. If this had taken place before his marriage, the young woman could be his wife-to-be. But he sounded as if he was having a good time with a different person. Who was she? Lifen?

"Ah, look at these legs," he said, sighing. "Look at these breasts, gorgeous. Aren't they fresh peaches? My goodness, how you're dazzling me! Oh, I'll have a heart attack tonight. I can't breathe." He smiled lewdly. "Oh, how come I'm so lucky! Am I dreaming or awake?"

So they definitely went to bed together. Since she had peachy breasts, she must be the same woman whose nipples tasted "like coffee candy," which I had heard him mention twice. When did this take place? Long ago? Or recently? If only he had revealed some clue to the time, then I might be able to figure out what was going on. Could this—

He cut my guessing short. "Don't think I'm a bad man. It's true I'm not a good man, but I'm not a bad man either. To be honest, you're the second woman I've ever touched in my whole life. So don't take me for a shameless, dirty old goat. I'm just an ordinary man who's fond of pretty women. But most women don't like me. I never thought that someone like you, charming and full of life, would be interested in me. If only I were twenty years younger . . ."

After a sigh, he subsided into silence.

He had made love to only two women in his life? That meant that besides Mrs. Yang, this was the only woman he had gotten intimate with, so she might have been Lifen, of whom he still dreamed from time to time. By now I was certain that Lifen didn't live in Shanning City and that they couldn't have met regularly. If he didn't love his wife, he must have gone through a good part of his life without the company of a woman he really loved. In other words, though married, he must have lived an emotionally barren life. His confession reminded me of a handsome, strapping graduate student in the History Department, a Casanova who often boasted that he would not consider marriage until he had "tried it out" with one hundred women. He was so bold that he'd accost a stranger girl, saying, "May I invite you to coffee or tea?" If she replied, "I already have a boyfriend," he'd tell her, "It won't hurt to do some comparison." In this way he often succeeded in securing a date. A friend of his told me that he was reaching his target of bedding a hundred women and would look for a wife soon. I often wondered why he had never encountered a woman outraged enough to harm him.

Then it crossed my mind that Mr. Yang's last sentence, "If only I were twenty years younger," might suggest that he had been with a young woman in recent years. What did he mean exactly? If he were that much younger, he would have known better how to love a woman? Or more capable in bed? Or able to spend more time with her? Or he would have left his wife? He was fifty-nine now. Assuming their intimate meeting had taken place recently, which was very plausible, then the woman should be under forty, roughly twenty years younger than he. That's to say she couldn't be Lifen, whose age should be close to his. Then who was she?

Mr. Yang coughed dryly and went on to say in a clear voice, "Weiya, don't you think I'm silly? Sometimes I feel I'd like to grow potatoes at the foot of a mountain rather than teach literature. I could live a happy life if I were a farmer. With knowledge comes misery and grief. Why are you smiling? You think I'm too mawkish? Or too quixotic?"

Heavens, Weiya was his mistress! My scalp tightened and I closed my eyes. A feeling of being betrayed surged up in me while my nose turned stuffy. I shook my head as if a hard object had hit it. Who betrayed you? I asked myself. Probably both Mr. Yang and Weiya had.

On the other hand, I was quite ridiculous — how could they have included me in their liaison? Weiya had never wanted a triangle, so I couldn't possibly fill an emotional corner in her heart. I remembered Banping had told me that Weiya often came to see Mr. Yang in the mornings and that she was "very emotional." Why wouldn't she visit him in the afternoons when I was here? Did she deliberately avoid me?

"If I were a farmer in another life," Mr. Yang went on, smiling mischievously, "say a cabbage or soybean grower, would you live with me as my wife?" He paused, his face radiating childlike innocence. "Don't smile, Weiya," he said. "I'm serious. We can't be together in this life, but we may in the next life when I won't be a bibliophile feeding on paper every day. I will be a man capable of honest work and worthy of a woman like you . . ."

They even discussed marriage! Did she really love him that much? He seemed absolutely serious about this relationship. Did his wife get a whiff of it? She might have. That must be why she had left for Tibet.

"Don't say love," Mr. Yang said fretfully. "I hate the word 'love.' People say they love each other, but they'll change their hearts later on. Love is a chameleon. No, worse than any reptile, it can be sold and bought with power, money, Party membership, and even food coupons. So just say you want to be with me, or you are attached to me. That makes more sense." He stopped as if waiting for Weiya to say something.

"So am I to you," he said in reply. "But heaven always contradicts human wishes. I'm too old to deserve a woman as young and as good-hearted as you. I'm so sorry, if only I could marry you."

She actually loved him? She was willing to marry him? Why wouldn't she mind the twenty-eight-year age difference between them? He could have been older than her deceased father. Maybe she just wanted to have a fatherly man. Somehow I often had difficulty with women who were only fond of older men. Four years ago at Jilin University where I got my B.A., I'd had a crush on a girl and even proposed to her, with full expectation that she would accept me, but she declared to me that she'd never marry a man younger than herself and that she could *trust* but not love me. She wanted to continue our friendship, which I refused, because it hurt me to see her date an older fellow, who was a mere half-wit, a braggart, though he headed a student poetry group called Open Road.

Mr. Yang was wordless now. He seemed to be dozing away, still whining faintly.

How could Weiya fall for such an old man? What made him so attractive to her? Could it be his acute mind? Not likely. There were other men who had perceptive minds too, even younger and quicker than his, if not deeper. Then what could draw her to him? His erudition? His limited power as the director of graduate studies? His reputation? His eloquence? None of these was thinkable to me.

To my mind, his only quality that might have attracted Weiya was his disposition. I had noticed a kind of hidden melancholy in him. Although he seldom expressed his emotions in front of his students, his voice occasionally betrayed some kind of misery that seemed peculiar to him, as though he had been born with it. Weiya didn't live a happy life either. Her maternal grandfather used to be an accomplished epigraphist in Tianjin City, owning a Japanese bungalow, which later was confiscated by the Communist government. She told me that her father, an architect in a construction company, unable to endure the torture inflicted by the revolutionary masses in the summer of 1967, had killed himself by jumping out of an office building. Some years later she was sent to the remote Yunnan Province to be reeducated on a rubber plantation. She might have lost her virginity there if Mr. Yang's remark about it was true. A woman of her experience and background could hardly view life with cheerful eyes anymore and must have been very sensitive to the melancholy that arose from Mr. Yang's disposition. Actually some people might enjoy sadness and suffering, because their lives have been nourished only by miserable feelings. They can endure anything but happiness, which is alien to their systems. Mr. Yang seemed to be one of those people; so did Weiya. This must be the grounds for their mutual sympathy, attraction, and affection.

Whether there had been genuine love between them, I wasn't sure. Didn't Weiya tell me that she had outgrown love? Was she really serious about their affair? She might have been at first, but now she seemed quite eager to hit it off with Yuman Tan. She couldn't be a novice when it came to a romance, could she? Mr. Yang must have been too naive about her.

To some extent, I felt mortified as I realized why Weiya had treated me, a man only five years her junior, as a nonfactor in her love life, as if I belonged to the younger generation. Perhaps her relationship with Mr. Yang psychologically prevented her from counting me as a man. Yes, this might be a hidden meaning in her statement that she wouldn't do Meimei "a nasty turn": if one day Mr. Yang recovered, divorced his wife and married her, she would become Meimei's stepmother and my stepmother-in-law. She'd be a generation older indeed.

Then I remembered the virginal heart she had claimed for herself. What did she mean? Did she anticipate that I might find out about her affair with our teacher? Very possible. Then why wouldn't she wait until Mr. Yang recovered or died and then see what she should do? Why had she left him for Yuman Tan in such a hurry? This wasn't very becoming for a woman with a virginal heart, was it? Maybe her liaison with our teacher was just a fling for her, but why did he take it as earnestly as though she were his only soul mate?

These questions puzzled me. Yet one thing seemed true: Weiya might be less serious about their affair than Mr. Yang.

On the other hand, I shouldn't be too critical of her. She understood their relationship would lead nowhere, as he had made it clear to her that he couldn't marry her. She had no choice but to look for another man.

Somebody knocked on the door. Before I could get to my feet, Nurse Chen breezed in, carrying a round aluminum tray that held Mr. Yang's dinner — a bowl of custard, a cup of soybean milk, and seven or eight slices of vegetarian sausage in a dish.

"Din-din," she announced pleasantly. This also meant that my shift was over and that from now on she would look after him.

"I don't want to eat dinner," Mr. Yang replied, still in delirium. "I want to eat you. You're my best meat, palatable." He grinned suggestively without opening his eyes.

I was embarrassed, fearful that Mali Chen would take offense, but she didn't seem to mind his nonsense at all. Instead, she turned to me, smiling knowingly and batting her eyes. It flashed through my mind that she must have heard similar words from his mouth so many times that she was used to them. Her smile suggested that she knew no less than I about my teacher's private life, as if it meant to say, "Boy, you have no idea what it's like at night. This is nothing by comparison." It was as though both of us had been grave robbers, but she had outsmarted me by digging deeper and at richer spots and had found much more treasure. She was a superior thief!

Never had I imagined that she too had been prying into Mr. Yang's mind. She might already have drilled, mined, and excavated the whole terrain of his blasted brain. How I hated her! But all I could bring out was "I wish he were dead!"

"How could you say such an awful thing?" Wide-eyed she froze, still holding the tray.

I felt giddy and nauseated. Without another word I snatched up my bag and rushed out the door.

21

Weiya Su came to see Mr. Yang the next afternoon. He was sleeping when she knocked on the door. I was surprised to see her because she seemed to me a different person now, difficult for me to understand. Her right arm was hooked around something heavy in a white cloth sack, pressed against her flank. She gave me a smile, which was so familiar and so good-natured that it induced me to say, "Come in. Why stand there?" The previous afternoon I had shaved Mr. Yang, washed his hair, and applied some lotion to his hands and cracked lips, so he looked presentable now, though his face was still puffy, like a loaf of stale bread.

"How is he today?" Weiya asked rather timidly.

"He's okay, very quiet."

"We shouldn't wake him up."

"All right, we won't."

To my amazement, she took a watermelon out of the sack, not a large one, but a seven- or eight-pounder. Where on earth did she get this? I asked myself. It was springtime, not the season for watermelons. At this time of the year, most fruit stores in town had only dried and canned fruits for sale except for fresh apricots and overripe plantains. The latter came from the tropical Hainan Island, very expensive.

Weiya noticed the surprise on my face and said of the watermelon, "I bought it at Swans."

I nodded without speaking. Swans was a supermarket owned by a Hong Kong man who had invested millions of dollars in Shanning City, mainly in restaurants and retail businesses. The supermarket was the first one on the Western model opened here. I had never been there, but heard that it offered many kinds of fresh produce, all at a tripled or quadrupled price. It wasn't a place where people living on regular wages would go shopping. I was amazed Weiya could be so openhanded; she had only a meager stipend like mine.

She stepped closer to Mr. Yang and bent forward a little to inspect his swollen face, which had lost its energetic features. She went on biting the tip of her tongue and opened her mouth from time to time, as if trying to say something but unable to get it out. Her eyes darkened, their lids flickering. She kept her hands on her sides the whole time, and her fingers twisted in her green sweater. Then her egg-shaped face softened, a smile emerging like a child's, as if she intended to invoke some response from Mr. Yang, who remained expressionless, still asleep. Noiselessly I slipped out and closed the door behind me. I meant to leave them alone out of respect for their privacy. I had done this without a second thought.

The moment I was in the corridor I regretted having left stealthily, because Weiya might construe my deliberate withdrawal as an insinuation that I knew about their affair. In other words, I had treated her as his mistress rather than his student. I felt stupid, hoping I hadn't offended her. On the other hand, if I had kept her company, I might have observed her too openly.

I loitered in the hospital building, just to while away an hour. There were so many patients that outside some offices people waited in lines to see doctors. Numerous patients were lying on planks or stretchers on the floor. Nurses in white robes and caps passed by like ghosts, most of them wearing broad gauze masks. A chair with ill-oiled wheels was pushed past, in which sat a disheveled young woman moaning vaguely, her legs encased in plaster. The air stank of a mixture of urine, phenol, and Lysol; there was also a whiff of decaying flesh. At the end of the hall a man was quarreling with a woman doctor, calling her a harridan, while she yelled back at him. Some people gathered there to watch.

By accident I wandered into a dark corridor. As I walked, I heard some women groaning. My eyes were not yet attuned to the dimness when a shriek rang out from somewhere on my right. I stopped to look into a room, which was curtained off.

When my eyes were fully adjusted, I saw a long line of beds set against the wall along the corridor. On them lay about a dozen women in labor, moaning in fear and pain. A few were crying for help. Some were motionless, their swelling bellies uncovered, but none seemed concerned about the presence of the men around them. Since there weren't enough delivery rooms, it seemed that some of them might have to give birth here. Most of the husbands stood with their backs against the opposite wall, and looked downcast with dull faces. Two were chatting in whispers; one was reading a picture storybook while nibbling the end of his long mustache.

An old nurse in horn-rimmed glasses turned up and stretched out her shriveled arm to bar my way. "What's your wife's name, young man?" she asked severely. Her other hand held a glossy purple folder, which must have contained information on the patients.

"I — I don't have a wife yet," I fumbled.

"Then why are you here?"

"Just looking around."

"What? You came to see these women without their pants on? Shameless. Get out of here!"

I flinched. She raised her withered hand and put two fingers against her thumb, as if to pull me away by the nose. I swung around and took flight.

As I was approaching the door through which I had come, from behind suddenly arose the squealing of a baby, mixed with hearty laughter and chattering. "It's a boy!" cried a man.

Coming out of the maternity ward with a burning face, I saw a large mirror on the wall, beside a white tank of boiled water set on a wooden stand for public use. I stopped to see how I blushed. To my horror, in the defective mirror the right side of my face appeared larger than the left — I had different-sized eyes and ears. Hurriedly I went out of the building and sat down on the concrete steps at its front. A cool breeze wafted, soothing my feverish head a little. In the copper-gray sky a helicopter was flitting away like a giant dragonfly, its rotor ticking faintly. Somewhere a female voice shouted through a bullhorn, "Eradicate corruption!" Then, "Reform to the end!" Students were demonstrating in town again. A brass band started blasting out the Internationale.

When I returned to Mr. Yang's room, he was sitting on the bed with his legs curled up, his lips wet and glistening. At the sight of me Weiya jumped up from the bedside, stuttering to me as if in self-defense, "He — he woke up himself."

"Don't worry. He slept enough."

My words put her at ease. She asked me with a childlike smile, "He's better than last week, don't you think?"

"I think so."

The amiable look on her face made me relax. Apparently she wasn't miffed at all. Nothing had changed in her manner except that her eyes were a little brighter. She didn't seem very upset. She unfolded her pink handkerchief and wiped Mr. Yang's mouth twice. He smiled serenely.

On the bedside cabinet sat the watermelon, cut in half, and a stainless steel spoon stood in the red pulp. She had fed him! She didn't even bother to conceal their relationship. I was touched and upset at the same time. A feeling of isolation overcame me, as though she had been the only person I could turn to for a bit of solace, but she too had gone beyond my reach. I had planned to ask her about how she was getting on with Yuman Tan, but now there was no need to be so inquisitive. In her eyes I must be either a lad or a eunuch, never having amounted to a man. I remained silent, feeling hurt.

"I should be leaving," she said to both me and Mr. Yang. Then she turned to me. "Please help him with the watermelon when he wants it."

"Sure, trust me, I won't partake of any of it." I tried hard to be funny.

"You can have a bite if you want." She gave a smile, the same shy, sweet smile. "Good-bye, Mr. Yang." She waved her small hand at him.

"See you later, Weiya," he muttered. Evidently her visit had calmed him down; he looked so gentle now.

Having taken leave of me, she made toward the door. Her lustrous hair, loosely tied into a ponytail, swayed against her pea-green sweater and almost reached her curvy waist. Her slim legs and hips were swinging a little in her long jeans, whose cuffs almost touched the floor, covering her red vinyl sandals. When she had disappeared beyond the door, I closed my eyes and couldn't help but think of the words our teacher had used to describe her body.

"What have you been doing?" Mr. Yang interrupted my thoughts.

"I—I've been preparing for the exams," I answered him, though I hadn't opened a textbook lately.

"What exams?" he asked.

"For the Ph.D. program."

"You should learn how to grow millet instead."

"Why?"

"The more you know, the crazier you'll go, like me. Intellect makes life insufferable. It's better to be an ordinary man working honestly with your hands."

I kept quiet, afraid he might throw another fit. Soon he began hiccuping spasmodically like a sick rooster unable to crow.

Weiya's visit puzzled me in an odd way. Usually a mistress wouldn't bring a watermelon to her lover's sickbed and feed him without any trace of unease, but Weiya had done that as if it were a natural thing for her to do. Her manner revealed a good deal of innocence. What really motivated her? In some way she acted like a child, as if she were performing a filial duty. Yes, "filial" might be the right word to describe her manner. She behaved like a daughter dutifully caring for her sick parent.

It dawned on me that she must have seen a father figure in our teacher to compensate for the father she had lost long ago. From Mr. Yang she might have sought not only intimacy and love but also consolation and assurance. Whether she herself had been aware of the true nature of their affair, I couldn't tell, but I believed my guess was close to the truth. This also explained why no matter how friendly we were, she had never been interested in me as a man and I had always remained a big boy in her eyes. She couldn't possibly be attracted to a man younger than herself.

If only I were ten years older.

22

At lunch Little Owl was delivering a speech again. He always wore his blue jacket and pants whose legs had lost their original color, whitish and stained with grease in places. A stout fountain pen was stuck in his breast pocket, just above a large blotch of dried ink and a crust of snot. He had never worn underclothes or socks, not even in freezing weather, when he would just put on a quilted, felt-collared overcoat. Winter and summer alike, his feet were sheathed in the same pair of suede shoes, which were often broken but always patched up for him by someone. Today he was babbling about artillery and tanks, every now and again shouting, "Bang-bang-bang!"

"Comrades, more than a dozen Russian tanks are coming across the frozen river," he went on. "They're crawling toward our position like giant turtles. Bang-bang-bang, our cannons fire at them, but they won't stop. They are all shaped like an egg, so our artillery shells cannot damage them — even our armor-piercing rounds cannot penetrate them. One by one the shots slip off their turrets as they're coming closer and closer. But our brave soldiers are not intimidated by the Russian Big Noses. They hide in the trenches covered by snow, waiting for the steel turtles. Not until the tanks get within twenty feet do our men fire their bazookas, bang-bang-bang. Launched so close, every shell finishes off a damn tank. . . ."

What he was describing was a battle between Chinese and Russian troops on the Wusuli River twenty years before. Although most of the students in the dining hall knew little about the battle, they paid no attention to the madman's ranting.

When I was a little boy, I had dreamed of becoming an officer in the People's Liberation Army someday, though my father's problematic political status would have disqualified me for army service; so I had often browsed through some old magazines that carried reports and pictures of battles. The tanks Little Owl referred to were T-62s, whose oval, streamlined bodies were almost impervious to the Chinese cannons. But some of them were destroyed by bazooka shells launched from an extremely short distance. One soldier, who later became a national hero, fired his bazooka within twenty feet of a tank. The explosion not only shattered the track shoe of the T-62 but also knocked him out. Although he was saved and hospitalized for half a year, he lost his hearing for good. I remembered reading in an article that the Russians, fearing that their most advanced tanks might fall into the hands of the Chinese, had shelled the ice around those disabled tanks to sink them into the river, but under cover of darkness the Chinese troops and militia hauled one of the tanks ashore and shipped it inland. After taking it apart and studying the tech-

nology, the Chinese made our own model of the tank, which I
heard had less armor but a similar cannon.

Tired of Little Owl's old story, I picked up my lunch and
went out, despite a wall of heat already rising outside. Somehow he seemed to have an eye on me these days. As I was
passing him, he brandished his tiny fist, shouting, "Down,
down with this Russian Chauvinist!" He even shoved my
shoulder from behind. My radish soup spilled, and a slice of
pork the size of a rose petal landed on the dirt floor. A few
girls in the Foreign Languages Department giggled. I turned
around, about to curse him, but his glowing eyes invoked so
much pity in me that I went out without a word. Meanwhile
he kept yelling, "Put down your arms, we'll spare you!"

"Knock it off!" shouted my roommate Mantao. That made
the madman turn on him.

I squatted down with my back to a brick wall, on which
remained Chairman Mao's instruction in gigantic characters:
BE UNITED, ALERT, EARNEST, LIVELY. I was eating
alone and unhurriedly, but in no time Little Owl began to
bother me again, calling me a running dog of the new Tsar. I
pretended I had heard nothing. Now and then he fired a shot
in my direction. I decided to eat at a food stand or a noodle
joint for a few days, so that he might forget me. There was no
way to call a truce with him. Full of belligerence, he was
always looking for an enemy, ready to hurl invective.

Dr. Wu had instructed us to let Mr. Yang sit at least a few
times a day as a kind of exercise. During my shift, besides sitting him up, I always made him lie on his stomach for half an
hour and rubbed him with a warm towel. Recently he often

complained of lumbago, probably because he had remained in bed too long; I tried to massage his lower back every afternoon, which seemed to help ease his pain. In the morning, sunlight often fell in through the window, so I told Banping to make Mr. Yang sun himself a little whenever it was possible. I believed sunlight would do him good.

Early Friday afternoon a group of undergraduates came to visit him. They brought along a box of almond cookies, a small net bag of apricots, and a bunch of golden daisies that they must have picked on the slope east of our school. With the youngsters around him, Mr. Yang changed altogether. He was no longer a crazed patient, but instead returned to his former self — a powerful, wise, fatherly teacher. It was as if there were a switch in his head which he could flip on and off to alternate his personalities. The students put the fruit and the cookies on the cabinet and the flowers into a glass jar on the windowsill.

"How are you, Professor Yang?" two girls asked almost simultaneously.

"Not bad."

"Do you feel better?" A boy touched the quilt over his legs.

"Of course I'm better. I'll be back to school in a couple of weeks." He smiled confidently.

Before he was ill, he had been a kind of guru to some undergraduates, who believed everything he said in class and were simply spellbound by his eloquence, vast learning, and lecturing style. Once after his seminar in traditional aesthetics, a sophomore girl went up to him and gushed, "Professor Yang, every sentence you said is full of truth!" I overheard her and was somewhat embarrassed by her naïveté, but that didn't bother my teacher, who smiled at her indulgently. He wouldn't deny that he was an authority on truth.

Look at him now. He conducted himself as if he were in a classroom. He knew every one of these students by name, and talked with them in a voice full of assumed kindness and consideration. *Damn it!* I cursed mentally. *Even with his blasted brain he still can play the game.*

He called a delicate girl Small Lili and asked her, "How are you going to prepare for your political test this time? Memorizing the entire textbook again?"

"No," she said, shaking her bobbed hair. "I have too much to remember this semester." Her voice invited you to pamper her.

A boy in glasses explained, "We've invented a new method of handling the brain-cracking test. Thank goodness this is my last one."

"Everybody seems to hate the political science class. Why? I don't understand," Mr. Yang wondered.

"It's a waste of time," said Small Lili. "After every test I still have no idea what I've learned in the course, although I always get an A. I understand the words in the textbooks all right, but the ideas simply won't stay in my head."

"We prefer literature to politics," a fat girl chipped in.

The nearsighted boy said, "The teacher of our political science class is really dumb. I doubt whether he believes in the stuff he's selling us and whether he's a Marxist himself." He mimicked the teacher's squeaky voice. "'Comrades, Marxism is the only compass for our course of action.'"

Some of them laughed. A girl nudged a boy aside so that she could get closer to their teacher.

"That's not a proper attitude," Mr. Yang criticized. "Human beings have always lived in some kind of political environment, so we ought to study political science, some knowledge of which I believe is necessary and invaluable."

"We don't deny that," the boy said, "but Marxism isn't everything in political science."

"Of course not," Mr. Yang conceded. "Still, Marxism is a powerful theory that can explain social structures and the evolution of human society. When I started reading Engels's *On Feuerbach,* I had headaches, but I stuck to it. Believe it or not, little by little I grew to be fond of the book. After that, I went on to study Marx's and Engels's works, one after another. I read *Manifesto of the Communist Party; On German Ideology; Socialist: Utopian and Scientific; The Origin of the Family, Private Property, and the State;* and the three volumes of *Das Kapital.* I enjoyed their writings a great deal, but I'm not an out-and-out Marxist. I respect their passionate arguments and their profoundly speculating minds." Ignoring that these youngsters knew nothing about those titles, he talked without pause and got carried away by his own discourse, just as in his class, where I had often felt that he was addressing a visualized world beyond the reach of the audience. Unlike other experienced teachers, who would modulate their tones and rhythms and pound their points home, Mr. Yang would simply speak with great gusto and without any calculation, as if possessed by a spirit. I had always admired him as a born lecturer, though I was afraid that his voice might interfere with my own teaching. As a matter of fact, one of my students had once said to his classmates that I tried to imitate my teacher. "A cat plays the tiger" was the actual remark. Yes, Professor Yang was their "tiger." The undergraduates adored him mainly because they couldn't always understand him.

The bespectacled boy admitted to Mr. Yang, "What you said makes sense, but we're going to take several tests and have no time to read any of Marx's books. At most we can only spit out what the teacher has fed us."

"I know," Mr. Yang said. "All I'm saying is that Marxism is a powerful theory in social sciences, which you may like or dislike, but you cannot simply dismiss it as charlatanism."

"I didn't say that," protested the boy.

"But you implied that. 'The stuff he's selling us,' what does this phrase mean? See, I caught you, my boy." He gave a belly laugh.

Everybody cracked up except the nearsighted boy, who grinned, scratching the back of his head.

Arms folded, I stood in a corner and observed them with loathing. Nobody seemed aware of my presence. They prattled on and on, their topics moving from Tang poetry to contemporary fiction, from the cases in German grammar and French verbal inflections to English tenses, from painting to calligraphy, from the food quality to the dormitory conditions at different schools. They also talked about the student demonstrations in Beijing and other cities. Mr. Yang assured them in all seriousness that the government would resolve this crisis reasonably; he advised them not to act like hotheads.

I was amazed that he blended in with them so well, like a leader of a student association. He even looked healthy and happy now.

Why did he need to do this? He didn't have to pull such a trick. They all knew he had suffered a stroke and wouldn't have thought ill of him even if he had shown them his true condition. He was just addicted to wearing masks.

Never had he betrayed to me any knowledge of Marxism before, and I hadn't seen a single volume of Marx's or

Engels's writings in his home or office. God knew if he had actually read those titles he just now mentioned. I couldn't imagine him spending months, or even years, poring over *Das Kapital*. But these undergraduates simply lapped up whatever he gave them. Although Mr. Yang knew German well and could read French, he didn't know English at all; at most, his knowledge of this alphabet was merely a smattering deduced from his knowledge of the other two European languages; very often when he came across an English sentence in his reading, he'd ask me to translate it for him. How come he had the temerity to talk about the English subjunctive mood and its future perfect tense? Some of these undergraduates had studied this language since middle school, but they were too fascinated by him to question the truthfulness of his words. They loved being duped.

I was sick of him, sick of his chicanery, sick of his nonsense, sick of these ignoramuses, sick of academia, sick of the hospital! I was sick of everything!

At long last the students were ready to leave. They said, "See you soon in class, Professor Yang."

He smiled and promised, "Sure, see you later." He even lifted his swollen hand halfway, waving at them slowly.

Passing by, Small Lili turned and locked her eyes on me. I recognized the meaning of her gaze—she envied my good fortune in accompanying their great teacher, their demigod. It was as if just by staying with him in this room I were crowned with an aureole and achieved a sort of apotheosis, attractive to girls despite my unremarkable face.

The door closed, leaving him and me alone. I wondered what he was going to say. I waited patiently for him to explain why he had acted like a fraud.

"Why do you keep looking at me like that?" he asked without turning his face to me.

I stared at him sullenly.

He broke into tears. He bent down and buried his face partly in the right arm of his hospital gown. He wept almost without noise for a while. Then he moaned, "Oh, how can I get out of this suffocating room, this indestructible cocoon, this absolute coffin? How can I liberate my soul? I don't want to die like a worm."

I realized he was referring to the dark rubber-surfaced room he had talked about some time ago. My anger abated a little, but still I felt embittered.

"I want to use my office, I want to teach," he whimpered timidly.

I made no response. He cried in gasps, "Ah, I know you're de-disgusted with me. You think I'm an . . . an arch-hypocrite, don't you?"

I kept silent. He went on, "I feel the same about myself, sick of the sound of my own voice. Oh, how repulsive I am! I'm a worm, a maggot, a coward, and a feckless crook! Why, why should I live? I have wasted my life and others' lives. Why should I continue like this? Oh, if only I could quit this world!"

His self-hatred shocked me. Still, I wouldn't speak.

23

Yuman Tan came to see Mr. Yang the next day. He was a bony man with a shock of hair falling over his forehead. His sallow but intelligent face, slightly pitted, had large, whitish eyes that were often bleary as though he was underslept. Today he wore leather bluchers, a beige shirt, and buff pants held by a belt with a shiny brass buckle. In such a light-colored outfit he looked less skinny, as if he had gained a coating of flesh.

Although to me Weiya deserved a better man than him, from his standpoint she might not be the best choice. There were a good number of unmarried women among the faculty, and I was told that two of them were actively after him. What's more, he often received letters from female fans of his essays, some of whom even sent him their photos. But in my opinion, his writing tended to be verbose and pretentious. He indulged too much in self-display and overused ah's and oh's as if they were punctuation marks; he was so fond of the adverb "very" that it would appear four or five times on a single page; besides, he tried too hard to titillate his readers.

Mr. Yang's collapse had presented a rare opportunity to Yuman Tan, who in a way was Professor Song's right-hand man. By now he was fully in charge of the journal *Studies in Classical Literature,* though Mr. Yang in name remained its editor in chief. After I let him in, I wondered why he had come. Despite respecting Mr. Yang in appearance, he had never been close to him. He sat down, opened his leatherette briefcase, and said, with his eyes shifting between my teacher and me, "Professor Yang, I'm here to see how you're doing. Do you feel better?"

"No, I'm getting worse," Mr. Yang snorted without moving his head. His right hand was fingering the elastic waist of his new pajamas.

"Professor Yang, may I report to you on the editorial plan for the next issue of the journal?"

"What journal?"

"The one you've been editing."

"That's a pamphlet."

"Okay, whatever you call it. So far we have picked eight papers for the next issue. Two of them are on the regulated verse, one on Ming fiction, one on ancient folk songs, two on—"

"Why are you talking to me about this propaganda stuff? I'm not a clerk anymore."

Yuman Tan looked confused, then turned to me searchingly. I forced a smile while my forefinger was cranking my temple. "Well," he answered Mr. Yang, "because you're the editor in chief, I'm just your assistant, and you have the final say."

"I quit long ago so that I can take a trip."

"A trip? Where to?" Yuman Tan closed the briefcase and put it on his lap.

"To Canada."

"Why Canada? Isn't it very cold there?" He sucked his breath as if feeling a sensitive tooth.

"No. Every room is heated in Vancouver, warm inside."

"Doesn't it snow a lot in winter?"

"Snow can clean the air and purify your spirit."

"I don't get it, Professor Yang. Don't you get laryngitis when it's cold?"

"This country is a pickle vat and I don't want to be marinated in this filth anymore. Like the lotus flower, I came out of the mud but will not be soiled by it."

That made me panic, because Yuman Tan might report Mr. Yang's twaddle to the leaders. He said unctuously, "You can't desert us like this, Professor Yang. We need your guidance and leadership. Without you we'd be totally lost."

"You should leave this place too. In such a pickle vat even a stone can be marinated and lose its original color and begin to stink. You should find a peaceful place that has clean water and fresh air, good for the health of your soul."

Yuman Tan frowned, but immediately his face softened. He turned to me and said under his breath, "Maybe I shouldn't bother him with this trifle for the time being."

I replied, "Yes. He can't think clearly now."

"Don't badmouth me!" Mr. Yang snapped.

"All right," said Yuman Tan, "Professor Yang, you're very tired today. We'll talk about the editorial stuff another time. Take good care of yourself." He stood up, stepped forward, and patted the back of Mr. Yang's hand. Then he turned to me and said, "I'd better get going."

Mr. Yang said crossly, apropos of nothing, "I shall forgive none of you. You all hate me, but I don't care. I shall leave this mousetrap soon, for good."

Shocked, Yuman Tan furrowed his forehead, but he didn't say a word. I followed him out of the room. In the corridor I begged him, "Please don't take Mr. Yang at his word. He's beside himself today. You know he loves our country."

"No doubt about it. Don't worry." He put on a smile that showed some smugness.

As he headed toward the stairwell, I wondered why he looked so happy. Was it because my teacher's wretched condition might assure him that the journal would be in his hands permanently? There seemed more to it than that. What else motivated him to come here? I stood at the broad window and thought about the visit of this crafty man, who appeared younger than his age and quite spirited today.

I craned my neck to look out of the building. Yuman Tan was coming out the front door. Hurriedly descending the concrete steps, he walked away with a bouncing gait. He even skipped briskly as if jumping an invisible rope. A few swallows were darting back and forth in front of him, making tinny squeaks while catching gnats. He waved at the birds, as if inviting them to land on his shoulders. He was more than happy, he was elated. Why?

Then it dawned on me that he had come mainly to find out whether Mr. Yang could recover from the stroke. Now obviously to him my teacher was beyond convalescence. This must be why the little upstart was so ecstatic: Mr. Yang's permanent absence from the department would create a new quota for a professorship, to which Yuman Tan was very likely to be promoted, since he was on good terms with both the Party secretary and the chairman and had published a good deal. How mysterious life was! The two men used to have nothing to do with each other, but Mr. Yang's misfortune had produced windfalls for Yuman Tan, who was now editing his journal, busy carrying off his mistress, and might soon rise to the rank of associate professor. Did he know about the affair between Weiya and Mr. Yang? Probably not. It crossed my mind that perhaps Weiya had decided to go with him because she was afraid that the secret might come to light someday, which would make her completely unmarriageable. She had better rush to get a man. Maybe Secretary Peng already knew about the affair; that must be the truth Weiya had withheld from me when she said Ying Peng could hurt her badly.

Then the thought occurred to me that Vice Principal Huang might have known about the affair as well. His words to Mr. Yang — "Let her decide what to do herself, all right?" — now began to make sense. He must have been referring to Weiya. No wonder she feared that she might get kicked out of the university.

Mr. Yang had been reciting poetry while I was away. When I came back, he was chanting an ancient lyric:

> *Beyond the curtain the rain drizzles.*
> *Spring is fading.*
> *A satin quilt cannot keep out*
> *The cold of a tattered night.*
> *In dream I have forgotten I'm a guest,*
> *Still indulging in merriment.*

Do not lean upon the balustrade alone.
Oh, the boundless rivers and mountains,
How easy it was to leave them,
How hard it is to see them again!

Spring is gone with fallen
Flowers in flowing streams —
A difference like heaven and earth.

"What a sad poem, heartbreakingly sad," he muttered. "Like the spring, I must be leaving too."

"Where are you going?" I asked.

"Canada."

"What will you do there?"

"I shall write a book on Ezra Pound. Have you heard of him?"

"Yes, he translated some of Li Po's poems."

"Correct. He also translated *Book of Songs* in its entirety with little knowledge of Chinese. My friend at UC-Berkeley told me that there were hundreds of mistakes in the translation, so I'm going to write a book entitled *Ezra Pound: A Multitude of Fallacies.*"

He was ludicrous and again possessed by the academic hysteria that often prompted scholars to trash one another's books and papers. I asked him, "Why not go to the United States? You may find more material for such a book there."

"Canada is a larger country, and my soul needs more space."

I kept quiet and wondered why he talked so much about his soul and Canada lately. He used to insist that he was a dialectical materialist who didn't believe in the soul. Had he changed into an idealist? Or had he become religious at heart? Or had his physical deterioration intensified his awareness of the spiritual life? In any case, he appeared to be struggling to take possession of his soul, yearning for some free, unsullied space, which in his case, absurd as it seems, might be symbolized by Canada.

24

At last Meimei's letter arrived, which upset me. She wrote:

May 17, 1989

Jian:

I'm appalled to hear you want to withdraw from the exams. If you do, you will make an egregious mistake you will live to regret. Why should you squander your time and energy like this? For a whole year you studied for the exams, but now, approaching the final moment, you quail and stop trying. I cannot help but conclude that you are either out of your mind or have lost confidence. If you try and don't succeed, I won't blame you, for you have made your effort. But without giving it a fight, you want to call off the battle. I have to believe that you're not serious about our relationship. It hurts me to say this, yet the fact is clear: you're willing to let go of the only opportunity for us to be together in Beijing. How can I think otherwise?

You have your choices, and I won't pressure you to decide on anything. But please cherish our relationship, cherish this unique opportunity in your life, cherish my father's expectations of you. Just imagine how happy he will be if you matriculate at Beijing University. Please stop loafing your time away and indulging in philosophical speculations. Now is the time for action. Put up a fight!

Whatever you choose to do, I'm adamant about my plan. I shall take the exams next week (the date remains unchanged). I want to live in the capital and pursue my medical career here. Please don't write to me if there's no good news. I don't want to be distracted before I slog through the whole thing.

Yours,

Meimei

PS: We are both educated grown-ups and shouldn't be too emotional about this sudden twist in our relationship. If we have to part, let us be candid and not hold each other back for long.

Her letters depressed me, not because she couldn't understand my predicament (as she hadn't fully witnessed her father's wretched condition) but because she seemed willing, as the postscript indicated, to break up with me if necessary. I used to think that since we had spent so much time together, she would treat me as more than just a boyfriend. I was her fiancé, expected to marry her within two years. But it looked like I was no longer indispensable to her. Normally in a situation like this, a woman would accuse her man of having changed heart or having found someone else, but Meimei seemed too proud to say anything like that. She must have felt superior to me. Admittedly, she was a better match. She was so pretty that men would turn to look after her in the street. Her self-confidence unnerved me.

Yet since I last wrote her, I had grown more determined to abandon the exams, which would be given in less than two weeks. Though I hadn't yet decided what to do after graduation, recently a voice went on in my head, "I won't live his kind of life!" I meant my teacher's.

That night my roommates and I listened to the Voice of America again. Martial law had been declared in Beijing. Thousands of hunger-striking students had occupied Tiananmen Square for days; some of them began to collapse and were being shipped to hospitals to be put on IVs. We could hear the sirens of ambulances screaming in the background. It was disturbing to learn that several field armies had assembled on the outskirts of Beijing, ready to implement martial law. The radio said more troops were on their way to the capital.

Mantao had heard that three weeks ago a few students had knelt before the People's Hall with a written petition raised above their heads, but no national leaders would come out to accept the letter, though a good number of them were at a conference inside the building. This piece of news evoked mixed feelings in me.

"Why were they so frightened of the students?" said Mantao, referring to the top leaders. "Nobody would bite them if they came out and said a few kind words to the petitioners."

"Now those old farts have become the target of the revolution started by themselves," said Huran.

I chimed in, "They must think the students want to share power with them. If they accepted the petition, they'd have to answer it soon. That would indirectly admit the existence of the student organization, which has never been recognized officially. They wouldn't set up a precedent with this case."

"Good point," said Huran. "But those students were clever, kneeling in front of that building for the sake of effect. They're not subjects of an emperor, but they acted as if they were, just to embarrass the officials."

I laughed. He was right. I had never knelt down to anybody in my life. The students indeed seemed to have overacted.

"Damn, I wish I were there," Mantao said with his eyebrows straightened. "More people should go to Beijing and smash 'the Imperial Court.'" He hated the Communists because his mother, when he was four, had drowned herself in a well, unable to endure beatings by the Red Guards. Ironically she had been a Party member, a middling official. Not until a few years ago had her name been rehabilitated.

"I hope the old fogies won't set the army on the students," I said.

"You think the troops were deployed there just for show?" Huran smiled, displaying his long teeth.

I wondered how Meimei could concentrate on her textbooks while the students in Beijing were engaged in such a historic struggle, which to many of them was a matter that would decide the nation's fate. She was really tough-minded, rational like a clock.

25

Banping left behind his *Jean-Christophe*. Gazing at the massive novel on the arm of the wicker chair, I wondered how he could still read for pleasure while looking after our crazed teacher here. Wasn't he eager to find out the secrets hidden in Mr. Yang's mind? He didn't seem interested in his ravings at all. Why was he so detached? He must be either too strong-minded or too thick-skinned. In a way, I wished I were as stolid as he.

Today five minutes after I sat down, Mr. Yang began speaking in his sleep. "As I told you last week, I cannot do anything more for your nephew. I'm not a professor of physics but I already wrote a recommendation for him. Who would believe what I said in the letter? The Canadian professors must take me to be a crook. I cannot put myself to shame again."

Then his voice wavered as he lisped something I couldn't quite catch. My interest was piqued. This was the first time I had heard him mention the letter of recommendation. A few days ago Banping had told me that during his shift Secretary

Peng often came to see Mr. Yang, talking with him privately. The young man must be *her* nephew, for whom our teacher had already written a letter. Yet the secretary seemed to have been pressing him for something more. What was it?

Though unable to figure that out, I realized why Ying Peng had been so helpful to Mr. Yang since he suffered the stroke. She wanted him to recover soon so that he could be as useful to her as before.

"Yes, I do know some people in Canada," Mr. Yang said again, "but they're all in comparative literature and East Asian studies. I have no connections in the science departments there. How could I help your nephew get a scholarship in physics? Out of the question." His nose whistled as he spoke.

At last it was clear that the young man wanted to attend a Canadian school as a graduate student, and that Secretary Peng had asked Mr. Yang to secure a scholarship for him. What a silly demand!

"You don't understand," Mr. Yang resumed impatiently. "Things are done differently in Canadian colleges, where every applicant has to compete with others on an equal footing."

How ridiculous Ying Peng was. She seemed unable to see that in Canadian and American schools scholarships were not something that could be procured only by pulling strings. Every applicant must reach some minimum standard, such as 1,800 in the GRE or 560 in the TOEFL, and would be evaluated by a committee of professors, none of whom alone could arrange the acceptance of a graduate student. The admission procedures were described clearly in the guidebooks to foreign colleges, and we all had read the descriptions before we applied. A dumb official, Secretary Peng didn't have any inkling of the admission process.

"That's entirely different," Mr. Yang said in answer. "I did write a letter for him, a very strong one. I wrote it not because he's going to be my son-in-law but because he's my student, whom I've known well and believed to be a promising scholar. You see, even if he's in my field, I cannot help him get a scholarship. He has to earn it by himself. That's why he cannot go to the University of Wisconsin."

Good heavens, he was talking about me! How had I gotten dragged into their dispute? It occurred to me that this wrangle must have taken place quite recently, because the University of Wisconsin had informed me of my acceptance only three months before.

I held my breath, listening attentively as he went on: "Believe me, Jian Wan can be an excellent scholar if he has the opportunity to do graduate work in an American school. That's the only reason I recommended him. As you know, he's a decent young fellow, serious and intelligent, though sometimes he's absentminded."

Mr. Yang's good words flattered me. Although he had more confidence in me than I in myself, he would never praise me to my face and instead often called me "my stupid young man." He once remonstrated with me about my unseemly handwriting, saying with his index finger pointed at my nose, "Your script is like your face to other scholars. I don't want my students to look ugly. If you write so sloppily again, do not show me your papers." Since then, I had been careful about my handwriting.

He sighed, then said testily, "You shouldn't mix my personal life with my professional life. If you think you can lord it over me, you are wrong. Besides, you have no evidence for that." After a pause, he faltered, "I ne-never thought you could be so unconscionable. You're very sneaky and even vile. You tried to trap me, didn't you?" Then his voice turned muffled. I listened hard, but to no avail.

He was so outspoken and even fearless, I was impressed. Did he actually confront Secretary Peng? I wondered. He might have. What did he challenge her to produce evidence for?

His voice grew audible again. "I'm well along in years, and my legs are already stuck in the grave, but Weiya Su is still young. Aren't you aware that your scurrilous words can destroy her life?" His face, on which drops of sweat stood out, looked dark. His chest was heaving for breath.

Now clearly, Ying Peng had known of the affair and used it to blackmail him into helping her nephew acquire a scholarship. How absurd this whole thing was! Even if Mr. Yang had interceded for the young man, he'd only have made a spectacle of himself. No physics professor would believe his words.

"Do whatever you like," he declared. "Remember, if anything happens to Weiya, you'll be responsible." A spasm of anger distorted his face.

The implication of his last sentence must have been that if Weiya committed suicide, as some young women had done when their romances were exposed, Secretary Peng would be held accountable for her death.

Knowing of his affair, I could feel the tremendous pressure he had suffered when he uttered those defiant words. If the accusation was proved true, it would ruin both his family and his academic life, and Weiya would become notorious as "a little broken shoe" and would be punished as well, at least kicked out of the university if not banished to a small town to teach elementary or middle school. No woman with such a lifestyle problem would be qualified to be a college teacher.

Mr. Yang must have been extremely anxious, fearful that the affair would be exposed. So this might have been the true cause of his stroke.

Not entirely. What he said next added something more. "Oh, I have no money!" he wailed. "Where on earth can I get so many dollars!"

Now, it seemed the secretary had resorted to the $1,800 too. How absurd the whole thing had become, totally out of proportion! Just for an imaginary scholarship, Ying Peng would do anything. Why couldn't she see the logic in his argument? What made her believe so firmly that he could get a scholarship for her nephew from a science department? This was almost like a joke.

"I have no money, no money at all!" Mr. Yang kept yelling and rocking his head. The boards of the bed were squeaking. "Leave me alone. I've already written a letter for him. Stop pestering me!"

I felt uneasy that he had stooped to producing the irrelevant recommendation. True, few faculty members here would hesitate to write such a thing, but Mr. Yang had always been regarded as a man of principle and a model scholar. Why had he joined the ranks of liars?

Speaking of recommendations, I had translated into English a good number of them for my fellow graduate students and had seen that the letters were all packed with hyperboles and lies, as if everybody were a genius and, once transplanted to foreign soil, would flourish into an Einstein or a Nabokov. Some of them, applying to American colleges, even fabricated their own recommendations and asked their friends or siblings to sign as their thesis advisers. No American school could tell or would bother to detect the fraud. I knew a young woman lecturer in the city's Institute of Industrial Arts and Crafts who had gotten admitted to a university in Louisiana on the strength of three letters of recommendation, all composed by her boyfriend and signed by him under different names and titles.

Mr. Yang was whimpering something incomprehensible. His nose was red and swollen, while bits of spit flecked his stubbly chin. I felt terrible for Weiya. With the knowledge of the affair, Ying Peng could easily have her under her thumb. Even if Yuman Tan married her someday, the secretary, possessing the secret unknown to the husband, could continue to control her. Undoubtedly Weiya was already in her clutches. This must be why she had to obey her, though she seemed to have turned the trap to her own advantage by dating Yuman Tan seriously.

Mr. Yang opened his eyes and yawned. "Meimei, is that you?" he asked.

I made no answer. He looked around slowly and fixed his eyes on me. Somehow my heart started palpitating. Then his dull gaze moved away and fell on *Jean-Christophe* on the armrest of the chair. "Why don't you throw that thing out the window?" he gruffed.

Bewildered, I remained speechless, unsure whether he knew it was a novel. He asked me again, "If I die today, do you know what words I'll leave you?"

"No, I don't."

"Well, I'll tell you to burn all your books and don't try to be a scholar."

"Why?"

"As a scholar, you're just a piece of meat on a chopping board, whereas others are cleavers and axes that can hack you at will."

I was shocked by the ferocity in his tone and made no response. He went on, "I tell you, it's no use studying books. Nothing is serious in the academic game, just a play of words and sophistries. There are no original ideas, only platitudes. All depends on how cleverly you can toss out the jargon." He paused to catch his breath, then asked, "Do you remember the man from Tanling University who gave a talk here last winter?"

"You mean Professor Miao?"

"Yes, Mr. Miao, the windbag, who's good at speaking in quotes. Only a moron like that can direct a comparative literature department. I know ten times more than he does."

Though that might be true, I felt uncomfortable about his haughtiness, which contradicted his usual self, a modest, affable scholar.

"Ah," he yawned to the whitewashed ceiling. "'With ten thousand books stored in my mind, / Why should I grovel in the wilds?'" He was quoting the couplet from an ancient poem. I watched him silently.

He seemed to be listening to something, then cried out, "Fakes, fakes, all are fakes! You must write a book to expose those fakes! Kick their butts in their own game!"

"But I've burned the books, burned them all. How could I write such a thing?" I said offhandedly.

"What? Save them! Save the books! They're not bourgeois poisonous weeds. You shouldn't take them away from me and feed them to the fire like dried leaves. Please don't confiscate my books, don't burn them. I'm kneeling down to you, little brothers and sisters. Oh, please have mercy! I beg you, comrades, please!"

I didn't expect my words would cause such an outburst. He must have remembered the scene of his home being ransacked by the Red Guards more than twenty years before. It was a well-known anecdote that he had knelt down at some Red Guards' feet, clasping his hands and imploring them not to seize his books and throw them into a bonfire in the playing field. They ignored him, of course.

"Water, water! Put out the fire!" he yelled, twisting as though surrounded by flames.

How I regretted having blurted out those spiteful words. Books were his life, and without them he would have been incapacitated. If he had been sane, the instruction "burn all your books" would never have come from him.

"Water, water! They're burning my soul," he groaned, still squirming.

I went over to see what was bothering him. "What's hurting?" I asked.

"Water, I want to pass water," he moaned.

My goodness, he was wobbling like this because of a full bladder. What an imaginative response to the visionary flames swallowing his books. I removed the blanket, raised the upper part of his body to make him sit up, and separated his legs. From under the bed I took out the flat enamel chamber pot and placed it between his thighs. Then I untied his pajamas, but he couldn't urinate in such a posture. Aware of the problem, slowly he moved forward into a more prostrate position with his elbows supporting his upper body. Having pulled down his pajamas, I helped him spread his legs so that a little cave was made under his abdomen. Thank heaven, he wasn't too fat; a larger belly would have left no room for the chamber pot. I moved the mouth of the pot under his penis, which had shrunk almost to nothing, a mere tiny knot with a ring of foreskin. Then slowly came out a line of yellowish urine, falling into the pot with a dull gurgle.

I had helped him relieve himself before, which hadn't bothered me much, but today somehow it revolted me. I felt giddy and like vomiting. Look at this mountain of anomalous flesh! Look at this ugly, impotent body! What a hideous fruit of the futile "clerical" life, disfigured by the times and misfortunes. He reminded me of a giant larva, boneless and lethargic. Though desperately I wanted to run away, I had to stay until he was done. The foul odor was scratching my nostrils, stifling me, and I tried not to breathe. Yet despite my revulsion, my horrified eyes never left him.

When he was finally finished, I removed the chamber pot and put it under the bed. I brushed a V-shaped pubic hair off the sheet and with gritted teeth helped him lie down on his back. Then I rushed out of the room. The second I got into the corridor, I began vomiting. The spinach and rice inside me churned and gushed out, splashing on the floor again and again until my stomach was empty and started aching. My legs buckled, and I put out my hand on the wall for support to get out of the building for some fresh air.

The breeze cooled me down a little, though my face still felt bloated and a buzzing went on in my ears. Something continued tugging at my insides. About fifty yards away, near the cypress hedge, a man in green rubber boots and a yellow jersey with the sleeves rolled up was hosing down an ambulance, the water dancing iridescently on the white hood. At the front entrance to the hospital a pair of red flags waved languidly. I had clenched my jaws so hard that my temples hurt.

26

Mrs. Yang came back from Tibet, but she could attend her husband only in the evening. During the day she had to go to work at her agricultural school in an eastern suburb. On the day after she returned, a distant cousin of Mr. Yang's, hired by our department, arrived from their hometown in Henan Province. This man, with gapped teeth and thinning hair, would take care of Mr. Yang in the daytime from now on, so Banping and I were relieved. However, I still went to see our teacher every day, usually after dinner in the evening, staying there about half an hour. Apart from seeing how he was doing, I was eager to seek information about Meimei, of which her mother could hardly give me any.

On Wednesday evening I arrived at the hospital later than usual. Mrs. Yang, needle in hand, was darning a calico shirt for her husband; on her middle finger was a gilt thimble like a broad ring. For the first time I saw her in reading glasses. Though the spectacles made her appear older, they brought out a kind of equanimity in her bearing that I hadn't noticed before. Her features were gentle and amiable, as if she were at their home — she looked like a devoted wife. Mr. Yang, sitting on the bed with his head drooping aside, was humming something, perhaps the tune of a folk song. I remained quiet with both hands in my pants pockets, my back leaning against the jamb of the window. Mrs. Yang lifted her half-gray head and gave me a smile, her face pallid and slightly bloated as though she were suffering from dropsy. She must have been very exhausted. On the windowsill sat a large cassette player; beside it were two tapes piled together. I recognized the contents of the top tape — *20 Most Popular Songs*, most of which had mellow tunes. Mrs. Yang must have played them to her husband to prevent him from chanting those belligerent songs.

Out of the blue Mr. Yang yelled, "Dance for me! Sway your hips!"

"What do you want, dear?" his wife asked with a start.

"I want you to dance for me."

"You know I can't dance."

"Of course you can, you do it for every man."

"Wh — why do you say that?"

"You did it when I was away, didn't you?"

"Did what?"

"You slept with him."

She lowered her head, her face livid though her hands kept stitching the collar of his shirt. I was too taken aback to say anything.

He began crooning an old song, which was on the tape. He sang in a feminine voice:

I lift the saucers clinking them.
Ditties are easy to sing
But my mouth is hard to open.
Line by line I cannot lament enough
Human suffering, yet my songs
Please the rich and powerful.

The hook of a crescent shines
On high mansions, every one
Of which was built by poor men.
But in the teeth of winter
The wealthy smile gleefully
While the needy freeze in grief.

My head went numb as a shiver ran down my spine. I regretted having come to see him this evening, to be caught in such a flash of domestic madness. Noiselessly I tiptoed over to Mrs. Yang and whispered, "We can ask the nurse to calm him down. Do you want me to do that?"

"No need." She shook her head in despair. "Let him get his anger out. It'll make him feel better." Her tone of voice revealed that she was already familiar with this kind of rage and abuse. Although she sounded very rational, her eyes were wet. She looked mortified as she raised the shirt to her mouth to nip off the mending thread.

"Dance for me, bare your shameless thighs!" he yelled.

I looked at his wife, whose face was taut in agony, her thin jaws clenched. I felt so awful I said to her, "I should be going." Without waiting for her reply, I hurried out of the room.

I stayed a while outside the door and overheard Mrs. Yang shout at him, "Don't ever do this to me again, Shenmin! You mustn't pour out your hogwash in front of others! You made a buffoon of yourself. Now stop that! Stop smiling like an imbecile!"

In response he hit on another song, singing with some gusto. She began sobbing.

For some reason Mr. Yang had grown more delirious and more obstreperous these days. He often yelled at others, especially at his cousin, who never talked back. Apparently he didn't recognize the man as a relative, though the poor fellow always called him Elder Brother. Two days ago Mr. Yang had even refused to eat, and the nurses tied him up so that they could give him an intravenous drip of glucose. However hard his wife tried, she couldn't placate him.

On Thursday morning I ran into Professor Song in the classroom building, though lately I had avoided crossing his path. He told me to devote myself completely to the last leg of the preparation for the Ph.D. exams, which were just a week away. I thanked him halfheartedly.

Despite having time now, I couldn't concentrate on anything. Whenever I picked up a book, my mind would wander. For two weeks I had been in a quandary, unable to muster my resolve either to cancel my application officially or to resume preparing for the exams. I often went swimming in the afternoons. I missed Meimei terribly but dared not write to her.

Strange to say, Secretary Peng assigned me some new work. The Party branch of our department was considering inducting Banping Fang into the Party and was investigating the personal history of his immediate relatives to make sure his family background was clear. Ying Peng wanted me to help with the investigation. This assignment was quite odd because I wasn't a Party member and shouldn't have been involved in it. As a rule, trips of this kind were entrusted only to the faculty members in the Party, not to a graduate student like me. What was Ying Peng hatching? If only I could have seen through her machinations. Though doubtful, I had to accept the job.

"According to regulations we shouldn't let you go to Yimeng County," Secretary Peng said to me in her office. "But we don't have anyone else available at the moment. Besides, it's an easy job and will take you only two or three days."

I nodded to show my gratitude for her seeming trust, though I wondered all the while why she deliberately interrupted my preparation for the exams, which she still believed I was going to take.

She told me, "Three months ago, we sent an investigation letter to Hanlong Commune where Banping's uncle lives, but we haven't gotten a word back yet. We need an answer immediately. Your task is to go there and get the reply from the local Party branch. There's a form in the letter. Make sure they fill it out properly. You see, it's very simple, just a procedural thing."

"Sounds good, thanks," I said.

"I know you're busy now, but our Party branch must give final consideration to Banping's application for membership before he graduates. You're his friend and should help him."

"Of course, I'd love to go to Yimeng County for a couple of days. Mr. Yang's illness has really gotten to me and turned me into an insomniac. A trip to the countryside will definitely help, and I'll come back with a fresh mind." The moment I finished the last sentence, I realized my tongue had gone loose. She might intend to undo me. This trip was by no means just "a procedural thing"; it must be a move in her scheme of things, which I couldn't figure out yet.

Her sparse eyebrows joined and her forehead puckered as though she had smelled something unpleasant, then a smile broke on her large face. She said, "That's fine. I hope the trip will put your mind back in good order. But don't let Banping know where you're going. Keep this secret, we trust you."

"I won't breathe a word."

"Good."

With a black fountain pen she wrote me an official letter, which informed the Party branch in the countryside about my mission and would enable me to obtain board and lodging on the way. "Here, you're all set. You can leave tomorrow morning. Have a pleasant trip." She smiled as a double chin appeared at her throat.

Having left her office, I wondered why Professor Song as the chairman of the department hadn't mentioned my new assignment this morning when I bumped into him. Maybe it wasn't the Party branch, of which Mr. Song was also a leader, but Ying Peng herself who was sending me on the trip. By rule, she ought to have informed Professor Song of my new work. Why did she keep this so underhanded? Why was she so interested in me? I had never applied for Party membership, and politically I was a straggler, the last person who should participate in this business. She had never trusted me. Then why would she let me take part in the investigation?

27

Although I boarded the bus at 9:30 the next morning, it didn't depart until an hour later. The driver did not show up for work, having drunk too much at a wedding the night before, so the company had to call up another driver. In the bus all the passengers sat quietly. Many of their faces were sullen, but nobody dared say a word for fear that the supervisor on duty, a scratchy-voiced woman, might hold the bus forever. Not until we pulled out did people begin complaining; some even cursed the drunken driver and the rude personnel at the station.

The crowded bus crawled through the vast Yellow River Plain, which looked parched, gray, and dusty. The torrid heat made the late-spring morning feel like a sweltering summer day. The pale blue sky curved toward the horizon mottled by green-and-white patches of small villages. The lethargic clouds hung so low that they almost touched the fields, in which corn stood over two feet high and millet about one foot high. Here and there peasants were hoeing, all in conical straw hats. Once in a while some of them stopped to watch us passing by, and a few young men would let out meaningless shouts.

Farther to the north the Yellow River curved away eastward. Though the spring drought had shrunk the water, the river still looked like a broad highway, on which lines of black barges towed by tugboats crept west at a snail's pace. The river is said to be the cradle of Chinese civilization and to possess a legendary power. But for some reason the sight of it reminded me of a poem by Mantao. It began like this:

> While the rickety ferryboat
> Is crossing the Yellow River,
> I, under an urgent call,
> Rush into its toilet,
> Open my pants and hunker down
> Watching my golden bombs
> Pop at the sandy water. . . .

Nothing was sacred to Mantao, such a defiant man. Yet the poem gained some popularity for him on campus. Unlike me, he often went to literary gatherings, at which budding poets and fiction writers would talk about their theories and writings and argue heatedly. These days, however, they all discussed politics instead of literature, thanks to the crisis in Beijing.

Now in the immense plain everything seemed inert except for our six-wheeler wobbling and jolting along. The bus was so full that four men had to stand with their backs bent, patiently waiting for someone to disembark so that a seat would become available. The window near me rattled without stopping, but because of the heat I dared not roll it all the way up. The passengers behind me would have complained. A carsick girl, seated two rows ahead of me, vomited into a plastic bag time and again, making such a racking noise that I thought she might hurt her larynx. But between her vomiting bouts, she would chatter and laugh with her pals excitedly as if nothing was bothering her. *Country girls are tough*, I said to myself.

As the plain grew hilly, the road became bumpier. The bus lurched along slopes and curves and swung at elbow turns like a boat, rocking most of the passengers into a drowse. We passed village after village and town after town. I dozed away most of the time. Though it was unpleasant to travel like this, my mind was relaxed. This was a change nonetheless.

It took almost five hours to arrive at Hanlong, a small town in Yimeng County. Its dirt streets were rutty in places, flecked with animal droppings and bits of cornstalk spilled from fodder sacks carried by ox and horse carts. Most houses here were built of adobe and a few of brownish rocks. Many chimneys were belching out white smoke; the air smelled of charcoal, and bellows croaked one after another. Before a larger house, which boasted two show windows and a roof of cement tiles and looked like a department store, three knots of small boys were waging mantis fights, their cries and curses sputtering. Most of them were barefoot, running about nimbly.

Since it was too late to go to the Commune Administration, I found the town guesthouse and checked in for the night. I told myself, *Take it easy, tomorrow you'll have a whole day for the investigation letter.*

Even dinner was a change, too. In the dining room of the guesthouse I bought a bowl of sorghum porridge, a plate of stewed tofu, and a large chunk of sponge bread made of cornmeal and wheat flour mixed together. I disliked corn stuff, which was thought of as "coarse food," but the bread was the only kind offered here. It was soft and sweetened with saccharin; somehow it tasted surprisingly good, and I ate it with relish. The tofu was fresh, different from the sour thing sold in my school's dining hall. More interesting, at the other end of the low-ceilinged room a banquet was under way. I couldn't see the attendees because a line of sky-blue screens separated them from us, the common diners. The banquet was boisterous — laughter and shouts surged up from time to time. I ate slowly on purpose, curious to find out what the country banquet was like. Soon my appetite for my dinner began dwindling, as the spicy, meaty smell of some dishes served at the feast pervaded the room, caressing my nostrils.

"To your health, Magistrate Chang!" a thick voice proposed loudly beyond the screens.

"Yes, he can swallow a lake!" added another man. *What an odd way of praising someone's capacity for alcohol,* I thought.

"Drink up!"

"Hoo-ha-ha, raise your cup, everybody!"

"No one here should leave the table without getting drunk. Come on, drain your cup."

"Who'll take us home if we can't walk?"

"We have plenty of rooms here."

"Besides, his wife doesn't want him back tonight."

"Shut up, you bigmouth!"

Peals of laughter rang out and made some of the diners on this side of the room turn toward the screens, which carried the figures of prancing tigers and frolicking dragons. The creatures were golden, painted against the sky-blue backdrop. Then six waitresses in red aprons and orange pants and short-sleeved shirts stepped out of the kitchen, where burst forth the sizzle of a wok searing meat and the sound of a spatula scraping a cauldron briskly. They each held a large tureen containing a steamed turtle, on whose black carapace were stuck cooked garlic cloves and scallion stalks that made the dish look slimy. The second the waitresses entered the screened area, a commotion went up. "Goodness, we're doing turtle!" cried a man.

"Armored fish!" several voices shouted. The air beyond the screens was almost gray with tobacco smoke.

Then came the clatter of ladles, porcelain spoons, and bowls. One of the waitresses gave a little shrill laugh and said, "Thank you, I don't drink."

"Come on, just a sip!" invited a man.

"That's a good girl," another voice piped in.

A rotund man eating at my table said to us, "That's an expensive dinner, isn't it?" He pulled a piece of gristle out of his mouth and threw it on the dirt floor.

A young fellow, who looked like a salesman, said over a bowl held under his chin, "They're eating the peasants' blood." He slurped his cabbage soup.

Soon after the waitresses came out of the screened area, some men at the banquet began playing a finger-guessing game, and the room at once sounded like a marketplace. Several voices chanted together:

> There's a large red rooster
> With a fluffy tail.
> He digs into dirt like a miner
> But won't touch a snail.

His hens cry, "Stop, mister!"
Still he won't give a damn.
No matter how they holler
He eats turd like yam. . . .

The smell of tobacco and alcohol grew so thick that I felt a little woozy. Hurriedly I finished dinner and left the table. Fascinated by the ditties they had been chanting, I sashayed to the entrance of the screened area in hopes of catching a glimpse of the finger-guessing game. But a beefy guard stood there with his arms crossed before his chest, his hands invisible as if holding concealed weapons. I dared not step closer, and instead headed away for the door. Before I could walk out, a balding, husky official, apparently coming back from the public latrine in the backyard, wobbled over from the opposite direction, holding a bottle of Five Star beer. He came up to me and put his free hand on my shoulder, saying with an obscene smile, "Come, take a swig, my pretty girl." His face was as crimson as a boiled shrimp, dark goo around his lips.

I was perplexed, then realized he took me for one of the waitresses, perhaps because of my long hair and my yellowish short-sleeved shirt. I spat on the floor and cursed, "Pig!"

He guffawed, slapping his gut, and said, "Between pigs and men I don't see any difference."

As I was reaching the doorway, the waitresses came out of the kitchen again, each holding a platter of fried silkworm pupas. I turned away in disgust, despite knowing the dish was a kind of delicacy to the country people.

A crew from Shanning Film Studio was staying at the guesthouse. They had come to this mountainous area to shoot a movie. The two young fellows sharing the room with me were cameramen on the team. They told me they were making a movie about the historical figure Heng Zhang, who had been an upright official and an expert in earthquake forecasting in the Han Dynasty, about two thousand years ago.

"Why did you pick this place?" I asked the shorter man, who seemed better tempered than his hulking colleague.

"Because this is one of the poorest areas. Look at the landscape." He waved his squarish hand as if he were sitting in the open air. "Rocky valleys and barren hills, they're perfect scenery for the movie. The soil's so poor it looks like even rabbits won't shit here."

I knew the story of Heng Zhang, but I couldn't picture what the film would be like. I didn't go to the movies very often and instead read books, so I was not terribly interested in what they were making. I picked up the washbasin from under my bed, fetched some hot water, and bathed my feet in it. My only desire now was to get some sleep. I went to bed early despite the two men chattering without cease. Exhausted by the trip, I slept soundly that night.

28

It turned out that Hanlong Commune had been disbanded a few years before. The investigation letter from our school had been addressed to the former commune; that was why it had gone astray. A typical case of bureaucratic negligence.

A woman clerk at the Town Government told me that the best way to carry out my mission was to go directly to Sandy Rock, the village where Banping's uncle lived, to get a reply from the Party branch there. She assured me that if the letter had ever arrived at Hanlong, it must already have been forwarded to the village, so I'd better go to Sandy Rock personally. It was four miles away to the north. Not far; I could walk. But having wasted a solid hour at the Town Government, I couldn't set out until ten o'clock.

The walking was pleasant in the beginning as the road was flat and the air fresh. I liked the chirrup of the grasshoppers, the scent of wormwood, and the sight of the furry soybeans that were just about four inches tall. But as the road grew more sloping, I started puffing a little. From time to time sand got into my shoes, and I stopped to take them off and tip it out. The sun was blazing right overhead; there were neither clouds nor breeze. It was so dry that most fields had become tawny, the young corn, sorghum, and millet drooping with curled leaves. Far away, some dwarf trees clustered on the surrounding hills, whose tops were mostly bare rocks. Occasionally a cart, drawn by oxen or horses or by a mixed team of both, would emerge from the opposite direction, coming up and halting away toward Hanlong Town. The drivers nodded off behind the haunches of the shaft animals with their backs against loads of rocks or bricks or oil cakes; without exception each held a long whip in the crook of his arm.

Soon I felt thirsty and looked around for water, but there was no stream or spring in view. So I kept walking. As I was approaching a crossroads, a teenage boy appeared from the road on the right, coming my way. He carried two buckets of water on a shoulder pole shiny from use. Because of the heavy load, which seemed to weigh more than himself, he moved much faster than I, almost rushing forward in a tottering gait. After the crossing point, I slackened my pace.

When he caught up with me, I said to him, "May I have a drink of water, little brother? I'm so parched."

He looked reluctant, but stopped and put down the load, gasping for breath. Staring at me with his sparkling eyes, he nodded yes. I took my mug out of my bag, scooped up some water from the front bucket, and drank it. It tasted slightly salty and must have had a lot of sulfur in it. After two mugfuls I still felt thirsty.

Without a word he shouldered the load and went on his way. He looked about fifteen, and his thin shoulders showed no muscles. He didn't wear shoes, his bare feet large and broad compared with his lean calves. I watched him swaying his left arm rhythmically as he hastened away. Gradually I lagged farther behind. At the mouth of a granite quarry he turned away from my road, heading west.

It took me an hour and a half to reach Sandy Rock. Approaching the village, I heard a child crying in the distance. The screaming, which I had at first mistaken for a reed pipe being played by a tyro, was sharp and staccato, growing more guttural as I walked closer. I wasn't sure if the crier was a boy or a girl. The voice seemed to come from the hill in the northwest; it rose and subsided, but never fully stopped.

The village consisted of more than sixty houses, most of them adobe and thatched with wheat straw. Every front yard was surrounded by a low wall made of rocks piled together. An unusual hush enveloped this place as if it were deserted, and I wondered where the people had gone. As I walked around a bit looking for the village office, a few foraging sheep bleated from behind wattle gates. In the distance the child was still crying, rather furiously. By now I was sure it was a boy, whose screams came from the hillside.

Without much difficulty I found the village office, a little tumbledown house with a decaying roof, in which sat the man temporarily in charge of the daily affairs of the Party branch. His family name was Hao, and he must have been a small cadre in the former production brigade here, for he spoke with a manner of authority, though without any arrogance. The low-pitched room resembled a tiny barn; slender, crooked rafters supported bundles of sorghum stalks that formed the lining of the roof. A few cracks meandered on the north wall like rivers on a map; one of them was so wide that it could let in a thumb. Sitting opposite me at the only desk,

Hao told me, after searching through the drawers, that the investigation letter had never arrived. I felt at a loss and kept scratching the warped desktop, which was glossy and must have been painted recently. I turned my head away. On the west wall was pasted a portrait of Deng Xiaoping in a pork-pie hat, smiling and holding a cigar between his forefinger and thumb, and on either side of the portrait was a strip of calligraphy. One said, "Poverty Is Not Socialism"; the other, "We Must Liberate Our Minds." Near the door hung a clock, whose face looked rusty, its long pendulum swaying, with a lazy clack.

What should I do? I wondered, my eyes resting on an oil lamp made of a small amber bottle.

Though upset, I didn't show my disappointment to Hao, who had a narrow forehead and a broken front tooth. His caterpillar brows and rheumy eyes made him look ill, but he seemed good-natured. His blue jacket had a large rectangular patch on the right shoulder. His hands were huge, sinewy, and chafed. *Maybe he can help me,* I thought.

My guess proved correct. After I said I couldn't go back empty-handed, he assured me, "No need to worry. There's something we can do. I know the format of this kind of letters. They're all the same." He kept fanning himself with a folded newspaper.

"Can you fill out a form for me?" I asked.

"Well, I can write you a letter and put in all the information you need. I know the Fang clan well and can answer all the general questions. How would you like that?"

"Great, please do it! That will save my skin!" I said with relief.

He put down the newspaper, took out a sheet of stationery with a scarlet seal at its bottom, dipped a pen into a lumpy glass inkwell, and started writing. The steel nib scratched the paper with a rapid rustle. I was impressed by how dexterously he handled the pen despite his massive hand. Evidently he was quite literate, familiar with this kind of writing and with Banping's uncle's life, but I had no idea what he put into the letter or whether he answered the right questions. I didn't care. As long as I could bring back a letter, my mission would be completed.

"Rest assured, there's no problem with Wanmin Fang," Hao said about Banping's uncle, and put down the pen on the desk. "He's from a poor peasant family, always active in political movements. He's a Party member too." He told me this probably because he assumed I also belonged to the Party. I nodded to show my appreciation.

Having stuck the letter into a manila envelope without sealing it, he handed it to me and said, "You're all set."

I picked up the glue bottle on the desk and sealed the flap of the envelope. He rose to his feet, took an earthenware teapot from the windowsill, and poured some tea into a ceramic mug. "Here, have some tea. You must be thirsty." He placed the mug before me.

"Thanks." I lifted the tea, which looked thin and brownish, and took a gulp. *Yech, what tea is this?* It tasted bitter, a bit oily, like a medicinal decoction.

Hao saw the surprise on my face and smiled with some embarrassment. "It's pomegranate tea, good against the summer heat," he explained.

"Er . . . thanks."

Many years ago I had heard that some country people were so poor they couldn't afford to drink tea, so they used some kinds of tree leaves instead. Call this stuff whatever you liked, it wasn't tea at all. They might just want the brown color from pomegranate leaves. Heaven knew whether this substitute actually could help relieve internal heat like real tea. What astonished me was that never had I imagined that people here still drank this stuff. I tried to appear unsurprised, lifting the mug and taking a sip again.

"How's Old Fang's nephew doing?" Hao asked me.

"Banping's fine."

"The Fangs used to be one of the poorest clans in this area. That boy had no shoes to wear for school when it snowed. Every winter his hands were frostbitten, swollen like rotten taters."

"They were that poor?"

"Yes, in the year when the locusts came and ate up all our crops, his whole family had only one jacket. Whoever was going out put it on."

It was incredible that Banping had lived through that kind of hardship. No wonder he was so tough and phlegmatic. I said, "He's doing well now, quite rich actually. His wife just bought a Flying Pigeon bicycle. He'll start to work at the Provincial Administration next month."

"You don't say so! Who could tell he'd go to college and become a big official? A phoenix hatched in a chicken coop indeed. He's really something." Hao kept shaking his stubbled head, a bald patch on his crown. "That boy was smart, a quick hand at the abacus."

"Really? I didn't know that."

"He was very good at numbers. No matter how poor the Fangs were, they wouldn't take him out of school. In those days schooling was free, you know. After middle school, he became our accountant and didn't have to go to the fields like the others. That's how he got the time to study for the college exams. 'Education, education is the thing,' I always tell my younger brothers this."

I felt hungry, so I fished out of my bag half a corn bun, left over from breakfast, and began chewing it. I meant to appear natural in front of him. "Do you mind if I'm eating while we talk?" I asked, intending to show how I enjoyed the food they ate every day.

"No, go ahead. I should've invited you to lunch, but all the folks have gone to the shooting."

"What shooting?"

"You don't know? Some people came here and want us to take part in a movie they're making. I've no idea what it's about, though."

The clock struck two. The door opened and in came a woman holding a toddler, a boy with a runny nose. She wore a fuchsia shirt that was so soiled it looked almost purple. One of her blue cloth shoes had a hole in its front, her big toe peeping out. The baby was wearing a clean bib that carried on its front the large words LOVE PEACE. His hand held a chunk of black bun like a stone.

"This is my wife, Fulan," Hao introduced.

"How do you do? I'm Jian," I said and almost stretched out my hand. She looked at least ten years older than her husband, as if in her fifties; but seen closely, she must have been in her early thirties, without a single gray hair. In spite of her leathery face and flat chest, she had thick arms, muscular like a man's.

"Welcome," she said in a shy voice. I realized that women in the countryside usually were not addressed formally by a male stranger.

Meanwhile, the baby boy fixed his watery eyes on the corn bun in my hand. "Yellow cake," he cried, his hooked fingers pointing to my bun. "Yellow cake, Mama, I want yellow cake."

"Don't be naughty. I'll bake you a big yellow cake this evening. Be a good boy." She rocked the child from side to side to stop him.

"No, I want yellow cake now." He looked at me ravenously.

"All right, let's trade." I got up and put the corn bun into his hand and took his black chunk away. "How's that?" I smiled at him.

He nodded assent, then started munching the bun.

"Thank Uncle," his mother ordered, smiling with curvy eyes.

"Thank you," he mumbled.

"What a good boy," I said and put the piece of black bun into my bag. "Old Hao, please don't let Wanmin Fang know I came. I was told to keep this secret."

"Sure, I won't tell him. It's the Party's rule, I understand." He grinned.

Although I had said good-bye, Hao walked me outside of the yard. I had told him several times not to come farther; still he wouldn't turn back, accompanying me all the way out of the village. He seemed to enjoy talking with me.

On the distant hillside the boy was still crying, his voice fierce like the buzz of cicadas. I saw a few goats grazing almost motionlessly on the slope, but I couldn't see the child.

Why did he scream without stopping? I asked Hao, "What's wrong with that boy?"

"What boy?"

"Don't you hear him crying over there?" I pointed to the hillside in the northwest.

"Oh, he may've been stung by a scorpion."

"What? A scorpion can make him cry for hours nonstop?"

"It can make a man cry too." The corners of his mouth stretched aside as if he had just been stung.

"Why don't his parents help him? They can at least cover the sting with some ointment or give him a sleeping pill, just stop him from screaming in the heat."

"Easier said than done. Where can his folks get the drug and the ointment? We have no money for those fancy things. Many kids are hurt by scorpions when they look after sheep on the mountain. My daughter got bitten last fall. Oh, she hollered her head off, hoarse for a month afterward."

"How long will he cry?"

"He'll be all right before dark. Don't worry."

This meant the boy would continue to scream for another few hours. My heart sank, but I kept silent. As we went out of the village, a hen burst into cackling behind us, triumphantly announcing that she had just laid an egg. Ahead of us, about five hundred yards away in the south, stretched a barren slope narrowing into a valley between two knolls. Many people were gathered there, some standing and some sitting on yellowish boulders.

Hao said, "They're shooting the picture there. Why don't we go have a look?"

"All right, let's go." I realized why he had accompanied me all the way here — he wanted to see the shooting.

Up on the slope the two men who shared my room at the guesthouse were busy working on their camera. This was indeed an ideal setting for an earthquake scene. The slope was strewn with boulders and rocks, and there were no trees anywhere. Only a little grass spread on the edges of some dried ditches. The tops of the two knolls were plantless too, baring patches of granite. Farther up in the valley, at the foot of the eastern hillock, sat a small temple, before which stood a flagpole, whose upper half was missing. Around the temple, nearly all the gravestones had toppled over, as if an earthquake had just struck this area and tossed everything into a mess.

A few guards, hired from the local militia, stopped us and said we were allowed to watch the shooting only from a distance of thirty yards. So we had to stay where we were. In the meantime, a few members of the crew were assembling the villagers for a scene.

More than a hundred country people knelt down. Men, women, and children all were in straw sandals and ancient ragged clothes. A few shaggy men carried bedrolls slung over their shoulders. Beyond the villagers, about sixty yards up the slope, stood a two-wheeled carriage in which sat the figure of Heng Zhang, a tall, stately official. The sunlight lit up his ruddy face, glittering on the golden tassels hanging on his black hat.

A spare man with ratty gray whiskers and a mustard-colored cap, who must have been the director, shouted to the villagers, "If you don't do it right this time, I won't pay you. Understood?"

"Yes sir," replied some voices.

He went behind a lop-eared young man kneeling on the ground and stepped on his calf. "Ouch!" the fellow cried, then gave a muffled moan.

"Don't spread your legs like a crippled duck," the director rapped out.

"I won't, sir."

Then the bigwig went over to an old man, who was skinny and hunchbacked. He grabbed a tuft of his white hair and shoved his head down, which hit the ground so hard that the man groaned and would have keeled over if he hadn't put out his right hand to break his fall. The director ordered, "Let your head touch the dirt when you kowtow. Got it?"

"Yes sir."

"Now ready?" The big boss turned around and saw Hao and me. He shouted, "Hey, you two over there, get away. Hide in the gully."

The guards pushed us away while the short cameraman recognized me and gave me a military salute, though he was bareheaded.

Hiding in the ditch, Hao and I couldn't help but poke out our heads to watch. The director instructed the villagers loudly, "This time you must all knock your heads on the ground and cry like your parents just died." He raised his slim-fingered hand and called, "Ready?"

All the crew nodded.

"Action!"

The carriage, drawn by two white ponies that looked like twins, began rolling down the narrow trail. The four men walking beside it looked sweaty and exhausted, slightly staggering; one of them was carrying across his back a long sword with a red tassel. Down the slope the villagers kow-towed and cried in singsong voices, "Savior! Our Savior is descending!"

"Heaven has eyes!"

"Oh, we're saved at last!"

"Our Lord, our great Lord is coming!"

In no time their cries grew chaotic, but they had really got-ten into the drama. Some were swaying their heads from side to side as they found release in wailing. Many of them were shedding tears of joy as if the new arrival were the real Heng Zhang, a legendary savior expected by millions of down-trodden people for two thousand years. Following their par-ents, the children bawled and kowtowed too — they looked like chickens pecking at grain seeds. I was shocked by the emotion they had worked up. They were enacting their roles much more earnestly than the professionals. As if entranced, some of them were sobbing, some sniffling, and some moaning.

Heng Zhang rose a little in the carriage and clasped his hands before his chest, smiling and nodding at the people down the slope. He then stroked his long but scanty beard, as though his mind was full of wise plans. As the vehicle slowed to a stop, all the people sprang to their feet and ran up to him, car-rying baskets of foods and fruits and gourds of wine and water.

"Cut!" the director shouted and flung up his hand. "This is the fourth time today, and still you haven't done it right. I told you not to get up too soon. Why is this so difficult? I've never met people as stupid as you. What can I do with you? All right, get your money from her." He pointed at a young woman in a white gob hat and sunglasses, then went on, "Go home now. Come back tomorrow morning at ten o'clock, and we'll try again."

The villagers, still dazed despite the interruption, began gathering around the woman, who was calling out their names and handing out cash.

After dusting ourselves off, Hao and I came out of the ditch. I asked him, "How much do they pay each person?"

"One yuan a day."

"What?" I couldn't believe my ears.

"One yuan a day, the same for the kids."

My head started throbbing as I tried to control myself. Never had I thought these people could be so poor that for a pittance of one yuan they'd allow that director to do whatever he wanted with them. Some of them must never have seen a movie before and couldn't possibly enjoy the prospect of having their faces shown on the screen. My heart was shaking, filled with pity, dismay, and disgust. Feeling queasy, I squatted down. Hao explained, "That's good money for us, you know. I can't get the money myself because my dad and daughter are already there. Each family is allowed only two members in this business. Folks like us rarely have a chance to make one yuan a day. You have to sell five eggs to get that much."

Not wanting him to see my emotion, I buried my face in my palms while breathing heavily, my elbows resting on my knees. I remained this way for over a minute.

A group of teenage girls emerged from the valley, each carrying two buckets of water on a curved shoulder pole. Their loads were crushing, and they hurried down the trail unsteadily. As I wondered how this would fit in the movie, one of them lost her balance. With a clack she fell on her behind, and her buckets clanked all the way down until they hit a huge rock. She broke into a woeful cry. A young man rushed over to help her up, but she refused to budge. Her face was smeared with dust, sweat, and tears; she was wailing shamelessly with her mouth wide open like a frog. The other girls stopped and put down their loads, but they seemed too exhausted to respond to her crying. They were just watching.

"Get away!" the director shouted. He held up the camera, busy shooting. Two guards pushed the people aside. The man went on filming the crying girl, whose eyes were shut and whose voice was croaky. She even kicked her heels on the wet spot, the soles of her rubber sneakers caked with mud.

"This is it, great!" the director said rapturously, working the camera with his left eye closed.

"My dad will whack me again!" the girl shrieked. "Oh, it's too late to go back and fetch another load."

A square-faced girl yelled at her, "Shut up! Shame on you. I'll give you a bucket. Get up now."

"She's new. Everybody's like this in the beginning," a female voice whispered behind me. I watched but couldn't make sense of this scene.

Finally the girl stopped wailing. The director turned off the camera and handed it back to the short fellow. "This is real stuff," he said, beaming with his snaggleteeth flashing. Then he turned to the villagers. "You all saw it. Tomorrow when I say 'Action,' you must cry like her. Got it?"

Nobody answered.

The girl was helped to her feet. She picked up her shoulder pole and buckets, which somebody had recovered for her, and began leaving with the other girls. As she was passing the director, he took out a two-yuan bill from his wallet and gave it to her. She accepted the money without a word. Meanwhile, the film crew was packing to move to another spot deep in the valley. A cleated plank slanted up to the rear of their truck.

I figured they must have arranged the last scene, so I asked Hao, "Did they hire those girls too?"

"Nope. Can't you see that the girl hurt for real?"

"Why was she so mad over two buckets of water?"

"Why so mad?" He sounded a little crazy too, his eyes ablaze. "She carried the whole load from Sweet Fount Village three miles away. When she had almost reached home, the water was suddenly all lost. Why so mad? Her folks were waiting for the water to cook supper with. She was too tired and it was too late to go back to fetch another two buckets. Her dad is going to beat and cuss her this evening and the whole village will hear him. Don't you see now, why so mad?"

"She has to go that far for water? Isn't there a closer place?" I asked with a tremor in my voice.

"Nope. There're two wells in Peach Village, but you can't drink the water from them. It stinks like piss and can only be used for laundering and watering livestock. Folks have to go to Sweet Fount for good water."

"If only I had known all this!" I said, hot with rage.

"Then what?"

"I might've bashed in that old bastard's snout!" I meant the director's.

"That wouldn't help, wouldn't change anything." Hao licked his front teeth. His candid words, like a slap on my face, rendered me speechless.

A moment later I asked, "Have you folks ever sunk a well here?"

"Yes, but we don't have a deep well, so we often run out of water in summer."

"Why didn't you sink a deep well?"

"We have no machinery."

"Why not get some?"

"No money."

His answers were so simple that they made me feel like a raging fool. I looked around and saw that indeed the entire area of six or seven villages had no electricity. Actually there weren't enough trees on the hills whose trunks could be used as electrical poles.

Having taken leave of Hao, I walked back to Hanlong Town. The scorpion-stung boy still cried at the foot of the mountain, though no longer continuously. He wailed falteringly, now stopped awhile, now resumed. I fished the piece of black bun out of my bag and took a bite. It was bitter, sticky, and coarse, made of millet husks, acacia blossoms, and sweet-potato flour. It tasted like an herbal bolus, but I chewed on it. Nothing could abate the bitterness in my heart.

29

The morning after I returned from the countryside, I went to Secretary Peng's office to deliver the letter and also to inform her that I had decided to go to the Policy Office at the Provincial Administration.

I had made up my mind to pursue an official career not because I fancied I could become a savior of the country people. No, I wasn't that simpleminded. I just wanted to be a man more useful than a lightweight clerk — a scholar. If I had the power to distribute resources and funds, I would help children like the screaming boy stung by a scorpion and the downtrodden folks like those at Sandy Rock. There was work to do in this province, for which I was finally ready. My trip to the countryside made me realize that like myself, the poor villagers were also meat on the chopping board. Now I was determined to become a knife or an ax, so that someday I could cut down a few corrupt officials. In addition, this move was also a way for me to have a life different from my teacher's. I wanted to live actively and meaningfully.

As I was about to knock at the door of Secretary Peng's office, somebody shouted from inside, "You've tortured him ever since he's been ill!" I recognized Mrs. Yang's voice.

"No," countered Ying Peng. "I've helped him all along. Anybody with good eyes can see how much I've done for him. You should be more grateful to me."

"You helped him? By going to the hospital to blackmail him again and again?"

"Watch your tongue, Nanyan. Your words are wide of the mark." She called Mrs. Yang by her first name.

"Didn't you demand that he get a scholarship for your nephew?"

"Who told you that?"

"Never mind how I found out. You mean to torture him to death, don't you?"

"Nanyan, how can you accuse me like I was a criminal? I tell you, he promised me to secure a scholarship for my nephew before he went to Canada last year."

"No, he didn't."

"Of course he did."

"Liar!"

"Listen, if he hadn't promised me, I wouldn't have granted him permission to visit Canada. Do you think he could've gotten the funding without my support? To put it bluntly, he owes me a scholarship."

"You're shameless."

"Tell me, how much is shame worth? I'm a practical person, a dialectical materialist."

"You're like an animal."

"At least I've never gone back on my word like what your

husband did. I hate two kinds of people most: ingrates and promise breakers. He's both."

I tried to think of a case in which Ying Peng had failed to make good on her word, but I couldn't recall one. Strangely enough, she did seem to have a clean record on that score.

The secretary spoke to Mrs. Yang again. "Heaven knows how much I've done for him and you."

"For me?"

"Yes."

"Like what?"

"I took steps to keep him from sinking deeper into an illicit affair with his student. Don't you see that you're a beneficiary of my effort too? I helped save your marriage. Shouldn't you be more grateful to me?"

Silence ensued. At last I understood why Ying Peng had yoked Weiya to Yuman Tan — she meant to separate her from Mr. Yang so as to stop their relationship and protect our teacher and his reputation. In other words, she might indeed have intended to help him out of a troublesome situation, although at the same time she had used this knowledge to coerce him into working for her nephew. From her standpoint, her effort did constitute a huge favor, for she could have exposed him and turned him in anytime, but instead, she had the affair hushed up and dissolved within the department. Heavens, she would do anything to get the imagined scholarship. How ludicrous and convoluted this whole thing was! I was flabbergasted beyond words.

I knocked on the frosted glass on the door. "Come in," called the secretary.

Both women were surprised to see me. Mrs. Yang's face

was dilated with emotion, her round eyes fierce and her chest heaving. Her hands, with the fingers interlaced, kept rubbing each other. I gave Ying Peng the envelope that contained the investigation letter and my application for the position at the Policy Office.

Then quietly I left the room without exchanging glances with Meimei's mother, fearing Secretary Peng might suspect that it was I who had informed Mrs. Yang of the letter of recommendation and the scholarship. Yet in Ying Peng's glowering eyes I detected some suspicion. In fact, I had never mentioned this matter to Mrs. Yang. The only person who could have provided her with the information was Banping. Or Mr. Yang himself in his delirium.

Because of the trip I hadn't listened to the Voice of America. Mantao told me that some army units had attempted to enter Beijing City to clear the hunger-striking students out of Tiananmen Square, but they were blocked on the streets by the civilians. Although most of the soldiers were unarmed, tanks and artillery were assembling on the outskirts of the capital. I was disconcerted by the news, but I couldn't imagine that the government would dare to unleash military force on the citizens and students, especially with so many foreign reporters still in Beijing, who had gone there for the Soviet leader Mikhail Gorbachev's visit about two weeks before. Some undergraduates on campus were exasperated and restless, eager to leave for the capital to join forces with the students there. Mantao was considering if he should go with them.

Early that afternoon a phone call came from the hospital. With a sob Mrs. Yang said to me that my teacher's condition had turned critical and I should come as soon as possible.

Hanging up, I hurried to the dormitory building to inform

Weiya of this sudden development, but she was not in. Without further delay I set out for the hospital. It was said that recently Weiya went to paint in Yuman Tan's apartment almost every afternoon, and that one of her paintings had been selected for an exhibition of works by young artists in the province. In my heart I still resented her getting so thick with that man in a time like this. Our teacher, her old inamorato, wasn't dead yet, why couldn't she wait a while? Bicycling townward, I couldn't stop thinking about what Mrs. Yang had told me on the phone. That morning, when she was quarreling with Ying Peng in her office, my teacher had fallen out of bed and hit his head on the edge of the cabinet. After emergency treatment he came to, but he still had suffered a severe concussion and a cerebral hemorrhage.

When I arrived at the hospital, Mrs. Yang, Banping, Mali Chen, and several others were in the sickroom. Dr. Wu was there too, wearing a grimy stethoscope around his neck, a cigarette in a jade holder clamped between his teeth. At the sight of me the nurses stepped aside to let me get to the bedside. My teacher looked lifeless, his face ghastly and a large bandage on his right temple. From the evasive look in the doctor's eyes I could tell that no medication would help Mr. Yang anymore, though an IV bottle still hung on an iron stand beside the bed, whitish liquid dripping listlessly into the brown rubber tube.

Mr. Yang's lips moved, but his voice was inaudible. Slowly he opened his eyes, which gradually expanded into an earnest look. "Nanyan," he murmured.

"I'm here, Shenmin." Mrs. Yang held his hand in both of hers.

"I'm sorry, truly sorry," he said.

"Don't talk like this, please!" she begged tearfully.

"Forgive me, dear."

"You mustn't think of leaving me, Shenmin!"

"Too late," he mumbled and closed his eyes.

A heavy hush descended in the room, and everyone watched him intently. A moment later, he opened his eyes again. His face showed an intense effort, as though he was struggling to suppress some pain. His eyes searched around slowly but with eagerness. "Tell me what you want, Shenmin," his wife asked, sobbing.

His lips stirred again; he was saying something none of us could make out. He turned his head a little, his gaze fixed on the window half draped with green chintz curtains. On the sill sat Brecht's *Good Woman of Szechwan,* which hadn't vanished perhaps because few people here could understand the play. I went over, picked up the book, and waved it at Mr. Yang. Sluggishly he shook his head. I put it down and drew the curtains together to block out the daylight; the room at once became darker, but he shook his head again. I pushed the curtains aside to let in the light. He nodded, so I opened the window too. He observed the outside world with a distant look in his glazed eyes, his face almost vacant. Beyond the mountain of anthracite the sky was pale with smog, an elongated, underlit cloud gliding over the aspen crowns whose leaves were flickering in the breeze. Somewhere pigeons were cooing. Blankly Mr. Yang stared at the outside; he seemed disappointed, maybe already unable to see anything clearly. He went on shaking his chin as though irritated by something. A gust of wind tossed up a small cloud of coal dust; then a ray of sunlight fell on one of the concrete smokestacks and bounced slantwise toward the window. For a moment the room was brighter, but Mr. Yang didn't seem to notice any change. He withdrew his eyes from the window and closed them, facing the ceiling and murmuring something again.

Both Mrs. Yang and I stepped closer and bent down to listen, but again couldn't understand his words. So I straightened up and joined the others, standing stupefied and watching him while his wife wept, her hand on his upper arm.

"It was awful yesterday afternoon," Banping whispered to me. "He recited poetry without a stop."

"What poetry?" I asked.

"Mainly Dante, I guess."

"What part of Dante? *Inferno* or *Paradiso*?"

"I don't know, I've never read Dante."

Mr. Yang heard my voice and moaned faintly, "Jian, Jian—"

All eyes turned to me as I stepped closer and leaned over him. "Mr. Yang, I'm here. This is Jian." I held his cold hand in my fingers.

"Save me, save my soul!" he gasped.

"I'm with you, Mr. Yang."

"I'm scared."

"We're all here, nobody can hurt you."

"Oh, don't touch me!"

I let go of his hand. "What do you want me to do, Mr. Yang?"

"Keep them away from us!"

"Who?"

"Save her."

"Who are you talking about?"

He didn't answer. I was on the point of asking "You mean Weiya?" but checked my tongue.

His lips still quivered, his voice tapering off. He seemed to be uttering something desperately while I strove to listen, but I couldn't hear a thing. I observed him for a minute or two. Then he made some audible sounds again, and I put my right ear to his mouth. Now his voice was clearer. He said while exhaling feebly, "Jian, Jian—"

"Yes, I'm here."

"Be good to Meimei."

"I will."

"Remember, avenge me and . . . don't forgive any one of them. K-kill them all!" His eyes suddenly opened, glinted fiercely, then closed, for good.

I was stunned by his last words, of which I could make nothing. I hunched over the bed with a blank mind, my eyes fastened on him. His mouth was half open as though he were still struggling to inhale, and his face gradually stiffened. Behind his parched lips, his teeth were yellow and dark along the gums. Two of his molars had gold fillings.

I was still in a daze as Mrs. Yang broke into short, rapid sobs. Mali Chen held my arm and pulled me away so that the other nurses could disconnect the apparatus from him. Not until now did I begin weeping. Tears ran down my face while something was writhing in my chest; I was sobbing shamelessly like a wretched small boy. Except for Banping, who looked sideways at me now and again, nobody seemed surprised by my crying. None understood why I had suddenly given way to my emotions. Even I myself couldn't explain my feelings until some time later. A middle-aged woman said to Nurse Jiang about me, "He must love his teacher dearly like a father." Two other nurses tried consoling Mrs. Yang in the opposite corner of the room.

Mali Chen handed me a clean towel. "Don't be so heart-broken, Jian," she said with wet eyes. "He often called to you at night. He must've been relieved to see you before he passed away."

"Thanks," I mumbled.

Then Banping held my elbow and led me out of the room. My head was swimming, unable to understand the full meaning of Nurse Chen's words. The stains of drying tears were still stinging my lower lids.

In the hallway Banping sighed and patted me on the shoulder. "Don't be too sad, Jian. Maybe it was time for him to go. He suffered enough."

His words brought me back to my senses to a degree. As we walked along the corridor, I said to him, "It was an awful, awful death!"

"Come, it's normal," he said impassively. "All the dead have the same ending. Death is the ultimate equalizer."

"How can you say that?" I couldn't help staring at him.

"All I mean is that he died naturally. A lot of people are bedridden for years before making their final exits. By comparison, our teacher didn't suffer that much. We should be grateful for that."

"Do you know what his last words were?"

"What were they?"

"He told me to kill all his enemies!"

With the same unperturbed face he replied, "Considering he wasn't himself anymore and what he'd gone through, that isn't too outrageous. We all have our enemies and shouldn't judge the dead too harshly. We should forgive him for saying that."

I realized it was impossible to make him see the monstrosity of our teacher's death, because he thought of suffering only in the physical sense. What a callous mind he had! As an educated man, why did he seem to have no spiritual dimension in his mind at all? He had heard Mr. Yang sing songs and recite poems and had witnessed his struggle to save his soul, but nothing could touch him deeply or enable him to commiserate with our teacher beyond the level of bodily pain. He only understood the suffering of the flesh. No wonder he was so at home in this world, where callousness is a source of strength, essential for survival, and where most people are obsessed only with the health and longevity of the body. I took the Rose cigarette he lit for me, dragging on it relentlessly.

To me the worst part of Mr. Yang's death was that he had died in hatred. Did he save his soul? Probably not. Possessed by the desire for vengeance, he couldn't possibly have attained the spiritual ascent he had striven for. He failed to liberate his soul from the yoke of malevolence. His soul must still have bogged down in the muck of this life.

His death shook me to the core. In my mind a voice kept dictating, "At all costs you mustn't die a death like his!" This sentence reverberated in my head for the rest of the day. It wasn't just about death. It presupposed that I must live differently in order to avoid a virulent end. As a human being, I should spend my life in such a way that at the final hour I could feel fulfillment and contentment, as if I had completed a task or a journey. One doesn't have to be an accomplished scientist, or a consequential official, or a billionaire, or a great artist to feel that death is no more than a natural change like a sleep after a long day's work. In short, death should be a comedy, not a tragedy. This realization strengthened my resolve to leave the university for the Policy Office.

30

For most of the next day I lay in bed thinking about Mr. Yang's last moment and about how to talk to Meimei when she got back. It rained the whole morning, frogs croaking like crazy outside. In the afternoon the sun came out, but it was so muggy that the bamboo mat underneath me remained sticky. I hated this enervating climate. Unlike my hometown in the Northeast, there was seldom a brisk breeze here in spring or summer.

Toward dinnertime, when the loudspeaker began to play the song "Both Hands Water Happy Flowers," my stomach at last rumbled, reminding me that I had not eaten lunch. I wouldn't go to the dining hall because Little Owl might pick on me again; instead, I went to Deli Bite, a noodle joint nearby that had opened recently. It stood next to a grand Gothic church, built by German missionaries in the nineteenth century, which had served as a depot for cotton yarn for over three decades. A year ago the church had been renovated and reopened; now hundreds of people went to it on

Sunday mornings. As I walked toward the church, I noticed that its windows, formerly glassless, were all glazed now, some of the panes flashing in the setting sun. The peaked towers looked awesome, though the belfry was still empty.

Through the window of Deli Bite I saw two large wicker baskets sitting on the glass countertop, both covered with white quilts. They must have contained twisted rolls and wheaten cakes stuffed with pork and chives. I'd heard that noodles here were especially good, so I bought a radish soup and a plate of noodles fried with slivers of lean pork and mung bean sprouts. At an empty table in a corner I sat down, eating unhurriedly.

The owner of this place was a middle-aged woman, who was so stout that she had no neck and her bare arms resembled two long loaves of bread. Her small eyes were almost buried in their hanging lids. She was fiddling with the beads on an abacus; once in a while she slapped at a fly with a leather swatter. Although she looked cranky, I liked this place. Different from state-owned restaurants, it was relatively clean and quiet here. Besides, it offered cheaper food.

As I was eating, a squat man sauntered in. He must have been a peasant, in his mid-forties, having a mud-colored face, piggy eyes, a severe underbite, and cupped ears. He was stripped to the waist and wearing only black slacks, secured above his hips with a band made of the same cotton cloth as that of his trousers. His triangular breasts jiggled a little as he walked. His body reminded me of a Buddha's, though his pudgy face showed no benevolence.

"A bowl of noodles with fried soya paste," he drawled as if speaking through his nose, and handed a banknote to the woman behind the counter.

In a little while a large bowl of noodles with a pair of connected chopsticks standing in its middle was put before him. The woman stretched out her hand to deliver the change. The man counted the money, then his sparse eyebrows knotted together. "Why did you charge me five fen more?" He spoke loudly for everybody to hear. Besides me there was only one other customer eating in this place.

"Don't you have eyes?" the woman asked sharply.

"Why did you shortchange me?"

"No, I didn't."

"Give my five fen back, now!" He threw up his hands.

"Can't you see the pair of chopsticks on top of the noodles? That costs five fen. You're not blind, are you?"

"I don't want them chopsticks. You gave me that yourself." He pointed his index finger at the woman while his other hand took a green plastic spoon out of his cloth waistband. He waved it and said, "I have my spoon. Who wants your shit-digging sticks?"

"Watch your mouth!" she yelled. "I have no change for you. Clear out of here, will you?"

"Uh-uh, not till you give my money back."

"Okay, you stay here. I'll give you something for change. I've never met a customer cheaper than you."

"You're cheap, you gyp people."

Arms akimbo, he stood by the counter waiting patiently while the soybean paste atop the noodles was sending up steam. I was amazed that they were fighting over such a trifle, just five fen, which wasn't worth the anger they had worked up. I was curious to see how this squabble would end.

Then out of the kitchen came a tall young man in jeans, the cuffs of which were tucked in knee-high rubber boots. He looked savage, with sloping eyes and an athletic build; a knife scar curved at the corner of his mouth. "You're the bum that wants money?" he shouted, and went straight to the waiting customer, who was too petrified to make a peep. The man seized the peasant's hair with his left hand; with his right fist he started punching him in the face. "This is your change! Take this!" he kept saying through his teeth.

The peasant was groaning and stamping his foot. "Ow! Ow!" he yelled, trying in vain to cover his face with both hands. He struggled desperately but couldn't break loose from the thug, who was striking him harder and harder.

This was too much, worse than robbery. The other diner, an old lecturer in sociology, hurriedly finished his meal and made for the door. I stood up and went across to the brute. "Cool it! That's enough," I said firmly, glaring at him. He stopped and inadvertently let go of the peasant. "You mustn't beat your customer up like this," I added.

"Who the fuck do you think you are?" he exploded. "This is none of your business."

"It is my business to stop you from committing a *crime*," I insisted.

To my surprise, he turned and walked away toward the kitchen. He shouted at me over his shoulder, "You wait for me there! Damn you, you act like a ghost that's never afraid of death. I'm going to give you a test."

The peasant was still gasping with tears. Dark bruises appeared on his face, and his eyes had become puffy, almost sealed. He bent forward, loosened his waistband, and retied it. On the floor were his broken spoon and drops of blood from his nose. As soon as I handed him a piece of paper, the young thug rushed over with a cleaver in his hand. At the sight of the knife the peasant cringed, then dropped to his knees, begging, "Master, please spare my worthless life! I won't come to make trouble again." He clasped his hands before his chest and then put them down on the floor. Shamelessly he began to kowtow, knocking the concrete floor as if his head were a block of wood. I took a deep breath and tried to refrain from trembling.

Initially the brute had come for me, but the racket the peasant made invited him to deal with him first. He said to him with a wicked smirk, "Come again whenever you like. You're always welcome." He raised the cleaver over the man's head.

"No, Master! I won't cross your doorstep again. Please spare me. Oh help, help!"

The cleaver drew a circle in the air and came down onto the peasant's head, but as it was falling it twisted so that its side struck his crown with a crack. "Ouch!" He collapsed to the floor and instantly began crawling toward the door. The thug kicked him in the buttocks again and again until the squealing man rolled out into the street.

Now the brute came at me. He placed the cleaver on my shoulder, pulling and pushing it as if sawing my neck. The blade sent a chill down my body, but it wasn't sharp enough to draw blood. My right leg was shaking.

"See how stiff the shaft of your neck is?" He cracked a smile, half closing his lozenge eyes. His lips protruded, spit flying about as he spoke.

I couldn't say a word. As though my chest were jammed with sand, I could hardly breathe.

"You think you're mighty smart, huh?" he hissed. "Now feel this. I didn't expect you were that wild a moment ago.

How do you like this now, boy? Cold, eh? Why are you so tame?" His grin distorted his pimply face. Out of his nostrils came hot, alcoholic fumes, which kept brushing my forehead, but I wasn't sure if he was drunk.

I swallowed to catch my breath and remained unbudging, though the cleaver still rested on my shoulder. He said, "If I like, I can hack your noggin off and it'll drop to the floor like a rotten pumpkin."

How I wished I had taken off! Cold sweat was running down my back, my armpits were clammy, and my heart was lurching.

The thug snarled, "You think you're mighty gutsy to help that worm. Fact is, you're just a jackass. Where's he now? He doesn't care a hoot about how you'll end here, does he? He just crawled out the door to save his own ass. He's a dumb animal, a yellow-faced ape, and shouldn't be treated like a man." His words sent a sharp pang to my heart. "Knees!" he cried, pressing my shoulder with the side of the cleaver.

Heedless of his order, I said, "I'm going to have you arrested."

"What?" He tipped his head back and went off into loud laughter. Unwittingly withdrawing the cleaver, he kept on, "You, such a little book bag, have me nabbed? Boy, you never fail to amaze me."

"I'll do it soon."

"All right, I'm going to let your noggin stay on your neck for a while so I'll see how you can nab me. Now, get out of here. Your grandpa's tired of handling you today — I don't want to soil my hands to beat the shit out of you. Do you hear me? Get out of my face!" He still held the knife before his chest. There was dried pig's blood on the blade.

I braced myself to say to both him and the fat owner of this place, "I'm going to work in the Policy Office at the Provincial Administration. The first thing I shall do is have your business closed."

He turned to look at the woman, who was visibly stunned by my words. Flaring his nostrils, he let down the cleaver, which hung along his thigh lifelessly. Beads of sweat emerged on his nose and cheeks. I left without another word.

Scarcely had I stepped out the door when the woman caught up with me and pleaded, almost in tears, "Please don't have my business shut down. Have mercy, comrade! My brother's just an asshole. He didn't know who he was dealing with. He has eyes but they're only rotten meatballs in their sockets, so he can't see a high official in front of him. I'll ask him to apologize to you. This place's all we have. Please don't wreck us. You can eat here for free . . ."

I walked away without giving her a look, though she followed at my elbow for about fifty yards. I was shivering with fear and excitement; an itchy laugh was mounting to my throat, but I suppressed it. A long truck passed by carrying four concrete electrical poles, moaning fitfully and throwing up a cloud of dust. I was headed for the campus, amazed by the effect I had produced just by mentioning my future job. On the other hand, I was embittered, as the thug's remark about the peasant rankled me more now. How right he was about him! I had intended to rescue that man, but he wouldn't have had second thoughts about letting me be butchered alone. I felt betrayed, realizing he was one of those people I meant to help.

31

The memorial service for Mr. Yang was held the following day at New Wind Crematorium, which was at the foot of One Thousand Buddhas Mountain, two miles south of the city. Meimei had come back the night before and attended the service. Most of the faculty of our department were present; so were several school officials. Mrs. Yang, Meimei, and I wore black armbands and white roses made of gauze on our chests. People came to us and gave their condolences. Meimei wiped her eyes with a foulard handkerchief the whole time and kept saying if only she had been with her father when he was dying. I stood beside her as though I already belonged to her family. And most people shook my hand too.

Mr. Yang lay in a massive coffin, which most of the dead shipped here would occupy for a few hours or a day before being pushed into the furnace at the back of the house. On either side of the coffin stood a thick white candle, shedding bronze light on the long strips of paper attached to the wreaths that stretched away toward the side walls. The strips carried elegiac words, such as *In life you were a man of distinction; in death, an immortal spirit! Boundless glory to you! Your noble soul will never perish! You will live in our memory forever!* Mr. Yang looked awful, his face shiny with a thick layer of rouge and his bloodless lips slightly apart. A fat fly crept into his mouth and a moment later came out, zigzagging on his chin. All his wrinkles had disappeared, but his features didn't seem to have relaxed; he looked as though still thinking hard about something. His hair seemed wet, combed back neatly and parted in the middle, and it exuded an odor like ammonia water.

Professor Song, as the departmental chair, delivered the memorial speech. He praised Mr. Yang as a diligent, erudite scholar and a model teacher, who had loved the people and the Party with "a pure heart like a newborn baby's," and whose death was a great loss to the university and to our country. He wanted all the mourners to transform our grief into energy and strength so as to carry on my teacher's cause, which was to build a first-rate literature department that would eventually offer a Ph.D. program. He concluded with a small sob, "Comrade Shenmin Yang, may you sleep in peace. Your heroic spirit will always remain with us."

Then the pair of black loudspeakers hung up in the corners of the hall bellowed out the mourning music as loudly as though some monsters had broken loose and were haunting this place. People lined up to pay their last respects to Mr. Yang. Among them were Weiya and Kailing. When it was Kailing's turn, she burst into tears at the foot end of the coffin, crying, "Professor Yang, we still have many books to translate together. Why did you leave so soon?" She wailed with abandon, hands holding her sides. No one seemed surprised, probably because she had a reputation for being visceral. I stole a glance at Mrs. Yang, whose face remained unchanged, sad but dignified.

A few women teachers of the Literature Department shed tears, too; even some men had wet eyes. Weiya stood by a half-moon window, motionless as if lost in thought. She didn't show much emotion, though she seemed ill, colorless, her cheeks more prominent. I couldn't help but look askance at her. She was unaware of my observation and absently held something in her hand, perhaps a key or a tiny pen. However, as she went to the coffin and bowed deeply to Mr. Yang, I noticed a solitary tear hanging on her right lower lid. The tear didn't move, as though congealed. She turned and hurried away, her face rather haggard, bonier than before. Approaching the door, she covered her mouth with her palm, and her shoulders trembled. With lurching steps she left alone before the others.

Secretary Peng was also at the memorial service. I talked with her briefly and found out that she had seen my application for the position at the Policy Office, but the crematorium wasn't a proper place to talk about such a matter, since I was obligated to keep Meimei and her mother company throughout the memorial service.

The day after the funeral, Meimei and I had a talk. We met in her father's office, whose single window faced a huge weeping willow. I left the door ajar so that nobody could accuse me of using Mr. Yang's office for smooching. Already there were grumbles in the department about my access to this office. In fact I seldom entered it these days. Some faculty members must have coveted this room, which was more spacious than theirs, and they were afraid I might occupy it permanently.

The heat coming in from the outside was palpable. Through the screen window the thrumming of cicadas could be heard, and from time to time a droning bee bumped into the iron mesh with a tiny thud. After Mr. Yang was hospitalized, I had kept everything in place here. His ink bottle, Plexiglas paperweight, tobacco box, and porcelain teacup all remained in their original places on his desk. On the wall, in the very place once occupied by Weiya's painting of the smiley monk eating figs, now hung a large framed photo, in which Mr. Yang, wearing a huge red paper flower on his chest, was accepting an award for his scholarly accomplishment from the director of the Provincial Education Department. The prize was a bulky dictionary, *Origins of Words,* and a blue satin case containing a Hero fountain pen. On either side of the picture were two certificates pasted to the wall, commending his teaching. He had been elected an outstanding teacher four times.

Meimei and I sat face to face, with the desk between us. I tried to relax some, my heels resting on the crosspiece under the table. She wore a honey-colored dress with a bateau neck. A pair of sunglasses clasped the front of her thick hair. Despite her nonchalant manner, she looked exhausted, not having slept well several nights in a row. Her cheeks had lost their glow and her face was a bit sickly. She must have worked very hard lately; even her eyes looked tired, not as vivid as before. The moment she received the telegram, she had rushed to the train station and caught an express back to Shanning. By then she had finished her exams, in which she believed she had done well. Apparently she was still upset about my decision to withdraw from the exams, which would be given in two days.

"It's not too late yet, Jian," she said in her contralto voice. "Please take them, just for me."

I swallowed, but managed to reply, "Forgive me, Meimei, I've made up my mind. Don't try to bring me around." I hated to say that. This was the first time I had ever refused to listen to her.

"I don't understand why you changed your mind all of a sudden," she said vexedly, pursing her lips.

"It's hard to explain in a few words. I spent weeks at your father's bedside and he made me think a lot. Let me just say I don't want to live an intellectual's life anymore."

"What's wrong with that?" she insisted, her upturned nose quivering, which usually foreshadowed a rage.

"It's a waste of life. Every intellectual is a clerk in our country."

"That's malicious! How come you've become such a crude cynic?"

"Your father told me that."

"He taught you many things, why have you forgotten them all except this spiteful idea? He must've said that when he wasn't in his right mind."

"But that's the most truthful thing he ever said."

She looked me straight in the face, her large eyes full of doubts, which gradually turned into annoyance. Her long eyelashes flickered. "So you definitely won't come to Beijing?" she asked deliberately.

"Not as a student."

"Can you come in another way?"

"I don't know."

"What are you going to do then?"

"I've written to Ying Peng and informed her that I want to work in the Policy Office at the Provincial Administration."

"You mean to be an official?" she said in disbelief.

"Yes, a real clerk."

"You have betrayed my father."

Surprised, I raised my voice. "You don't understand your father at all. You don't know how miserably he suffered his whole life. He wanted to be an official too, but he didn't have an —"

"Don't blaspheme my father!"

I thought of telling her about the absurd letter of recommendation and the scholarship her father had promised Secretary Peng, but I bit my tongue. Then it dawned on me that Mr. Yang's desire to become a scholar-official might not have originated only from empleomania. Driven to despair, he too must have thought of officialdom as the only possible way to live a life different from a futile intellectual's. In other words, if in my place, he would have made the same choice. Though struck by this realization, I didn't know how to explain it to Meimei. All I could say was "Believe me, you really don't understand your father."

"I'm his daughter. At least I know what kind of man he'd like to have had as his son-in-law."

"What do you mean?"

"You can figure it out by yourself."

"So I'm disqualified?" My heart twinged, but I kept calm and forced a smile.

"What else can I say?" she replied.

"Why?"

"Because you're too greedy and don't know your place in the world."

"What is my place?"

"My father taught you to be a scholar in poetics so that you could go to Beijing and study there. Also, in that way we could be together. If he were alive, he would never allow you to get involved in politics."

"But he told me not to be a scholar before he died. He told me to quit studying books. He even said I'd be better off growing millet."

"That's all rubbish. He couldn't have meant what he said."

"How can you be so sure?"

"You ought to look at his entire life for an answer. Didn't he say he'd be happy if we got married and settled down in Beijing? Tell me, what kind of life is better than a scholar's? It can be peaceful, rewarding, detached, and even nurturing. I don't believe that my father, a disinterested man, ever regretted having lived such a life. If I were you, it would be my only choice."

"You have no idea how awful and wretched your father's life actually was! You don't know how crazily he ranted during his last days!"

"Don't disturb the dead! Let him rest in peace."

"Believe it or not, a scholar's life is the last thing I want."

"You know what's wrong with you?"

"What?"

She said, with flushed cheeks, "You're hungry for power and greedy for material comforts. That's why you want to become an official like Banping, to get rich by taking bribes. I never thought you had such a peasant's narrow outlook too."

"That's not fair! If I craved material comforts, I would go

to Beijing where living conditions are better than elsewhere. I just want to live a useful life."

"Tell me, what is a useful life?"

"Not to be a piece of meat on the chopping board for others to cut. No, let me put it this way: I want to take my fate in my own hands, and when I die, I want to end with the feeling of content and fulfillment. In other words, I don't want to feel that my life should have been used otherwise."

"You're silly if not megalomaniac. Even Hamlet, a prince, cannot control his own fate. Who ever can?"

"You don't understand. I mean to make my own choices in life."

"You always have your choices."

"All right, let me just say I want to be a knife instead of a piece of meat."

"You're crazy, you want to hurt others?"

"No, I want to live an active life. You will understand what I mean someday."

She gave a wry smile, her nose wrinkled. "What makes you think there's still a future tense for us?"

My heart shrank in pain, but I managed to say, "Meimei, you know how much I love you."

"Love alone is not enough." She was biting the left corner of her mouth, her eyes dimmed.

"What else do you want?"

"I want to make my life in Beijing. How can you join me there if you give up this only opportunity?"

I couldn't answer.

She got to her feet and bent down to pull up her nylon anklets. "You still have a day to decide whether you'll take the exams," she said without looking at me.

"That's out of the question."

"All right then, let's stop here. Good luck with your official career." She stepped toward the door and held its handle. She seemed to be hesitating whether to walk out. I noticed that she had gained some weight, probably six or seven pounds, but she was still slim with a thin waist and a straight back.

Before I could stand up, she spun around and took two steps toward me. She said almost furiously, "I know why you've given up."

"Why?"

"Because there're all kinds of talents in the capital, and you're afraid to compete with others in your field. You're such a *coward* that you don't have the guts to go to Beijing!"

Gagging, I started to cough, hunching over the desk with my hand rubbing my chest. I wanted to yell at her to defend myself, but couldn't get a word out. She stared at me for a few seconds, then walked out the door.

"Wait, stay a while, Meimei!" I brought out finally. No response came from the corridor.

I lurched to my feet, biting back the cry that was fighting its way through my cramped throat. The sound of her footsteps faded away, then vanished. I flopped down on the chair and buried my face in my arms on the glass desktop.

Before she returned from Beijing, I had planned to make love to her, assuming that our intimacy could help me persuade her or at least induce her to see my view. I even bought a packet of "extra-sensitive" condoms. But once she was back, the ambience of mourning prevented me from getting intimate with her. I dared not even sneak a kiss when we were with others. I only managed to squeeze her hand a few times and pat her behind twice after the memorial service. Besides fear and propriety, I simply couldn't get hold of her—she was never home.

Finally I realized that she had just issued me an ultimatum. I felt wounded. She had changed, become colder or more rational than before, though I was unsure whether the change had stemmed from her heart or was a mere pose she had struck to deal with me. What upset me more was that she wouldn't even consider my position at all. Whatever I said had seemed to make no sense to her. Worst of all, her word *coward* stung me to the heart.

32

Seeing me, Ying Peng said, "You did a fabulous job with the investigation letter, Jian. Banping owes you a dinner now. I'll let him know about your help after he joins the Party." She patted her hair and apparently remembered something. "Oh yes, I want to talk to you."

I knew this was about my new decision, so I broached the topic indirectly. "Secretary Peng, I have changed my mind about the exams. I've decided not to take them."

"Are you sure?" Her face glowed so happily that the large, hairy mole on her chin seemed mobile.

"Absolutely," I said.

"All right. In that case I'm going to call the Graduate School to withdraw your application. But I have to tell you that you can't work at the Policy Office."

"Why?" I was astounded.

"Let me be candid about this, Jian. The Policy Office wants a Party member for that position, because they have access to lots of classified documents. At least you must be a prospective Party member, like Banping, for them to consider you for that job."

I was stupefied and for a while couldn't say a word. Three weeks ago the office hadn't required Party membership for the position at all; why such a new restriction? It must be Ying Peng herself who had brought about the change.

"I'm sorry, Jian," she went on. "If only I could be more helpful. You've never applied for Party membership. It's impossible to consider you for that job even if you turn in your application now." Despite her regret, she seemed unable to contain her happiness. Even her voice had grown crisp.

I swung around and staggered out of the office, my head reeling. The instant I closed the door, I overheard her pick up the phone and call the Graduate School to cancel my name as an examinee. Never had I imagined that the most crucial decision in my life was based on a shaky assumption, on a mirage. What a swellheaded fool I was! Why had I never doubted the feasibility of changing myself from a piece of meat into "a knife"? And why was I never seriously concerned about all the odds against my entering officialdom if I didn't belong to the Party? Meimei was right—I hadn't known my place in this world.

For a whole day I couldn't do anything. My chest was so full that I felt as if I were suffocating; I couldn't stop hiccuping, filled with gas. Should I take the exams tomorrow? I didn't feel like it. Besides, Ying Peng had already withdrawn my name. If I wanted to reenter, I would have to get her approval first, which she was unlikely to give. Why was she so eager and so glad to have my candidacy revoked? I wished I had known.

Having heartburn, I didn't eat lunch. Yet however hard I castigated myself for my foolhardiness, I still believed in living a life different from Mr. Yang's. I would never go to Beijing through Ph.D. candidacy. At the same time I felt trapped, all at sea about what to do. If only I could have made up with Meimei. I wouldn't mind admitting to her that I had been a high-minded fool. I needed her and mustn't lose her. In my heart there was the burning desire to win her back, though I was uncertain what I could offer her so that we could be reconciled.

After dinner I went to the Yangs' to look for Meimei. Her mother answered the door. Mrs. Yang looked tired, a little unkempt. Yet her face lit up as she talked to me. She wore a yellow shirt and a maroon skirt, her bare feet in a pair of mauve sponge-rubber slippers. She didn't seem very grief-stricken over her husband's death.

After she poured me a cup of tea, I asked her if Meimei was in. She looked surprised and said, "You didn't see her today?"

"No."

"I thought she was with you."

"The last time I saw her was yesterday afternoon."

"Really? She went out this morning and won't come back till midnight, she told me."

Something must have gone awry. *With whom is Meimei spending her time today?* I wondered. *Does she have some friends in town?*

A pang suddenly seized my heart and my nose turned stuffy, but I took hold of myself. I told Mrs. Yang that there was some friction between Meimei and me, mainly caused by my decision not to take the exams. Without comment she listened to me explaining my thoughts; now and again her eyes flashed at me sympathetically. She didn't seem to disapprove of my decision, though I was unsure how much she understood of my reasons.

After I was done talking, for a moment the room fell into silence. I remembered something that had weighed on my mind for a long time. Regardless of propriety, I asked her, "Do you know a woman by the name of Lifen?"

Her eyes expanded. "What about her?"

"Mr. Yang often mentioned her when he was delirious." I tried to keep calm, though my heart was thumping.

"I've never met her and don't know if she's dead or alive," she said in a level voice.

"Mr. Yang talked a lot about her, saying that finally he met her again."

"That's just his fantasy. He didn't know her whereabouts either, I'm positive about that."

Misery overcame me. I grew quiet, uncertain whether I should talk more about this unpleasant subject, which I shouldn't have brought up with her.

"Love is always a unilateral effort, ridiculous," she said. "That woman dumped him like a used dishrag, but he couldn't forget her all his life. I'm sure he loved her more than me. I was hopeless against her, my invisible enemy, and I couldn't find a way to win his heart, no matter how hard I tried." She grimaced, her chin wrinkled. Tears brimmed in her eyes.

I didn't say a word as I remembered how harshly Mr. Yang had rebuked her in his dreams.

She sighed. "I only hope Meimei won't repeat my mistake. What a hell a marriage can be."

"I love her," I said.

"I've known that from the very beginning."

Silence set in again. I wondered if I should leave.

Then she asked, "Do you want to see your teacher's ash box? I brought it back yesterday evening."

"Yes," I answered, amazed by her question. She was indeed a tough woman, not distraught by what I had just told her. She must have been hardened to thoughts of her loveless marriage.

I got up and followed her into my teacher's study, which was also their bedroom. On the wall hung a pair of calligraphic scrolls, one of which said *Learn with zest* and the other *Teach without fatigue.* The room smelled fusty, with a tang of tobacco. On the tiny desk, whose top was three by two feet, sat a cinerary casket with gilt corners and brass clasps. On the front of the box was a large photo of Mr. Yang wearing a woolen pullover, his hair combed tidily and less gray; his eyes bulged slightly, as though he had just cried; the wrinkles on his jaw looked so tight that they seemed about to vibrate. In this picture I could feel his determination to hold together his life and his world, though he might already have been verging on a breakdown.

Tears came to my eyes; I tried but couldn't force them back. I sat down on his chair and buried my face in my arms. Despite my shame of tears, I went on weeping noiselessly as Mrs. Yang put her palm on my head and patted it gently. "All I want is not to live a life like his," I said.

"I understand."

"I don't want to die full of hatred."

"I know he had an awful life."

"Do you think Meimei has lost faith in me?"

"Don't be silly. Pull yourself together, Jian. Give her some time, she'll come around."

Although not convinced by her words, I ordered myself, *Stop crying! She'll tell Meimei about this. Stop!*

A few minutes later I calmed down, wiping my face on my sleeve. Outside the window, alongside the fence made of wooden boards, the dozen sunflowers my teacher and I had planted together were half dead, their broad leaves wilted by the heat. I had watered them every other day before my trip to the countryside.

When I returned to the dorm, a letter from Meimei was lying on my bed. My roommates were not in, so I couldn't know when she had come. I opened the envelope and saw her squarish handwriting on the ruled paper.

> 6/1/1989
>
> Jian,
>
> It's time for us to part, since we have different dreams and have to travel separate ways. This is a painful decision for me, but it's necessary. Good luck with your life and career.
>
> Meimei

I was so upset that my brain turned numb, though my scalp went on smarting. I sat in the darkness for two hours on end, unable to think coherently. A pair of geckos were resting on the window screen like two question marks, growing bronze against the moonlight. Above them were some lace-wings, motionless as if glued to the mesh. It was so sultry that even mosquitoes were too exhausted to fly, although crickets were shrilling metallically outside. If only there had been someone I could talk with about this whole mess.

33

Y ou folks are disgusting!" Mantao said to me and spat on the concrete floor. "The People's Army's tanks have rolled into Beijing ready to attack the students, but you're still going to hold the dance party this evening."

"It's time to show a right political attitude, Comrade Jian Wan," Huran butted in. He was lying in bed wearing nothing but his underwear, while Mantao and I sat at our desk.

I said, "Even if they paid me a hundred yuan I wouldn't make an appearance there, but we were ordered to attend."

"If I had a bomb, I would plant it in that building," Mantao said. His chubby face puckered as though he had accidentally chewed on a grain of sand.

"Come on, don't be so nasty," I said, tapping my cigarette over a chipped cup that had a broken handle and served as our ashtray.

Despite strong opposition from some of us, the college had refused to reschedule the farewell party for the departing graduate students. Every department had taken measures to make sure there'd be enough attendees. The party was to be held in a small assembly hall in the basement of the main classroom building at seven o'clock.

When I arrived, many graduate students were already there. Above the door to the hall stretched a long scroll proclaiming GO ANYWHERE OUR MOTHERLAND NEEDS US! Inside the hall, colorful balloons and golden streamers hung from the ceiling, fluttering a little whenever somebody passed beneath them. Eight frosted-glass lampshades, affixed to gilt chains and resembling huge round loaves of bread, rendered the white walls yellowish. Some people sat on the slatted benches arranged in a large horseshoe, but most stood around, chitchatting with drinks in their hands. The room was droning like the inside of a train station.

Weiya was over there with a group of female graduate students, some of whom were drinking soda pop directly from the bottle. She had on a sleeveless black dress, with a tiny white chrysanthemum pinned to the right side of the bodice. Her outfit seemed to indicate that our teacher's death was still on her mind. As I was wondering where she had gotten the fresh flower, she saw me and smiled. I waved, then went over. Unwittingly she touched the mum on her chest, her hand thinner than before, as if translucent. Secretary Peng was in a corner talking with Professor Song, who was wearing an eyeshade over his left eye, having suffered a detached retina recently. She glanced at Weiya and me from time to time.

"Are you all right?" Weiya asked me in a concerned voice.

"Not really."

"You don't look like your usual self. What happened?"

"Meimei and I have broken up."

A lull followed while she gazed at me, her eyes dimming with feeling. She whispered, "I never thought Mr. Yang's death would affect both of us so much."

"My world has fallen apart," I said, wondering how differently her life had changed from mine. Probably for her the change was for the better. She had benefited from our teacher's death, hadn't she? At least his death had set her free. In spite of my bitter thoughts, I noticed that as I was talking with her, a peculiar kind of calm was settling over me, almost like the feeling of security. Whenever I was with her, the same kind of placidness would come upon me, whereas with Meimei I couldn't help but get excited and restless. This must be one of the reasons why I had felt drawn to Weiya. I understood she might have ended her relationship with Mr. Yang willingly, and nobody should blame her for that. What else could she have done? Still, I was amazed that she could be so at ease. She looked as innocent as a little girl, but on the other hand, she was a woman with a lot of self-assured grace. If only I could have despised her.

She leaned closer to me and said under her breath, "I'm leaving academia."

"What? You're going to work somewhere else?"

"No, I'll stay in town and do my own thing."

"What thing are you talking about?" I couldn't imagine she would abandon her regular job, which she had been so afraid to lose just a few weeks before.

"I'll sell my paintings to support myself. In fact, I sold two pieces last week. Mr. Yang's death made me think a lot about life. I'm already thirty-one. Heaven knows whether I can live another thirty years. Why should I continue to live under others' thumbs?"

"You're really brave." I realized that with Mr. Yang gone, there was indeed no reason for her to remain at this university. Besides, giving up her teaching position would be an effective way to get out of Ying Peng's clutches. Despite understanding the logic of her decision, I was still stunned; never had I thought she could be so strong-minded and so bold. "It's a stupendous move, I'm impressed," I said to her. "What does Yuman Tan say about this?"

"He supports me."

"That's good."

"By the way, I've painted a portrait of Mr. Yang. Would you like to stop by and see it?"

"Sure, where is it?"

"At Yuman's place."

"I'll stop by this weekend."

Somebody clapped loudly. "May I have your attention please," Vice Principal Huang said into the microphone. People quieted down, some taking seats. There weren't enough benches, and many of us remained on our feet. Yuman Tan appeared from behind Weiya and stood next to her; he was so happy today that his mouth seemed unable to close, smiling at everybody while his eyes darted in all directions. He looked rather silly with his hands thrust behind him like a smug official. I walked away to join Banping, still thinking about Weiya's decision. I was amazed that within such a short period of time she had been able to utilize Yuman Tan's apartment and make a breakthrough in her art. Heaven knew what she couldn't accomplish if given more opportunities.

The vice principal started delivering the farewell speech, his silvery hair shimmering as he read from a sheaf of paper with affected gusto. It was annoying to hear him click his tongue every two or three sentences. Bored by the tedious speech, Banping told his wife, who was waving a magazine as a fan, that he was going to have a smoke outside. He tugged my sleeve, so I left the hall with him. We hadn't met since Mr. Yang's funeral, and I wanted to talk with him too. His eyes were lackluster with whitish gum in their corners, perhaps because he had been working hard on his detective novel lately. As soon as we got into the foyer, he asked me why I hadn't taken the exams.

"Just didn't want to," I said sourly.

"Was it due to Mr. Yang's death?" he asked.

"What do you think?"

"I think you're too sensitive. You gave up too easily. If you don't go to Beijing, what's going to happen to your engagement to Meimei?"

"I've no idea." I bristled. Two weeks ago he himself had advised me to leave academia, assuring me that I didn't have to be a Party member to enter the Policy Office. Apparently he had heard that I, a non-Party man, was disqualified for the job. I wondered whether he knew how the new requirement for that position had come into existence.

Before I could ask him, Secretary Peng stepped out of the hall and said loudly, "Where have you been these days, Jian? I've been looking for you everywhere." She was pretending; she had seen me with Weiya just now.

"What for?" I asked.

"We need to know what courses you'd like to teach next semester."

"Anything."

She was taken aback and said, "I'm serious."

"I know how serious you have been."

"What's that supposed to mean?"

"You understand."

"No, I don't."

As I was about to say something more, Meimei and a tall young man appeared atop the stairs, holding hands. The man wore a brand-new tuxedo with a bow tie like a giant butterfly. I had seen tuxedoed men in some Western movies before, but had never met anyone in the flesh wearing such a jacket. Meimei had on a white dress with red polka dots on it, its middle cinched by a cream-colored leatherette belt, which outlined her strong but shapely waist. Her gauzy dress billowed out a little, through which her streamlined thighs and underthings were partly visible against the harsh light at the landing. This was the first time I had seen her made up — her face was delicately powdered, her lips rouged crimson, and her eyebrows, penciled in the arching Russian style, stretched from the root of her nose to her temples. This way she looked a few years older, but still glamorous like an actress. On the other hand, her two little braids, which barely reached the base of her neck, kept her less exotic. With all the makeup, her face was rather rigid, smiling at no one in particular. As she and the man were coming down toward the door of the hall, she let go of his hand. My breath tightened, but I tried to steel myself to face her. Secretary Peng and Banping waved at them. Apparently they knew the young man, who returned their greetings, baring his broad teeth in a grin. He asked, "Are we late, Aunt Peng?"

"No, just on time. The dance hasn't started yet," replied the secretary, smiling ingratiatingly.

I felt it strange that the man had addressed Ying Peng in such a familiar manner. Meimei walked nonchalantly, her chest out and her chin up, the heels of her stilettos clattering on the terrazzo floor crisply. I intended to greet her and even opened my mouth twice, but no word came out because she wouldn't deign to pay me a scrap of attention. It was as though I were a total stranger and she had spent many wild nights the previous summer not with me but with another man. I felt stupid and maimed.

The young man, lanky and dandified, had a horsy face and a sparse mustache. His hair, to which he must have applied a cup of pomade, was wet and shiny. They passed by, and Meimei left behind a minty scent. Though the fellow's black jacket looked very expensive, his dark blue pants were baggy and too long, the cuffs scraping the floor.

As Banping watched the couple pass, his mouth fell ajar. He shook his heavy chin at me. "Is all this because you won't go to Beijing?" he asked.

"Who is he?" I said almost in a shout.

"He's Vice Principal Huang's son, his only son. He teaches at Beijing Foreign Language Institute. He speaks French fluently. I heard he's going to do research at the Sorbonne this fall, but I didn't know he and Meimei were so close."

My temples were hammering as things began to swim before my eyes. Unconsciously I stretched out my hand to hold Banping for support.

"Easy, take it easy," said Ying Peng.

I regained my composure within seconds, though my heart was still shuddering. Shaky-footed, I hurried away to look for a place where I could be alone and untangle my thoughts.

I went out of the building and hid behind some lilac bushes. I sat against the wall beneath a window with my head in my hands. My neck hurt, stiff with a crick from the previous night. About fifty yards away, on a curved ramp, two girls were playing badminton with Ping-Pong paddles, which hit the birdie with rhythmic thuds. Somewhere people were laughing, and their laughter rose and fell in the gathering dusk.

Gradually my mind began working. So this was why Meimei had jilted me. The young man was in Beijing and must have been carrying on with her for a long time. At last I understood why Vice Principal Huang had visited Mr. Yang in the hospital—it was not about Weiya but about Meimei. He intended to help his son secure a relationship with my fiancée. This was the true meaning of his request "Let her decide what to do herself." He was asking my teacher not to interfere with his daughter's private life. I used to think that Mr. Yang's deathbed instruction, "Save her," referred to Weiya; now clearly he must have had his daughter in mind. But Meimei wasn't in any danger, was she? She had dumped me of her own free will. Probably she joined that man with an eye to making sure that she could remain in Beijing if the pediatric program didn't accept her. She knew how to take care of herself.

How did Ying Peng collude with Vice Principal Huang in this case? No doubt she'd been helping his son all along. She assigned me to tend Mr. Yang every afternoon in order to distract me from preparing for the exams. She dispatched me to the countryside with a view to wasting my time, too. Now I realized why she had been so delighted when I told her that I would withdraw my application for the Ph.D. program. She had been an accomplice of Vice Principal Huang all the while, and her task was to prevent me from passing the exams so that I couldn't join Meimei in Beijing.

Ever since the death of Mr. Yang, I had been wondering who were his enemies—those to be killed in his last wish. Now clearly Vice Principal Huang was one of them too.

Sitting in the deepening twilight, I felt like a small insect snared in a spiderweb. The harder I struggled, the tighter the strong, entwining filaments would enfold me, choking the life out of me little by little. Then came to mind the image of the dark, rubber-surfaced room described by Mr. Yang. I too felt trapped in such an indestructible cocoon, although I hadn't despaired of escape yet.

When I returned to the dormitory, Mantao declared, "I'm going to Beijing tomorrow morning with some undergrads to demonstrate in Tiananmen Square."

"He's going to join the revolution," Huran said to me. I made no comment.

"Do you want to come with us?" Mantao asked him.

"No way, not even for a thousand yuan," replied Huran. "I'm going to marry next month." He was joking. He didn't have a girlfriend yet.

"How about you, Jian?" Mantao asked.

"My wallet is empty and I can't pay for the train fare." I told him the truth.

"No problem, I can give you fifty yuan. Look, I have money." He pulled out a wad of banknotes from his pants pocket. Somebody must have given him the cash for the trip, because he was poorer than the other graduate students and often scrimped on food. Each month he would mail twenty-five yuan, almost half of his stipend, to his younger sister, who went to college in Wuhan City.

"My, he's so generous today. What a philanthropist," Huran put in.

Mantao said, "We've decided to join the struggle in Beijing. If we don't take part now, there'll be no hope for China anymore."

"I'll go with you," I said.

"Are you kidding?" Huran asked me.

"No."

"What made you interested in politics all of a sudden?" he kept on.

"It's too stuffy here, and I want to get some fresh air in Beijing."

"You may take in the smoke of gunpowder instead."

"Fine with me."

Mantao said with genuine emotion, "Jian, you're my friend, a real man!" He handed me a Tsingtao beer, which I downed in two swallows. Again a film veiled my eyes; I felt like sobbing, but restrained myself. Meantime Huran drank his beer silently, amazed by my outward insouciance.

That's how I decided to go to Beijing with Mantao and thirty-two undergraduates. Different from them, I had no grand purpose or dream of democracy and freedom; nor did I have the sense of responding to our national exigencies. My motive was mainly personal — I was driven by desperation, anger, madness, and stupidity. First, I meant to show Meimei that I was not a coward and could go to the capital at any time and in any way I chose. Second, I wanted to puncture a hole in this indestructible cocoon that caged me; somehow I felt that the right place to plunge a knife in was Beijing — the sick heart of this country. I was crazed, unable to think logically, and was possessed by an intense desire to prove that I was a man capable of action and choice. So I set out for the capital with a feverish head.

34

On the morning of June 3 we boarded the 5:30 train bound for Beijing. Through a light fog, the eastern sky was just turning pale. Two teachers saw us off at the platform. One was Kailing and the other a lecturer in physical education, our school's soccer coach, whose son was among us. Kailing was wearing sunglasses and a windbreaker. With a secretive air she whispered something to Mantao near the iron paling, about twenty yards away from us. Then she handed him a folded envelope, which I suspected contained cash. It was said that she had made quite a bit of money by translating modern German fiction, and that unlike most poor teachers, she hired a maid for cooking and housework. Ever since Mr. Yang's death, I had felt she was evasive whenever I ran into her, probably because she suspected I had my doubts about her relationship with him, which I was actually inclined to regard as mere friendship.

Both the teachers said good-bye to us when the train

started. It pulled out smoothly as if wafted away by dozens of hands waving along the platform.

Soon after we settled down in our seats, Mantao and I were elected the leaders of the group, because we two were the only graduate students among them. The undergraduates assumed that Mantao and I, four or five years older than themselves, were more knowledgeable about political struggles. I was reluctant to accept any leadership, but after they repeatedly begged me, I yielded. I felt uncomfortable about my new role. Whenever one of them called me Vice Chief Wan, a sour taste would come to my mouth.

The train chugged along a muddy lake in the north, whose surface was mottled with green and dark patches of reeds. A flock of domestic geese, like white dots, were floating almost motionlessly in the distant water, brightened by the rising sun. After we passed the lake, the landscape suddenly seemed narrowed. The fog was thinning away, though the windowpanes of the train still sweated, blurring the endless peanut and wheat fields divided by rows of stunted mulberry trees. A baby burst out crying at the front end of the car; however hard its mother tried to calm it down, it wouldn't stop. The baby's hollering, mixed with the soft Taiwanese music and the pungent tobacco smell, made my head swim a little. The floor was littered with pumpkinseed shells, candy wrappers, popsicle cartons, chicken bones. Under our feet the wheels were grinding rhythmically but with such a clatter that when talking, we had to strain our voices. Since conversation was hard, we remained silent most of the time except that once in a while we'd curse the government together. Many of the undergraduates had somber faces as though they had grown older all at once.

A spindly attendant in a blue, visored cap appeared, carrying a large kettle, and seat by seat he poured boiled water for the passengers. With a few exceptions, people all produced their mugs. Many of the undergraduates brewed black tea, which a boy had brought along. For breakfast, some of them broke instant noodles into their mugs to be soaked with hot water. The attendant knew we were going to Beijing to join the demonstrations, so he was very patient with us. Unlike them, I was too sleepy to bother about tea and food. It was getting hot, though overhead a miniature fan in a wire cage revolved without stopping. The soot-grimed window near me got stuck and couldn't be lifted up to let in fresh air. I was bored by the news blared out by the loudspeaker. Eyes shut, I leaned against the window frame, my head pillowed on my forearm. Soon I fell asleep.

Approaching the capital in the evening, we began to make plans for our next step. We decided to raise our flag, which had SHANNING UNIVERSITY printed on it, and march to a bus stop. From there, we would get on a bus going to Tiananmen Square. We were not sure what bus route we should take; some said Number 20, some said Number 14, and some said Number 1. But this shouldn't be a problem; we could always ask.

The train was two hours late, and we didn't get off until eight in the evening. Once out of the station, we were told that there was no bus service for the time being, because all vehicles had gone to barricade the streets to stop the army from entering the city. Even the subway was closed — rumor had it that the military was using the trains to transport troops downtown through the underground tunnels. A skinny young woman in a railroad uniform gave us each a handbill that contained mimeoed slogans, such as *Our motherland is in danger! This is our last struggle! Let us save the republic! Stop the army from entering the capital! End martial law! Down with the corrupt government!* I had a foreboding something hideous was unfolding in the distance. It was whispered that the army was going to clear Tiananmen Square tonight.

Bewildered, fatigued, and frightened, the undergraduates gathered around Mantao and me, expecting us to come up with a solution. Neither he nor I had ever been to Beijing before, so we were at a loss too. We didn't even know whether we should still head for Tiananmen Square as we had planned. Mantao kept grinning and assured the others that we'd find a way, but I could tell he was also nervous. He went away to make some phone calls, but fifteen minutes later he returned, rather downcast, saying he couldn't get hold of anyone at the headquarters of the Beijing Autonomous Student Union. His cheeks puffed up and the corners of his mouth fell.

A dignified-looking old man told us that in some areas the army had begun fighting its way into the city. "Students," he said, shaking his pockmarked face, "there's no hope for this country anymore. You'd better go home now. Don't waste your lives here. Those old bastards at the top won't bat an eye to have you erased. Go back, please!" He couldn't help his tears while speaking. Indeed, we heard quite a few gunshots coming from the west, where patches of pinkish light shimmered in the sky. After the man left, the woman who distributed the handbills told us that his son had been bludgeoned half dead by some policemen the night before.

What should we do? Sitting in a ring on the ground before the train station, we discussed our situation briefly and decided to set out on foot for Tiananmen Square. We would go in two groups, because we were not sure if all of us could get there and afraid that the police might stop us. Although we were unfamiliar with the city, it wouldn't be difficult to find our way to the square. We could ask for directions, and a lot of other people seemed to be going there too.

But before setting off, we noticed a white minivan parked at a bus stop. On its roof was a taxi sign, so we talked to the driver, a man in his early thirties who had a bell-cheeked face and a large wart between his left brow and eye. He would charge twenty yuan for a trip downtown, but hearing we wanted to go to Tiananmen Square, he smiled and said, "I can give you a ride free, but I'm not sure if I can get you there. Most streets are blocked."

"Please take us as far as you can," I begged. "None of us has ever been here before."

"All right, get in my car."

We thanked him profusely; several girls even called him Uncle. My group, composed of sixteen people, began climbing into the van, which couldn't hold more than fourteen passengers.

"All right, no more," cried the man. "This is an old car. I'll have a flat tire if it's overloaded."

So we left two boys with Mantao's group and headed townward. The streets were messy, here and there crowded with pedestrians and bicyclers. Some areas, apparently occupied by people during the day, were strewn with fruit cores, cigarette cases, leaflets, crates, glass bottles. Across a broad street four double-length buses stood parallel to one another, forming a barricade, and their tires were all deflated. We had to turn left into a small back street. The citizens here looked quite resolved to deter the army. The driver told me that he was a veteran and had quit his regular job at a steel mill a year ago, and that if he hadn't owned this minivan, he'd have joined the team of workers called Flying Tigers, which was most active in supporting the student movement. "It's funny, I feel the car owns me now," he said. "I can't afford to be as reckless as I used to be."

We had to stop and detour at many places. About half an hour later the driver gave up, saying to us, "You better get off here. There's no way I can take you to Tiananmen Square. I've tried three different routes, all blocked up. Actually the square isn't far from here, ten minutes' walk at the most, but I can't help you anymore."

We all alighted and thanked him again for the lift. Following his directions, we headed for Tiananmen. But about a hundred yards later, at a street corner, we ran into a huge crowd of people, at least two thousand strong, who were assembled around a column of army trucks, all the backs of which were under canvas. At the head of the contingent were six armored personnel carriers with heavy machine guns atop them. The civilians begged the soldiers not to go farther downtown to harm the students. Some of them shouted slogans, such as "The People's Army serves the people!" "We love our soldiers!" "Don't butcher the young!" By now the sky was umber beyond the high buildings, as if a fire was burning in the distance. Though I had told my group to stick together, we soon began to have stragglers. Two girls disappeared in the crowd, and try as I might, I couldn't find any trace of them. As I was thinking what to do, the crowd suddenly surged and pushed us in different directions. I looked around in panic — my group was scattered, most of them having vanished from sight, and none was with me.

No longer able to hold my team together, I elbowed my way forward through the people to see what the soldiers were like. I couldn't reach the front and stopped halfway. From there I saw a young man, flat-faced and with long hair covering his ears, standing at the rear door of the first personnel carrier. He looked like a college student. He was lecturing the dusty-faced troops inside the vehicle and telling them that they had been deceived by the government, and that the city was in good order and didn't need them here.

"They'll turn back like the group in the morning," a man in coveralls said to others about the soldiers.

"This must be a different unit, though."

"Do they belong to the Thirty-eighth Army too?"

"No way to tell."

"Yesterday an officer said they would never hurt civilians. He was a pretty good fellow."

"Yeah, he said that after we gave his men a hamper of cucumbers."

"But these men here look different."

"Yes, like a bunch of hoodlums."

A voice boomed at the people in the front, "Hey, ask them which army they're from."

"Yeah, ask them."

A moment later the student cried back, "They're from the Twenty-seventh Army. They said they didn't like going downtown either, but they were ordered to get to Tiananmen Square by any means."

"Tell them they'll have to kill us civilians before they can pass."

"Yes, we won't let them go there."

As people were talking, a jeep came up tooting its horn;

inside sat a square-faced colonel and two bodyguards, all in steel helmets. The civilians parted to make way for the car to reach the front, assuming that the officer would order his troops to retreat. Seizing this opportunity, I squeezed forward through the crowd and got closer to the first personnel carrier. The tall colonel jumped off the jeep and went up to the student who was still talking to the soldiers. I was impressed by the officer's handsome looks: broad eyes, thick brows, a straight nose, white, strong teeth, and a full chin. He looked like material for a general, at least in appearance. Different from his men, he wore a black necktie beneath his jacket, which had four pockets. His shoulder straps showed two stripes and one star. A purple belt tightened his waist, and a pair of binoculars hung on his left hip. Without a word he pulled out his pistol and shot the student in the head, who dropped to the ground kicking his legs, then stopped moving and breathing. Bits of his brain were splattered like crushed tofu on the asphalt. Steam was rising from his smashed skull.

Stunned, for two or three seconds we didn't react. Then people staggered back and the crowd began churning. Turning to his men, the colonel ordered in a shout, "Move ahead! Shoot anyone standing in your way. Teach this rabble a bloody lesson!" He raised his pistol and fired into the air.

The vehicles started snarling one after another, then lunged forward as people swung away, struggling to avoid being crushed. All the personnel carriers and trucks began rolling, unstoppable like a crazed dragon. In no time gunshots burst out. The troops were firing at the people who couldn't yet get out of their way and at us, the ones taking off.

"Real bullets!" a woman screamed.

"Oh, Mama!"

"Ah my leg!"

"Run for your lives, folks!"

"I'm killing all of you hooligans. Take this!" a soldier shouted and kept firing his AK-47. Some men in the same truck guffawed as they were shooting away.

"Now you see your grandpa's temper," cried another man while his rifle was cracking.

"No grenades!" ordered the colonel.

More guns were fired, and people broke into every direction. Not knowing where I could find safety, I just ran as fast as possible, following a young woman before me. She looked like a college teacher or a graduate student, wearing bobbed hair, brass-rimmed glasses, and a pastel dress with accordion pleats. As we were approaching a tall billboard, a volley of gunfire swept down a few people ahead of me. The young woman fell, then scrambled to her feet and zigzagged forward, shrieking, with both hands holding her bleeding left side. One of her shoes was missing, and her white stockings were soaked with blood. I pulled her aside to keep her from being trampled. She dropped down, but I dared not stop to carry her away because more bullets whizzed by, drawing blazing lines. I fled with the crowd, running and running until we ended in a small alley. My heart was beating so violently that I couldn't help trembling.

Calming down a little, people began cursing and crying. I wept too, but I was so shocked that the whole time I couldn't speak and my nose was dripping. A moment later someone shouted "Down with Fascism!" People followed him, roaring in unison. We went on howling "Down with Li Peng!" "People's Army go to hell!" "A tooth for a tooth and an eye for an eye." As we continued bellowing, bullets went on hitting the walls at the mouth of the alley, knocking chips of brick off the corners.

Having shouted ourselves hoarse, we stopped and began talking, trying to figure out why the army had suddenly gone on such a rampage. But as the enormity of the event sank in, many of us grew reticent. An amalgam of loneliness and grief overwhelmed me. I hadn't intended to come here to fight for democracy, but now I was caught up in a tragedy that didn't make sense to me at all. I shouldn't have been here to begin with. Then I remembered the wounded woman I had left behind; she must have died by now. Why hadn't I carried her away to a safe place? She must have bled or been trampled to death. *Coward!* I couldn't even prove to myself that I was above cowardice. This realization brought me to tears again. I wept wretchedly. An old woman patted my shoulder, saying to no one in particular, "Lord of Heaven, please save those kids in Tiananmen Square!"

Her words reminded me that the troops were headed for the square to get rid of the students there. So this was it! Again a numbing pain tautened my chest.

"I do Deng Xiaoping's mother!" cursed a man, his round eyes aflame. He had a bristly face, which had become murderous.

"Li Peng will have to pay for this with his life," a short woman cut in.

"I know where his daughter lives. I'll blow up her apartment one of these days."

"Yes, they are our class enemy now."

After a pause, someone added, "The troops must've been drugged."

"Yes, they looked crazy."

"I smelled alcohol on the colonel's breath."

"They're a different unit. I heard they'd been brought in from Datong or somewhere."

"A bunch of bandits."

After about an hour's cursing and talking, some people grew restless, eager to go home or look for their siblings and friends who had come out to stop the army too. But the instant they stepped out of the alley, volleys of bullets would force them back in. Apparently the army was determined to keep everybody off the street. A loudspeaker was ordering all civilians to obey martial law and stay indoors because the People's Liberation Army was suppressing the counterrevolutionary uprising so as to restore order in the city. The announcement brought out more curses among us.

A woman student, grazed in the arm by a bullet when she had attempted to get out into the street, sat on the ground blubbering hysterically. Now and then some people would stick their heads out of the alley to watch what was happening on the street. Units of tanks passed frequently, roaring fitfully. I searched through the hundred people trapped in the alley, but didn't find anyone of my group. I was worried about their safety and whereabouts.

Exhausted and hungry, I sat down in a corner and soon dropped off despite the crowd milling around. During my two or three hours' sleep, I vaguely heard that another person had been wounded while trying to leave and had been carried back into the alley. When I woke up, I couldn't help shivering; the night was chilly; if only I had brought a jacket. I went to the mouth of the alley, lay down, and stuck my head out to see what it was like out there. A puff of fireflies was flickering before my face. In the distant sky an orange glow pulsed while the sound of gunshots was rising from somewhere as though a battle was under way. Two or three armored personnel carriers stood at a nearby street corner; beyond them dozens of soldiers in fatigues and helmets crouched against trees or sat on the curbs, all with AK-47s or SKS carbines in their arms. One of them fired three shots up at a window of an apartment building from which some residents had called them names a moment ago.

As I watched, a boy suddenly appeared on the street. He threw an empty bottle at the soldiers, then dashed aside, running to a doorway; but before he could enter it, a gun fired. "Aiyah, I'm hit!" The boy fell, screaming for help. A few more heads joined me watching.

A group of soldiers ran over and kicked the boy in the chest and back. "Don't beat me, Uncle!" he begged, but they went on battering him with their gun butts. In no time he stopped making noise.

"We must save him," I said.

"Yes," agreed a young woman in a white blouse. "He may still be alive."

"The Benevolence Hospital isn't far away to the south," said an old bald man.

"Can you show us the way?" I asked him.

"How can I get out of here?"

I found a long bamboo broom, took off my white shirt, and raised it on the tip of the wooden handle like a flag. Stepping out of the alley, I cried at the soldiers, "Comrades, please don't shoot. I just want to save the boy's little life. He's only a kid. Please give him a chance!"

Though quaking all over, I walked straight toward the dark lump lying about eighty yards away. The soldiers didn't open fire. Then the young woman came out of the alley too, followed by a few others, one of whom carried a board dislodged from a wheelless flatbed tricycle.

"Only three people can come to take him away!" ordered an officer.

So the woman, the old man, and I went up to the boy together. His chest was crushed and his left thigh drilled by a bullet, but he was still breathing. He looked about thirteen, wearing a middle school badge. As I squatted down, about to use my shirt to bind his gun wound, the woman said, "We'll need that. Take this." She bit the bottom of her blouse, with one rip tore its hem off, and handed the broad strip of cloth to me. With it I tied up the boy's thigh to stanch the bleeding. Meanwhile, the old man shed his jacket and wrapped the boy's wound with it to prevent tetanus. We placed him on the board and carried him away.

Together we hurried toward the hospital. All the way the woman raised my shirt high so that the soldiers might not fire at us.

The boy wasn't heavy, about ninety pounds. Yet soon the old man at the front started panting and tottering, and we had to slow down a little. The street was strewn with caps, bags, shoes, bicycle bells, jackets, plastic ponchos. After three or four turns, we reached a broader street and saw buses and trucks in flames. In fact, by now it looked as though the whole city was burning, fires and smoke everywhere. At one place there was a pile of bicycles crushed by a tank or a personnel carrier — metal and bloody clothing all tangled in a mess. Not far away a group of double-length buses were smoldering, each having a wide gap in the middle, punched by a tank. Here and there were scattered concrete posts, steel bars, bicycle-lane dividers, lampposts, oil drums, even some propane cylinders.

We reached the hospital at about four o'clock. The building was swarming with wounded people, many of whom were dying. Some had already died before they arrived. The boy we had carried over was still breathing, but his heart stopped a few minutes after the nurses pushed him into the operating room. A head nurse told us woefully, "We didn't anticipate this carnage. We thought they'd use tear gas, so we stocked some eyedrops and cotton balls. Many people died because we didn't have the medicine and blood they needed."

I was astounded by the number of the wounded in the hospital. The corridors and the little front yard were crowded with stretchers loaded with people, some of whom held up IV bottles and tubes for themselves, waiting for treatment. A deranged young woman cried and laughed by turns, tearing at her hair and breasts, while her friends begged a nurse to give her an injection of sedative. I was told that there was a morgue here, but it was too small for all the bodies, so some of the dead were stored in a garage in the backyard. I went there to have a look. The tiny morgue happened to adjoin the garage, and three nurses were in there, busy listing the bodies and gathering information about the dead. An old couple were wailing, as they had just found their son lying among the corpses. Most of the dead were shot in the head or chest. I saw that a young man had three bayonet wounds in the belly and a knife gash in the hand. His mouth was wide open as though still striving to snap at something.

But the garage was an entirely different scene, where about twenty bodies, male and female, were piled together like slaughtered pigs. Several limbs stuck out from the heap; a red rubber band was still wrapped around the wrist of a teenage girl; a pair of eyes on a swollen face were still open, as though gazing at the unplastered wall. A few steps away from the mass of corpses lay a gray-haired woman on her side, a gaping hole in her back ringed with clots of blood. My knees buckled. Crouching down, I began retching, but couldn't bring anything up. On the ground sparks seemed to burst like fireworks as I slapped my chest with both hands to get my wind back.

Three or four minutes later I rose to my feet and staggered away. Reentering the hospital building, I was too exhausted and too numb to do anything, but was still lucid. I wondered whether I should stay in Beijing or return to Shanning. Since it was impossible to reassemble my group, I decided to go back as soon as I could. I asked a nurse for directions; it happened that the train station wasn't far away. She took off her robe and said, "Put this on. It's dangerous to be in your bloody clothes."

I looked down and found my undershirt and pants stained with the boy's blood. "Don't you need this?" I asked her about the robe.

"We have plenty."

I thanked her and slipped on the robe, which turned out to be more than helpful. On my way to the train station, the soldiers didn't question me, taking me for one of the medical personnel. By now it was already daylight, and the troops seemed too tired to move around. The farther south I walked, the more people appeared on the streets, some of which resembled a battlefield, littered with scraps of metal, bloody puddles, and burned trucks and personnel carriers. I was amazed that the civilians, without any real weapons in their hands, had somehow managed to disable so many army vehicles. Although few guns were fired now, smoke kept rising in the west.

Coming close to the train station, I saw a column of tanks standing along a street. Their cannons pointed north, their engines were idling, and their rears were emitting greasy fumes. The air was rife with diesel fuel. Some civilians were talking to the soldiers; many of them wept and scrunched up their faces. I stopped to watch. An officer in breeches was listening to the civilians attentively and went on sighing and shaking his head in disbelief. Among the crowd an old man held up a long placard that said PUNISH THE MURDERERS! A white banner displayed the slogan THE DEBT OF BLOOD HAS TO BE PAID IN BLOOD!

A young man standing beside me remarked with a thrill in his voice, "These tanks are the most advanced type our country has made, modeled after the Russian T-62. These fellows belong to the Thirty-eighth Army. They're good troops, moving in to shell those bastards from Datong."

"Long live the Thirty-eighth Army!" a male voice shouted.

People joined in, raising their fists.

"Wipe out the fascists!" broke from the same man.

Once more people roared together. Their voices quickened my heart a little, and my spirits began to lift. Then I noticed that all the muzzles of the tanks' cannons still wore canvas hoods, and that all the antiaircraft guns atop the tanks were covered too. My heart sagged again. When I was a small boy, my pals and I had often played near the barracks of an armored regiment garrisoned in my hometown. Occasionally we sneaked into the army's compound to pick up used batteries and cartridge cases. Whenever the tanks and self-propelled guns rolled out for a live ammunition exercise, they would shed all the canvas hoods and covers before they set off. So now I could tell that the troops in front of me were not prepared to fight a battle at all, and that probably they too had come to smash the "uprising." These civilians here were misled by their own wishful thinking. I wondered if I should tell them the truth, but decided not to.

Hurriedly I went to the train station, where I ran into two of the undergraduates from my group, a boy and a girl. At the sight of me they broke out sobbing. I had no idea how to comfort them and joined them in weeping.

"I'm going to write a novel to fix all the fascists on the page," announced the bespectacled girl, stamping her feet. Fierce light bounced off her glasses.

"Yes," the boy backed her up, "we must nail them to the pillory of history!"

I didn't know how to respond to that, unsure whether we could fight the brute force with words only, so I remained speechless. The girl was one of those budding poets who had often shown up at the literary gatherings on campus.

Around us were hundreds of students waiting for trains, many of which had been canceled. Some of the youngsters were wounded, weeping or cursing continually. Outside it began raining, the initial downpour pattering on the gray plaza, and whitish vapor leaped up, rolling like waves of smoke, so we couldn't go out to look for the rest of our group. In fact, we were too terrified to reenter the city. We stayed together in a corner of the waiting hall for a whole day until the first train was available.

35

Although I'd slept twelve hours since I came back from Beijing, I hadn't recovered from the trip yet. For a whole day I didn't go out except at noon, when I went to fetch some hot water and buy a few wheaten cakes at a food stand. When I walked, my legs still trembled a little, so I stayed in bed most of the time. Huran asked me again and again about the massacre in the capital. He had heard of it from the Voice of America, but he didn't seem surprised, saying he had expected such an outcome. Unlike him, most of the students in the dormitory houses were outraged, and a few brave ones even put on black armbands. Still in shock, I couldn't talk to Huran at length. I just repeated, "They killed lots of people, lots."

Mantao wasn't back yet, and I worried. Toward evening I went out to mail a letter to my family, telling them what I had seen in Beijing. On my way back I ran into an undergraduate who had been in Mantao's group and had returned that morning. He said they hadn't reached Tiananmen Square either. I asked him where Mantao was.

"You don't know?" His dreamy eyes gleamed.

"Know what?"

"He was shot in the face when he pitched a Molotov cocktail at a personnel carrier."

"Where is he now?"

"I've no idea. I heard he died on the way to the hospital."

My chest and throat contracted with pain, but I managed to ask, "How about the others in your group?"

"They're all right, I guess. Some of them haven't returned yet. Those who're back can't stop crying and cursing in the dorms. Old Ghost has a sprained arm."

Old Ghost was a skeletal fellow, an economics major. I walked away. Tears were flowing down my face. I wished I were an army commander, though I knew that even if I were, I couldn't have done a thing to avenge the dead, because it was the Party that controlled the army. In the indigo sky a skein of geese appeared, veering north while squawking gutturally. The sight of the birds reminded me of a squadron of superbombers. "Avenge me. . . . Kill them all!" Mr. Yang's last words suddenly reverberated in my mind. I shook my head forcefully to get rid of the haunting sounds.

Back in the dormitory, I dozed away in bed again. Whenever awake, I would listen to my shortwave radio, and tears welled up in my eyes from time to time. On the BBC a reporter said plaintively that an estimated five thousand people had been killed, that many students were crushed by the tanks and armored personnel carriers, that a civil war might break out anytime since more field armies were heading for Beijing, that forty million dollars had just been transferred to a Swiss bank by someone connected with the top national leaders, and that an airliner was reserved for them in case they needed to flee China. However, another reporter, a woman from Hong Kong, told a different story. She said composedly that at most about a thousand civilians had been killed, that the government was in firm control of the situation, that the police were rounding up the student leaders, and that dozens of intellectuals had been detained. The foreign reporters on the radio tended to contradict one another, whereas no mainland Chinese, except for the government's spokesman, Mu Yuan, and a lieutenant colonel in charge of clearing Tiananmen Square, dared to comment on the event. The officer repeatedly stressed that the People's Liberation Army had successfully quelled the counterrevolutionary uprising without killing a single civilian. I listened and dozed off by turns. The dormitory was noisy, and numerous radio sets were clamoring.

Ever since I boarded the train back, a terrible vision had tormented me. I saw China in the form of an old hag so decrepit and brainsick that she would devour her children to sustain herself. Insatiable, she had eaten many tender lives before, was gobbling new flesh and blood now, and would surely swallow more. Unable to suppress the horrible vision, all day I said to myself, "China is an old bitch that eats her own puppies!" How my head throbbed, and how my heart writhed and shuddered! With the commotion of two nights ago still in my ears, I feared I was going to lose my mind.

The next morning I didn't go out either. Toward noon, when I was lying on my bed and listening to the radio, somebody knocked on the door. I raised myself on one elbow and called, "Come in."

It was Yuman Tan. He wore a yellow V-necked sweater, which made him look like a different man, rather spirited. Seeing his bright-colored outfit, I almost flared up. He seemed anxious, and his eyes were scanning the closed mosquito nets over the other two beds, as if to make sure there wasn't another person in the room. I sat up and glared at him, believing he must be on an official errand. I grunted, "I'm alone here. What's up?"

He grinned and said, "Jian, I came to tell you that the city police are coming to arrest you this afternoon. You must go."

I was transfixed, then began to defend myself as if he were a police officer. I said almost in a cry, "I went to the capital only for personal reasons. Believe me, I was mad at Meimei and wanted to show her that I wasn't a coward and dared to go to Beijing whenever I liked. Honestly, I didn't mean to demand democracy and freedom and didn't even get to Tiananmen Square. You know I've never been politically active."

His face didn't change. "This makes no difference, Jian. They've already decided you're a counterrevolutionary."

"Why?"

"I'm not sure. Yesterday afternoon Ying Peng assigned me to prepare all the material about you. I overheard her telling the police on the phone this morning that if you hadn't lost your mind, you must be a counterrevolutionary. It's a hopeless case. She's made up her mind to send you either to prison or to a mental hospital. The police are coming for you early this afternoon. You'd better go now."

"I didn't do anything. Why should I run away?"

"Don't be stupid. This is no time to argue. They took Kailing Wang away yesterday. You must leave now, or at least hide somewhere for a few days."

"They arrested her? For what?"

"I've heard that she gave money to the students, or they couldn't have gone to Beijing."

At last his words sank in. I got up and began gathering things I'd take with me. He said anxiously, "I must be going. Don't let anyone know I told you this."

"All right, I won't."

Before he could head away, I said, "Wait a minute. Why did you run the risk of helping me?" I knew he disliked me as much as I despised him.

He blushed a little. "I told Weiya about your case at lunch. She wanted me to inform you immediately because she doesn't feel well and can't come herself."

"What happened to her?"

"She has taken to her bed since she heard that the army started attacking the students."

"But why do you look so happy? Because some of them are dead?" I couldn't help my derision.

"Come on, don't think I'm heartless. I cried together with Weiya when we heard the news, and I too have soaked my pillow with tears at night, but I have to put on a cheerful face in public. If I look happy, it's out of habit. A mask is necessary for survival."

Still I couldn't curb my anger. He had gained so much from Mr. Yang's death. Now he was officially the editor in chief of the journal, had Weiya in his palm, and surely would be promoted to professor soon. No wonder he was in high spirits. I said to him, "Listen, Weiya and I were Mr. Yang's students. To me she's more than a fellow grad, she's a friend. If you don't treat her well, I'll get even with you one of these days."

He was taken aback. His face fell as his eyes kept flickering. Yet he said rather solemnly, "Why are you so petulant, so hostile to me? What makes you believe I'm such a lucky man? Weiya and I have just been dating. You think we're going to get married tomorrow? I wish I were that lucky."

For a moment I was speechless, just gazing at him. He went on, "Weiya is a such a good girl that, to be honest, I feel I've just begun to learn how to love a woman." Seeing that I was still at a loss, he reminded me, "You must go now, Jian."

I forced myself to say, "Good luck."

"Thanks." He nodded, his eyes brightened.

After he left, I washed my face with cold water to refresh my mind a little. I had to act coolheadedly from now on.

Outside, in the scorching sun, Little Owl shouted with both fists thrust upward into the air, "Good news! Great news! The People's Liberation Army is executing counter-revolutionaries in Beijing. Bang-bang-bang-bang! All tanks are shelling those little bastards!" He was running on his bandy legs from one dormitory to another to spread the victorious news. Then came his wild bawling; somebody must be hitting him.

I dared not take too many of my belongings, because I wanted to give the police the impression that I was still around so they would wait for me to return. I placed my pocket Japanese dictionary and an English grammar on the desk and kept them both opened with a bunch of keys and a stack of flash cards. With two changes of clothes, my Panda radio, and a few books in my shoulder bag, including an English dictionary, I walked out, leaving the door unlocked.

Quickly I pedaled north to Black Brook, a rural town about seven miles away to the east. The police must have been combing trains at the downtown station for local student leaders and for those who had fled Beijing, so I'd better go to a small town.

Biking on the dirt road that had almost no traffic, I thought about Yuman Tan's visit. To me he used to be a mere toady, a flunky of Secretary Peng's; but now he seemed a different man. Today he showed a modicum of decency and even some dignity. More than that, I must admit that he acted as a respectable man, capable of honorable feelings. What happened to him? What caused the change?

Weiya, of course. She must have given him some hope and happiness. Yes, he even looked younger today, despite the national tragedy on his mind. So it was happiness and love for a worthy woman that had brought some human decency out of him. How often we hear people say that suffering can purify one's soul, ennoble one's heart, and strengthen one's moral fiber. How earnestly Mr. Yang had claimed on his sickbed, "I'm only afraid that I'm not worthy of my suffering!" Indeed, some great men and women are fortified and redeemed through their suffering, and they even seek sadness instead of happiness, just as van Gogh asserted, "Sorrow is better than joy," and Balzac declared, "Suffering is one's teacher." But these dicta are suitable only for extraordinary souls, the select few. For ordinary people like us, too much suffering can only make us meaner, crazier, pettier, and more wretched. In Yuman Tan's case, it was a little hope, happiness, and human warmth that made the seed of goodness sprout.

My thoughts turned to Secretary Peng. Why had she moved so swiftly to have me arrested? There were many more important "counterrevolutionaries" in this city; why would the police come for me in such a hurry? It flashed through my mind that Ying Peng must have been determined to get rid of me once and for all, and that she wanted to do this mainly for personal reasons. Although Vice Principal Huang's son was carrying on with Meimei, there was still a slight possibility that someday I might go to Beijing and rekindle the old flame in her heart. She couldn't leave for France with that man, who was going to the Sorbonne in the fall just for a year or two. Even if he decided to stay abroad afterward, legally she wouldn't be allowed to join him until he married her and made the amount of francs required for getting the visa for her. In other words, there would be a period of physical separation between them, so I would have time to step in to reclaim my fiancée. Ying Peng must have been aware of that possibility and knew I was in high dudgeon against her, so she had resolved to root me out now to forestall the trouble down the road. Probably Vice Principal Huang was involved in this scheme too.

This realization made me see how essential personal motives were in political activities. Just as I rushed to Beijing to demonstrate my bravado to Meimei, in the name of revolution people acted on the basis of all kinds of personal interests and reasons. But our history books on the Communist revolution have always left out individuals' motives. I remembered that when talking about why they joined the Red Army or the Communist Party, older revolutionaries had often said it was because they had wanted to escape an arranged marriage or to avoid debts or just to have enough food and clothes. It's personal interests that motivate the individual and therefore generate the dynamics of history.

In retrospect, Secretary Peng wasn't totally wrong about me. I indeed acted like a counterrevolutionary: I aspired not only to show my bravery to Meimei but also, like a free man capable of choice, to dislodge myself from the revolutionary machine. By so doing, I defied a prescribed fate like my teacher's.

An hour later I arrived at Black Brook. Having little money on me, I couldn't buy a train ticket for Guangzhou. It occurred to me that the only way to get some cash was to sell my Phoenix bicycle, which was still pretty new. Two years ago I had paid 196 yuan for it, so it was worth at least a hundred now. I walked along the clothing and food stands on the sidewalk of a wide street and asked a few people whether they wanted to buy my bicycle. Nobody was interested.

Finally at a fruit stand I offered it to an old vendor, who looked at it with a curious smirk. Hungry and thirsty, I could hardly take my eyes off the pile of apricots on a trestle table; my mouth was salivating, but I suppressed my craving and focused on selling him my bicycle. Asked again, he shook his gray head and kept waving his palm-leaf fan, though it wasn't hot at all. Then he gave me a peculiar smile, which seemed to insinuate that he had the cash but suspected the goods were ill-gotten.

I was desperate and pleaded, "Uncle, have pity! My sister is dying in Tianjin and I have to be there as soon as possible. But I don't have the money for the train fare. Come, take this bike. It's as sturdy as a mule."

He chased away a few bluebottles with his fan and shook his bullet-shaped head again.

"You think I'm a thief?" I pressed on.

He squinted at me, waggling his long eyebrows and clattering his carious teeth.

"You really think I'm a thief? Look, I'm a graduate student." I took my picture ID out of my trouser pocket and showed it to him. "See the big seal here? Absolutely the real thing."

He looked at the photo, then at me. "Seventy yuan," he said dryly, and blew his nose onto the ground with his thumb pressing his nostril.

"Plus some apricots," I responded, having no time to haggle for more.

He grinned, stood up, folded a piece of straw paper into a triangular bag, and put some apricots into it. "Here you are," he said.

I accepted the fruit. Then he handed me twelve fivers and ten greasy singles. Having given him the bicycle key, I left without delay. In the one-room train station I bought a ticket for Nanjing, where I would switch to an express bound for Guangzhou. I planned to sneak across the border into Hong Kong, though I didn't know how to do it exactly, unfamiliar with the terrain there. The photo of the woman attacked by a shark, which I had seen in the newspaper in Mr. Yang's sickroom a month ago, came to mind, but I was not daunted. If need be, I would attempt to swim across the shark-infested water. I was a good swimmer and with luck should be able to make it. From Hong Kong I would go to another country— Canada, or the United States, or Australia, or some place in Southeast Asia where Chinese is widely used.

The train wouldn't come for two hours. I walked east for about a hundred yards and found a quiet spot behind a stack of used ties. On one of them, a pair of rusted spikes still held a loosened plate. Lifting my eyes, I saw that the sidings and the main tracks all had ties made of concrete now, so these pieces of timber here must have become obsolete. In the distance two sets of shiny rails curved away and disappeared beyond a patch of young aspens. The air smelled of pungent asphalt oozing from the ties behind me. I sat down on a cinder block and began to eat the apricots, most of which were raw and sour; the only two sweet ones were wormy with deep holes in them. I couldn't stop sucking my breath. I knew I had been taken in. The old fruit seller must purposely have picked some unsalable apricots for me; otherwise he wouldn't have given them to me so willingly.

Done with the fruit, I noticed a barbershop at a street corner in the northwest, its signboard displaying a scissors, a hair clipper, and a pot of steaming water. With a black-headed match I burned my student ID, then rose to my feet and went to the shop to get a crew cut. Without my long hair my face would appear narrower, and from now on I would use a different name.

ACKNOWLEDGMENTS

My heartfelt thanks to Judith Grossman, who read an
initial draft of this book and convinced me that it
would become a novel; to LuAnn Walther for her advice
and suggestions; to Lane Zachary for her comments.
I am also grateful to Wallace–Reader's Digest
Funds for its generous support and to the
Ucross Foundation for a residency.